A Note to Readers

I am thrilled to bring you Beau Braden and Charlotte Sterling's love story! I have been excited to write Charlotte's book since I met her in *Story of Love* (Josh and Riley's wedding novella). When I met Beau in *Thrill of Love* (Ty and Aiyla's story. Aiyla is pronounced Eye-la), I knew he and Charlotte were perfect for each other. I hope you adore them as much as I do. If this is your first Melissa Foster book, all of my books are written to stand alone, so dive right in and enjoy the fun, sexy ride!

The best way to keep up to date with new releases, sales, and exclusive content is to sign up for my newsletter or download my free app.
www.MelissaFoster.com/News
www.MelissaFoster.com/app

Two Love in Bloom Worlds Become One!

Meet the Bradens & Montgomerys
(Pleasant Hill – Oak Falls)

The Bradens at Pleasant Hill and the Montgomerys have become one magnificent series! In book three, *Trails of Love*, the Montgomerys and the Bradens are going to be deeply intertwined. For that reason, I have combined the series to make it easier for readers to keep track of characters, weddings, babies, etc. What this means is that after the first two books (*Embracing Her Heart* and *Anything for Love*), you will see both worlds in most of the books. Some stories might weigh more heavily in one location than the other, but they are all going to cross over.

In book one, *Embracing Her Heart*, you met the Montgomerys, and in this book you will meet the Bradens. I hope you love these two close-knit, loving, and loyal families as much as I do!

About the Love in Bloom Big-Family Romance Collection

The Bradens & Montgomerys is just one of the series in the Love in Bloom big-family romance collection. Each Love in Bloom book is written to be enjoyed as a stand-alone novel or as part of the larger series. There are no cliffhangers and no unresolved issues. Characters from each series make appearances in future books, so you never miss an engagement, wedding, or birth. A complete list of all series titles is included at the end of this book, along with previews of upcoming publications.

Visit the Love in Bloom Reader Goodies page for free ebooks, checklists, family trees, and more!
www.MelissaFoster.com/RG

A Special Surprise for Fans!

If you have not heard the news yet, I am now part of a fantastic group of romance authors called the Ladies Who Write (LWW), and we have created a fun, sexy world just for you! In *Anything for Love* you will meet several fictional members of LWW, each of whom will have their own book written by me and the other authors of LWW. For more information on our group and to stay up to date on the release of LWW books, visit www.LadiesWhoWrite.com and sign up for our newsletter.

Anything For

LOVE

The Bradens & Montgomerys
(Pleasant Hill – Oak Falls)

Love in Bloom Series

Melissa Foster

ISBN-10: 1941480888
ISBN-13: 978-1941480885

Cover Design: Elizabeth Mackey Designs
Cover Photograph: Sara Eirew Photography

WORLD LITERARY PRESS
PRINTED IN THE UNITED STATES OF AMERICA

Chapter One

BEAU BRADEN GUIDED his rental truck around ruts and wild brush on the road that led to the Sterling House, a rustic inn located in the Colorado Mountains. He planned to spend the next four weeks shoring things up at the inn as a favor to his relatives Hal and Josh Braden. The umbrella of trees thickened, and sunlight splashed through in fits and spurts, eventually disappearing altogether, creating a tunnel-like expanse. It was like driving into a scene from *Where the Wild Things Are*. Beau had delayed his arrival for months, waiting to escape his hometown until the ghosts of his past came back to haunt, as they did every year at this time. It had been years since Sterling House had functioned as an inn, and the owner, Charlotte Sterling, didn't seem to mind the delay, though she'd taken forever to respond to phone calls, texts, and emails. He didn't know much about her, other than that she was a writer. Given the overgrown road, he was beginning to wonder if she actually lived there or if he'd have the place to himself.

He didn't care if he had to live among grizzlies. The job had gotten him the hell out of Pleasant Hill, Maryland.

The tree-bound tunnel birthed him into a virtual paradise. Beau stepped on the brakes at the top of a long driveway, taking in acres of sprawling meadows and picturesque mountains. Trees dotted the landscape, so vibrant and full they looked painted in place. At the end of the driveway, three stunning stories of glass, stone, and cedar overlooked a heart-shaped lake, with breathtaking views in all directions. Grand terraces adorned the structure like open-ended invitations, filled with possibilities.

He coasted down the empty driveway, thinking he might actually have the luxurious inn to himself after all. *Perfect.* There was a time when he'd thought his small hometown was the perfect mix of city life and rural surroundings. That had gone to hell in a handbasket a long time ago. But this? This was *nirvana.* Plenty of work, no family around to suffocate him, no dodging the haunted looks in friends' eyes. And four weeks from now he'd be on his way to Los Angeles for a job far away from the skeletons of his past.

As he stepped from the truck, he pulled out his phone and glanced at the waiting text messages from his family. He wasn't surprised to see several from Jillian and Jax, his younger twin siblings, the most emotional of them all. Each of his five younger siblings were different, ranging from the meticulous and thorough Graham, to too-macho-for-his-own-good Nick and wildcat Zev. As the oldest, Beau had always been the one to take care of his siblings, but this time of year they hovered—or rather *swarmed*—with well-meaning words and offers of distraction. He loved them, but nothing could take away his guilt for causing Tory Raznick to lose her life.

He pulled up Charlotte's text and read the cryptic instructions as he grabbed his bags. *Come whenever. I'll have a room ready for you. My wing is downstairs to the left. I'll be in my office. Knock first.* She'd added a winking emoji, making him wonder what kind of woman she was that she couldn't arrange whatever was going on behind closed doors around his arrival. Not that he was a saint, but self-control was not an issue.

He rang the doorbell, and when it went unanswered, he tried the door. Surprised to find it unlocked, he pushed it open and then tried the doorbell again, listening for the chime. Answered with silence, he mentally added it to his list of repairs and stepped inside the spacious mansion. He noticed a stairwell leading downstairs just off to his right and set his bags on the floor, taking a moment to get his bearings. Expansive stone and glass walls, exposed-beam ceilings, iron and antler chandeliers, and a beautiful stone fireplace added a wealth of character. His footfalls broke the silence as he walked by a study and dining room, both adorned in rich, dark wood. He admired a red-carpeted staircase leading up to the second floor. The ornate balusters had lost their shine, and he made a mental note to bring them back to life. He crossed the room and gazed out the doors to the terrace, trying the knob. *Unlocked.* It was easy to imagine the inn bustling with activity, children playing in the wildflowers while their parents mingled nearby. He meandered into the enormous kitchen, which was definitely in need of some TLC. Another unlocked door led to a terrace overlooking the rear of the property. He stepped outside and shook the railing, which was already on the list of repairs his relatives had given him.

Alone in such a peaceful location with nothing to do but the work he loved most?

Oh yeah, this is nirvana all right.

He headed inside, locking the door behind him. He'd have to remember to speak with Charlotte about security. He went back to the main entrance and headed downstairs to see if she had left him a note. He was surprised to hear hushed noises coming from down the hall. He lifted his hand to knock on what he assumed was her office door, hesitating as the sounds grew louder, clearer. The sounds of passion slipped through the crack in the door. The kind of noises that made a man's cock weep.

Beau cursed under his breath as he remembered her warning. *Knock first.*

He'd left his dog—and constant companion—Bandit, at home for this? This was *not* what he'd signed up for.

He rubbed the knot at the base of his neck and decided, *Fuck it.* He was doing this work for his relatives, and he wasn't going to let them down. It was a big inn. He could probably get away with avoiding Charlotte the entire time. Hell, given her untimely replies to his messages, she might not even notice he was there for a while.

He headed back the way he'd come to unload his truck and get things in order.

The door flew open behind him. "Damn it, Chris!" A petite brunette stormed out wearing a man's dress shirt rolled up at the cuffs. It hung so low, he had no idea if she had anything else on. Her tousled mane bounced over her shoulders as she stormed toward him in bare feet. Her cheeks were flushed, her eyes a mesmerizing mix of greens and browns, brighter than he'd expected after the lustful sounds he'd heard coming from behind that door. She had a rosebud of a mouth, small and so sweetly bowed he had a hard time looking away from it.

Those perfect lips blossomed into a radiant smile as she said, "Beau?" as happily as she'd been angry when she'd first stormed into the hall.

He was staring at her mouth, but his brain was too focused

on what she had—or *didn't have*—on under that shirt to say anything more than, "Yeah."

"I'm Charlotte. It's nice to meet you." She grabbed his arm, dragging him into another room. "Thanks for coming out." She opened a closet and huffed out a breath like the empty closet had upset her.

He leaned out of the room and peered down the hall, expecting a guy to come looking for her. "Is everything okay?"

"Fine." She grabbed his arm again and pulled him into the hall. "I'm looking for Chris. And by the way, they delivered your supplies. They're in the workshop down through the woods. I'll draw you a map later."

She flung open another door, traipsed into the room, and threw open the closet. Several blow-up dolls tumbled out.

What the...? Beau tried to hide his surprise as Charlotte appraised each doll's face and flung them on the bed.

"No. No. *No.*"

"I...um..." *Fuck.* This was a new experience. Could being alone too long in a rambling old place like this make a person crazy? Hal and Josh owed him big-time for this favor. He hiked his thumb toward the hall and said, "I'm just going to get my stuff from the truck. If you point me in the direction of my room, I'll get out of your hair."

"Your room!" She rolled her eyes. "Of course! That's where I left him. Chris Pine is *always* getting left behind. At least this time I think he's alone and not with the other guys. I hate when I leave those naughty boys alone for too long."

Damn. She's into some kinky shit. "Chris *Pine*? You can leave him there. There are plenty of other rooms I can stay in." Or maybe he'd stay in his truck. What the hell type of place was she running here? And who knew Chris Pine was into guys?

She waved her hand dismissively and strutted down the hall to the next door. "Don't be silly. I just need to find the key to the handcuffs."

Beau stopped in his tracks. Visions of *The Shining* danced in his head.

"THIS IS IT." Charlotte stood before the door to Beau's room and realized he was no longer beside her. She looked down the hall and found him standing outside her toy room.

"Beau?" As she closed the distance between them, she noticed what she'd been too distracted to see before. Her new houseguest had sun-kissed olive skin, short brown hair, and perfectly manicured scruff, which conflicted with his rugged vibe and rivaled the fictional heroes she created. She knew the Bradens had cornered the market on hot male genes, but darkly handsome Beau must have gotten a double dose, with his mile-wide shoulders, tree-trunk legs, and arms that could probably crush a man.

His expression grew even more serious as she approached. Geez, what was wrong with him? *She* was the one going crazy from writer's block for the first time in her life. She was behind on her deadline and everything she wrote about her characters fell flat. All *he* had to do was bang a few nails.

"Come on, Braden." She grabbed his hand, noticing how rough and big it was as she led him down the hall. She quickly tried to memorize the feel of it swallowing hers so she could use the details in her writing. His hand was so strong it made her feel feminine and small. *Submissive?* she wondered, an idea percolating in her mind. She loved the way that word sounded soft as a feather, and she enjoyed writing about submissive women. Sometimes she wondered what it would be like to be someone's submissive, which she was pretty sure she'd hate. But that was a thought for another day, because that required a living, breathing partner to hash out scenes with, and she had better things to do than worry about a man. *Like finishing my manuscript.*

There would be no *finishing* if she couldn't get past the first few chapters. Each of the four books in her Wicked Boys After Dark series followed a different alpha brother with secret sexual penchants. The stories had flowed from her like water from a tap, attracting so many ravenous erotic romance readers, she'd had to hire a personal assistant to handle her emails and social media and a public relations manager to handle media inquiries. Thank goodness for Becca and Luce. Without them she'd spend endless hours handling everything *other than* writing. She had no idea what had changed to cause sludge instead of eloquent, sinful words to come from that tap, but she hadn't even made a dent in the first book in her Nice Girls After Dark series, which followed four sisters who owned various businesses, including a sex club.

Oh! Maybe I should write about a woman who has no idea how to be a submissive!

"That's a great idea," she said absently.

"What is?" The muscles in his jaw bunched.

"Do you have a—" She snagged the pen sticking out of his shirt pocket and wrote *submissive* on her arm. Then she tucked the pen behind her ear and pushed open the door to his room. Her gaze fell to the mattress, where her blow-up doll lay handcuffed to the bed.

"There you are!" She climbed up and straddled the doll, searching the sheets around him for the key. "Poor Chris. I really need to stop forgetting where I leave him."

"*That's* Chris?" His dark brows slanted. "You *handcuffed* a blow-up doll to the bed?"

"Yes, Chris Pine. I can't exactly call my research partners by dorky names, can I? I'd *never* get in the mood to write erotic romance without a little inspiration." She had millions of fans to keep happy, and she felt pressure to make sure every book was better than the last and every character was unique. Inspiration was paramount. Especially now.

"Holy fu—"

"I just need to find that key, and then the room's all yours." Her gaze flicked up, meeting his baffled expression as she crawled off the bed. "What's wrong?"

He pointed to the hall. "Don't you have a real guy in your office, or whatever room that is down the hall, who you can work those things out with?"

"Real guy? Ha! No." She planted her hands on her hips and said, "I think I lost the key. I'll make up another room for you."

He cocked a brow like she was speaking another language. "You know you can just let the air out of your...*boyfriend*, right?"

"He is *not* my boyfriend." This guy was *way* too literal, but he was also super cute and ridiculously confused. Maybe she could get some emotions out of him to use in her writing. He was as big as her friend Cutter, who brought her groceries every few weeks and sometimes helped her work out scenes. Only Cutter was like a brother, which meant he was good for mechanics but not steamy emotions. She stepped closer and touched his chest, enjoying the feel of his muscles flexing against her fingers, and gauged his reaction.

Mm. That jaw clenching is hot.

"You need to lighten up, *baffled and burly Beau*," she said. "The dolls are for research purposes only. Fully dressed, mechanical research. Just like you might investigate how to build something, I need to explore positions for the stories I'm creating. I don't use them for gratification purposes. *Got it?* I'm not that lame." Unfortunately, she was even lamer. She wasn't about to tell him that she had a drawer full of adult toys or that there had been a time when she'd used them seeking satisfaction. But like with men, they'd let her down every time, and she'd given up on anything other than fictional sex.

"What you heard in my office was me acting out a scene so I could nail it down."

His lips quirked up in amusement. "Alone?"

"*No*, not alone. With Hugh Jackman." She dropped to her knees and peeked under the bed for the key to the handcuffs.

"Christ," he mumbled. He grabbed the back of her shirt, hauling her up to her knees.

"What?"

"You don't even know me and you stuck your ass up in the air like that? What if I was a creep?"

She folded her arms over her chest and smirked. "Hal and Josh Braden are the ones who asked you to come here, and they would never send a creep to my house."

He took her by the arm, helping her to her feet. Then he climbed onto the bed and grabbed one handcuff. "That's not the point." He squeezed the doll's hand and pushed it through the metal.

"Be careful," she pleaded. "Those dolls are expensive."

He slid her a *be serious* look. "Don't worry. I'm good with my hands."

"I bet you are," she said under her breath, earning another look that made her feel like a twelve-year-old scolded for cursing. The guy needed to lighten up. She coughed to cover her amusement as he pushed the other hand through the cuffs.

"Done." He climbed off the bed.

"But now you'll have handcuffs attached to your bed."

He clenched his jaw, and his serious eyes turned volcanic. A second later they morphed to *restrained*. It was freaking *hot*, and she wanted to remember every single detail for her book.

Maybe he would make the perfect research partner after all. Hot, hard-bodied, and best of all, *temporary*.

Chapter Two

LATER THAT AFTERNOON Charlotte stared at her computer screen, unsure if she should be thankful or irritated at her new muse. She usually wrote about five thousand words a day, many days even more than that. But over the last few *weeks* she'd written only twelve thousand words, four thousand of which she'd written after meeting über-serious and insanely handsome Beau. She'd never had to rely on anyone else to fill her creative well before, and the fact that he'd uncorked whatever had stopped up her pipes was bothering her.

She leaned back, propped her toes on the edge of her desk, and twisted her chair from side to side, trying to analyze the situation. After returning Chris Pine to her toy room, she'd shown Beau around the property. He'd remained just as serious and had taken pages of notes. She couldn't imagine what he'd seen that needed fixing. There hadn't been anything sexual about their interactions, although she had to admit she'd stolen a shameful number of glances at his gorgeous body. *For research purposes, of course.* And she'd come away with four thousand words worth of inspiration.

She gazed outside at the setting sun, and Beau came into view. He was carrying a ladder up from the workshop. *Shirtless.*

"Good Lord."

Her feet smacked the hardwood as she scrambled over to the window. Her eyes swept over the hard set of his chin, those ever-serious eyes focused on the path before him, and *heaven have mercy*, gorgeous planes of olive skin stretched tight over his muscular torso. She breathed faster with each of his determined steps. As he neared the corner of the building, she pressed her cheek to the glass, eking out the very last second of her view before he disappeared around the corner.

Turning her back to the window, she pressed her hand over her racing heart and closed her eyes. It had been *years* since a man had affected her this way. Although she didn't get many visitors, she opened the inn for a few weddings and charity events. During those times, the grounds were crawling with athletes, actors, and other wealthy, sharply dressed men. None of them had stolen her concentration for more than a passing glimpse of appreciation, but images of Beau taunted her—his pulsing jaw muscles, the weighty intensity of his eyes, and that curt nod that should turn her off but piqued her interest even more.

Was it *him* that had her so flustered, or was it that he'd provided the missing inspiration for her writing? Writing was not only her career, but it was her emotional lifeline. It had pulled her through the most devastating times of her life.

Surely her heart was racing because of the return of her muse. Of course that was it. She'd been so upset about having writer's block, her body was just celebrating the reprieve from it. That made perfect sense, except now she couldn't stop thinking about him and how virile he looked carrying that stupid ladder.

She needed to capitalize on it.

She slipped into writer mode, sat at her keyboard, and went

to work creating a scene to go with the ladder—and that man. As she hammered it out, she feared her muse would disappear again, and her pulse skyrocketed.

Yup. Definitely the muse and not the man.

She couldn't afford to lose this inspiration. She needed to keep feeding her muse so she could make up for lost time and write this book. The idea behind the four thousand words she'd written had hit her like a sensual slap in the butt when she'd made that comment about the handcuffs and his bed. Her fingers stilled over the keyboard as an idea formed. *A little harmless flirtation might lead to an incredible story.*

She grabbed a pen and paper and scribbled titles as they popped into her mind. *Nail Me. Hammer Time. Climb Me, Baby.*

Okay, maybe her muse was still a little off, but she was coming back! Now that she had a plan to keep her muse alive, she focused on creating the story of the sexy contractor and his enormous *tools.*

BEAU PRESSED HIS phone to his ear, pacing the lobby of the inn as he listened to his sister, Jillian, beg him to get an autograph from Charlotte. Jillian spoke a mile a minute, which reminded him of the sexy innkeeper.

"I heard that Charlotte has a new series coming out. Tempest said Riley told her Charlotte never leaves the inn…" Tempest was their cousin who lived in Peaceful Harbor, Maryland, and Riley was married to their cousin Josh.

Beau tuned Jillian out while she gossiped. She switched

topics like a hummingbird flew from flower to flower seeking nectar.

"Jilly," he interrupted.

"What? You're such an outdoors guy. I bet you can get Charlotte to go out…"

He stuffed his dirty shirt in his back pocket, waiting for her to take another breath as she offered suggestions of places for him to take Charlotte. He hadn't seen Charlotte since she showed him around hours ago, and he was starting to wonder if he'd imagined her altogether. The kitchen was completely void of food, which almost made sense, since Charlotte was the size of a pixie and probably existed on air.

"Tell me the truth, boo," Jillian said, pulling him from his thoughts. "How are you doing? Are you okay?"

Shit. He'd thought he'd avoided the interrogation. When she called him by the endearment she'd used as a little girl, it was hard for him to ignore her questions. This was his cue to get off the phone.

"Because I'll fly out there tomorrow and—"

"No, Jilly," he said firmly. "I'm good, and I really need to go, but I appreciate the call. I'll ask for her autograph." Even though he'd feel ridiculous doing so.

"Did you call Jax?"

Beau sighed. "Yeah. Jax, Mom, Dad…" He adored his family, but this time of year *close-knit* really meant *smothering*.

"I'm Skyping with Zev tonight. Want me to have him call you?"

"No." A spear of guilt sliced through him. "I mean, if he wants to talk to me, sure, but don't tell him to call me because…for any other reason." There was no need to mention the tenth anniversary of Tory's death. The whole fucking town had been affected by it.

"Fine," she said, a little clipped. "Are you really going to L.A. when you leave there, and not coming back for months?"

Beau had been offered a two-year contract as host of a reality television show called *Shack to Chic*, where he would travel around the United States renovating unique properties. He was flying out the week after the Mad Prix celebration, an annual wilderness race in which his brother Graham, an extreme sports fanatic, and their cousin Ty, a world-renowned mountain climber, were competing. The finish line was on the grounds of the inn, and the awards ceremony was scheduled for three weeks from Saturday. The week after the celebration, Beau was flying out to Los Angeles to sign the contract and meet the crew. If all went well, he wouldn't be coming back for a very long time.

"Because you should come back, you know," Jillian urged. "Duncan will be in town, and he always asks about you."

A-list actor Duncan—"Raz" to his fans—Raznick, Tory's older brother, had been Beau's best friend before Tory was killed. Beau hadn't seen him since her funeral, but he knew that just as Beau escaped Pleasant Hill around the anniversary of Tory's death, Duncan returned to spend time with his family.

"I can't, Jilly. I've got to be in L.A."

"How convenient," she said sarcastically. "Oh shoot! I've got to go. I've got a date."

"I thought you were Skyping with Zev tonight. Who are you going out with?" Even though Jillian was in her midtwenties, Beau's protective claws still came out.

"I'm Skyping with Zev at midnight because of the time difference from wherever he is this week. The guy I'm going out with is one of Tempe's friends. We're going to see Nick's show, so you can stop worrying. If he's a dick, after I give him hell,

Nicky will get rid of him."

Beau laughed. *Nicky.* Nick was a year younger than Beau and well over six feet tall, with muscles on top of muscles. He hadn't been *Nicky* since he was a toddler, except to Jillian.

"Good. I love you, sis, but I need to go find Charlotte and figure out where to get some grub."

"Take her out to dinner!" Jillian suggested. "All girls love to go out to dinner. Did you bring any nice clothes?"

"I'm here to work, Jilly, not entertain." Although there was no denying that despite being the first woman he'd ever met who actually *owned* blow-up dolls, Charlotte intrigued him. And it was more than just the way she'd awoken his body. He hadn't stopped thinking about her all day, wondering why a gorgeous, successful woman would want to hole up on this mountain so far away from civilization. *And why the hell does she need blow-up dolls?* Hell, if she strolled into a bar, she'd have more takers than she could ever want.

"What's that old saying about all work and no play?" Jillian asked, bringing him back to their conversation. "Oh yeah, it makes for wicked blue balls."

"Jesus, Jilly." He shook his head as she roared with laughter. "Nice talk from my baby sister."

"I heard Nicky say that to Jace," she said with barely restrained giggles. Jace Stone was a family friend and a tough biker who owned a custom motorcycle business. "At least try to have fun, okay? I worry about you."

"Thanks. And, sis?"

"Yeah?"

"*Don't* have too much fun tonight. And for the love of God, don't talk like that on your date."

She was still laughing when they ended the call.

Beau shoved the phone in his pocket and inhaled a deep, calming breath. Jillian always made him feel like he'd barely survived a hurricane and left him smiling despite it.

He headed downstairs to find Charlotte, slowing as he neared her open office door. The lights were off, and he listened intently for moans or other sexy sounds, trying *not* to envision her with a blow-up doll. *Christ.* What had he gotten himself into? And why was he so fascinated by her?

The clickity-clack of a keyboard came into focus, and he exhaled with relief. *Why are my hands sweating?* He wiped them on his jeans as he stepped into her office.

"Hey there."

She jumped up with a gasp. "Ohmygod! Beau!"

"Sorry. But um, what are you, a vampire? It's so dark in here." He flicked the light switch, but no lights came on.

"You scared the heck out of me." She leaned over her keyboard, giving him an eyeful of her narrow hips and the tiny cutoffs he hadn't been able to see earlier. She was still wearing the man's dress shirt, and he wondered whose button-down it was.

"Sorry. I didn't mean to scare you." He flicked the switch up and down again. "What's up with the light?"

"It's been burnt out since Christmas," she said absently, her back to him as she typed.

"It's been blown out for *five months*?" He looked around the room, and the blown lightbulb seemed to be the tip of the iceberg. Several of her book covers, each touting #1 NEW YORK TIMES BESTSELLER, hung framed and crooked on the walls. One of her book covers graced the cover of *Literary Focus* magazine. The frame dangled from a thin piece of string coiled around a large pushpin. Bookshelves were littered with stacks of papers, books, and photographs, interspersed with handcuffs, a ball gag, and a silk tie. Stacks of notebooks and loose papers lined the floor between the couch and the shelves. Two anatomically correct blow-up dolls lay on the couch.

He scoffed. They had nothing on him.

"No, not five months." *Type, type, type.*

He glanced at her desk, which was littered with empty water bottles, a half-eaten protein bar, candy wrappers, and a plethora of sticky notes and notebooks. Her trash can was overflowing, and a half-empty water bottle with a big purple straw sticking out of it sat precariously on the edge of a credenza beside her.

Charlotte straightened her spine, tossed her long dark hair over her shoulders and, still facing her computer, said, "It's been blown out since the Christmas before that."

"Wiring issue?" he asked, wondering if she had a critter problem and the wires had been gnawed through.

She shrugged as she turned to face him. The dress shirt she wore was open, revealing a tight T-shirt beneath. Her gaze landed on his chest, reminding him he was shirtless. Her eyes widened, as if she'd only just noticed he was a living, breathing person and not a doll.

"I'll take a look at it," he said to distract himself from how incredibly beautiful she was.

"The bulb died," she said a little breathlessly.

She couldn't change a lightbulb? Maybe she kept her light-bulbs in the same place she kept the handcuff key.

Her eyes trailed down his body, hovering around his groin before moving lower. She went doe-eyed, and her lips curved seductively. Thoughts of the lightbulb disappeared. Her gaze climbed slowly up his body, leaving a trail of hot pulses in all the areas where they lingered. She strolled toward him, those doe eyes locked on him. His body heated as she approached, stopping a few mere inches in front of him. She was at least a foot shorter than him, and when she tipped her face up, passion simmered in her eyes.

Fuuuck.

"Will you have to use your *big ladder*?" she asked in a sultry voice, emphasizing the last two words, which he heard as *big cock.*

What the hell kind of game was this?

She touched his cheek. Her fingers were warm and soft. He missed warm and soft. She studied his face as if she were noting every twitch.

Look lower, babe. You'll see a damn big twitch.

"Well?" she asked much too innocently. "Are you as good with your *ladder* as you are with your hands?"

He was skirting a dangerous line, wanting to throw her hot little body on that couch and show her how good a real man could make her feel. But he wasn't there to get mixed up with a woman who played with dolls and toyed with men. Not when she was friends with his relatives. And definitely not when painful memories could turn him into a raging asshole over the next few weeks. *Temporary* raging asshole, but a jerk all the same.

Jillian's blue balls joke trampled through his mind. She hadn't been far off.

Charlotte's fingers trailed down his neck to his chest, sending heat south. He grabbed her wrist, and heat or amusement sparked in her eyes. He couldn't tell which, and that pissed him off. He didn't like to be messed with.

"I only came in here because I was going to offer to whip something up for dinner," he said, more as a reminder to himself than for her benefit.

Her eyes narrowed seductively as she leaned forward, speaking just above a whisper in the dimly lit room. "I could eat…"

Jesus… His cock hardened at the thought of those rosebud lips wrapped around it. He forced his voice to work before he did something stupid. "I forgot to stop at the store on my way in. You've got a beautiful barbecue on the terrace. Looks like it hasn't been fired up in a while." Damn, that's how he felt about her, too. She had this innocent-minx thing going on, and it was killing him. "Do you have a couple steaks or something I can throw on?"

"Or something," she said with a daring grin.

Her eyes moved slowly over his face, openly assessing him. She placed her hand flat over his heart, and her pretty brows knitted in concentration. Just as he realized he was still holding her other wrist, she twisted out of his grip and hurried to her keyboard. She began typing even before her ass hit the seat, leaving him hot, hard, and fucking confused.

She waved her right hand without turning around and said, "Food's in my freezer. I figured we'd share my kitchen."

Gone was the heat and the seductive voice. She'd morphed into a typing machine, her fingers flying over the keys.

What the hell was that?

"Share your kitchen?" he said absently. "I'll knock before coming into your suite."

"Don't bother," she said as she typed. "Nothing good ever happens in there. You only need to knock on my office door if it's closed. Oh, and you won't find steak or anything. But you might find a can of soup and some crackers. Check the expiration dates. I'll put steak on the grocery list. I need to write, so you can go."

She glanced over her shoulder, her fingers still pecking away, and excitement brimmed in her eyes as she said, "You're way better than a blow-up doll."

Chapter Three

THE SUN CREPT into the sky like a sloth ascending a tree, unhurried and determined, pushing away the stubborn pre-dawn gray as the bright ball of fire rose toward the heavens. Ribbons of citrus splashed over the mountains, spilling into the fields. Light spread over the terrace where Beau stood leaning against the railing as he took in the gorgeous morning, thinking about Charlotte. She was a puzzle to him, like a set of architectural drawings that had been torn into bits and mixed up, in need of sorting. Her *wing* was more like an underequipped apartment. The entrance led directly into a living room, outfitted with standard resort-style furniture. It didn't feel like a home, or even like she hung out there. A quick glance had revealed no worn spots or dips in the cushions indicating her favorite place to chill. In a way, it reminded him of his own house, where he kept his things but never spent much time.

Her kitchen—if he could call it that—was just inside the door to her suite and off to the left. It was as sparse as her answers had been. She had a hot plate, a microwave, a coffee machine, and a small refrigerator, which was nearly empty save for a slew of water bottles, an insane amount of Luscious Leanna's Sweet Treats jam, a few containers of yogurt, and a bowl full of eggs. He'd poked around in the cabinets and found a container of instant coffee, a few packets of sugar, enough protein bars to feed a family of five, a box of pancake mix—*no syrup*—a few cans of soup, and half a sleeve of crackers. He'd heated up two cans of soup for dinner on the stone barbecue, but when he'd offered some to Charlotte, she'd waved him away and said, *Can't break my stride*, as she pounded that keyboard. He'd made the rounds of the inn, locking no less than nine doors in the process.

The woman needed a security system. Or at least a dog.

Or a man.

He sipped the acidic coffee. If ever a woman needed a man around, it was Charlotte. He'd never met anyone like her before. She had totally used him last night, or she was just enjoying fucking with him. Either way, he was nobody's fool. Two could play at that game. Hell, it might even be a good distraction from the memories he was trying to escape. The memories that had haunted him last night and had warred with fantasies of Charlotte straddling that damn blow-up doll. Except *he* was lying beneath her, and they were both naked. In the dark of night, a collage of terror and fantasies had played out in his mind. Tory's sweet face flashed seconds before the site of the accident that had stolen her life, and then Charlotte had appeared, skipping in a fucking meadow. What the hell that meant, he had no idea, but he'd woken up at the crack of dawn in a full sweat.

His thoughts turned to his to-do list, at the top of which was fixing the damage his cousins' wives had caused in the suite upstairs the weekend of Josh's wedding, which had taken place at the inn. From what Beau had been told, a few of Josh's sisters-in-law and his mother-in-law had consumed too much alcohol and had had an accidental run-in with brownies laced with marijuana. The women had taken it upon themselves to try to perform an exorcism on one of the supposedly haunted rooms on the second floor while the men slept. It sounded like something Jillian and her friends would do *without* the weed.

He quickly ran through more of his to-do list, which included cleaning up the main kitchen in the inn, so he had a place to prepare meals, and getting down the mountain to buy food. But first he needed to clear his head. A walk usually did the trick, calming the ghosts that trailed him like shadows.

He set his coffee cup in the kitchen to take care of later and descended the terrace steps to the yard. When Charlotte had shown him the workshop in one of the old barns yesterday, he'd noticed a few other trails and decided to check them out.

As he came around the side of the inn, he spotted Charlotte walking toward the woods a good distance ahead. She wore knee-high red rubber boots and an oversized gray sweater that hung off one shoulder, covering only to the middle of her butt, revealing maroon panties and sexy butt cheeks. Some of her hair was pulled up in a clip, but tangles stuck out like snakes trying to escape a nest, and a few long tresses dribbled down her back. She carried a basket in her right hand, swinging it as she walked through the long grass. She disappeared into the woods, and he quickened his pace, wondering where she could possibly be going dressed like that.

He followed the narrow trail over dead leaves and broken branches and heard her singing "Like a Prayer" loud and off-key. She sang about life being a mystery, and he could easily change those lyrics to *Charlotte is a mystery*. He chuckled, wondering what kind of alternate universe existed in her head for her to be so free and unencumbered, even if a little scattered.

Although, to be able to write hour after hour as she did, *scattered* didn't make sense.

She entered a clearing, and he hung back, watching her dance and twirl as she belted out the lyrics. Her arms floated up toward the sky like wings, lifting her sweater with it and flashing a few inches of enticing skin above her hip-hugging panties. When she sang the chorus, she broke into some sort of stomping breakdance.

Either that or she was possessed by the devil.

She tipped her chin up toward the sky, screech-singing about how she'd take him there like a prayer. He stood in the trees, mesmerized by her wild, frantic, carefree movements.

Suddenly she went silent. He listened more intently. She was humming and wiggling her shoulders and hips as she slipped through a band of bushes and disappeared out of sight.

"Charlotte?" He took off after her, needing to see more of her.

As he pushed through the bushes, she slammed into him with an *oomph!* His arms circled her, and their eyes connected with the force of lightning, earning a breathy gasp. It was the sexiest sound he'd ever heard. Her body was hot against him despite the cool morning air. Her lips parted, but she didn't say a word. Her gaze turned sultry, flooding his body with even more awareness of her softness, her sweet, feminine scent. He had the overwhelming urge to kiss her. Her tempting lips curved up in the same sinful smile she'd flashed last night—just before messing with his head. *Not this time, shortcake.* He tightened his hold on her.

Her eyes widened, and she clamped her mouth shut.

"Where are you going so scantily dressed?"

Her eyes narrowed again. "Where are *you* going so…?" Her

gaze dragged down his T-shirt to the waist of his jeans. "*Over*dressed?"

She was good, he'd give her that, but he was better. Holding her gaze, he pressed his hand flat against her back, bringing their bodies flush from leg to chest, and her eyes darkened.

"I forgot, you prefer your men *naked*." He reached over his back with one hand and tugged his shirt off, earning a lustful gasp. He dropped his shirt on top of a bush, enjoying the feel of her soft curves molding to his hard frame. "What do you call that thing you use to inflate your boy toys?" He lowered his face so their mouths were a whisper apart, and her breathing hitched. "Oh yeah. Your *mouth*."

She swallowed hard, her fingers pressing into his skin. She blinked several times, and then her gorgeous eyes narrowed and she said, "Good to know you have a thing for my mouth."

He was pretty sure she was fucking with him, and *still* his body flamed, turned on by her prurience as much as her sass and confidence. She had the sexiest mouth he'd ever seen, but this was a game to her, and he was about to show her who was King of the Mountain. He threaded his fingers into her hair and brushed his lips over her cheek, catching another whiff of her feminine scent.

"I wonder if you taste as sweet as you smell." He felt her shudder in his arms, and he slid his hand to the curve of her ass, earning a little squeak of shock. "I do have a thing for silk panties," he growled directly into her ear, and her fingernails dug into his flesh. "But you should think about the vibes you're giving off and the message you're sending me. I could strip you naked right here."

He let those words sink in, tightening his hold, though she wasn't trying to get away, and he continued his torturous game, driving his don't-fuck-with-me point home. "I could hold your hands down as I bury myself so deep inside you, you'll feel me tomorrow. Is that what you want, *shortcake?*"

He tugged gently on her hair, angling her glassy eyes up toward his. She had the look of a woman waiting to be kissed. Wanting to be taken. He had the urge to slide his fingers between her legs and feel how much she wanted him. But he was sure this was a game to her, and Beau didn't do games.

With his eyes locked on hers, he said, "I am not a man you want to fuck with."

He reluctantly released her, and the breath rushed from her lungs. She stumbled back, her hands hanging limply by her sides.

"I don't lose," he said sternly. "*Ever.*"

Only he had. *Once.* Guilt slithered through him like a viper waiting to strike.

He forced those ugly emotions down deep and said, "We need to have a talk about security."

Her eyes darted away. "Channing," she said breathlessly.

"No more games, Charlotte. You want my attention? You call me *Beau.*"

"No!" She pointed through the bush-lined path to a grassy area where a big white chicken was pecking at the ground. "Channing's loose! I have to get her!"

Three more chickens ran by, and Charlotte took off after them. "Oh no! All my Chickendales are loose!"

Beau uttered a curse and followed her. "*Chickendales?*"

Charlotte was chasing several chickens in front of a small stone coop with a too-short mint-colored door. A rustic chicken pen was attached to the side and back of the coop, framed with rough timber and wrapped in wire mesh. Branches ran in all directions between the frames to keep the mesh in place. Above the mesh-and-branch door to the pen was a wooden sunburst also made from branches and limbs. A quick sweep of the structure showed a hole in the front lower left. It looked like Charlotte had tried to patch it using leafy branches.

"Don't just stand there!" Charlotte pleaded. "I can't lose Channing, Matt, or Joe!"

"You do know these chickens are *female*, right?" he said as he strode toward her.

"Of course I know that! I named them after the *Magic Mike* characters."

A rooster crowed from somewhere off to the left, and Charlotte's face crumbled into genuine sadness that caused a twinge in Beau's chest.

"Oh no! Jason Momoa got out, too?" She ran in the direction of the sound.

Beau caught her around the waist with one arm, lifting her feet off the ground. "Hold up, shortcake."

"I have to get them before a predator does!"

"The more you run, the farther they'll scatter. Calm down."

She turned a death stare on him. "Do *not* tell a woman to calm down unless you want to be castrated." She pushed at his arm. "Let me go!"

"Jesus. Can you calm—*settle...relax* for one second?"

She crossed her arms in a huff, her legs dangling above the ground.

"We need a plan to corner them one by one and catch them."

She rolled her eyes. "Pantsers don't do plans."

"What do pants have to do with this? If you want my help, it starts with a plan. I'm going to set you on your feet, but you need to stay still or you'll scare them. Haven't they gotten out before?"

"Yes! That's why I need to get them. Last time it took me hours of chasing, until I finally gave up, and they…" Her voice trailed off.

"They…?"

She looked away and mumbled, "Came close enough for me to pick them up."

He chuckled as a big brown chicken came around the side of the coop.

"Oh no! Not Duncan!"

Beau's chest constricted. "Duncan," he repeated before he could stop himself.

"Duncan Raz!" She pushed at his arm belted around her waist. "You're holding me too tight. I can't breathe!"

BEAU'S FACE BLANCHED, and he dropped Charlotte like a hot potato, as opposed to the way he'd *reluctantly* released her in the bushes, when he'd looked like he'd wanted to do all the naughty things he'd described. Every inch of his body was strung tight and impressively hard. He'd made her completely forget that she was supposed to be taking mental notes about the things he did and said to use in her writing. And now he looked like she'd kicked him in the gut, making her forget her book altogether.

She touched his arm and he flinched. "Are you okay?"

"Fine. Let's get the chickens."

"*Chickendales*," she corrected, trying to make him smile, but he just ground his teeth together.

After what seemed like an eternity, but in reality was probably only a few minutes, Beau cleared his throat, his dark, calculating eyes taking in the location of each of the chickens and the rooster. Charlotte watched in amazement as he formulated, and carried out, the simplest of plans: throwing feed on the ground, then plucking up the chickens one by one as they ate. He closed the opening between the coop and the pen and put them in the coop. Then he strode toward her, shirtless and authoritative.

"Thank you," she said, looking around for her basket. "I can't believe they got out again."

"You thought those branches would keep them in? Or keep a predator out?"

She set her hands on her hips, challenging the *silly girl* lilt in his voice. "It was a temporary fix, but yes. I saw my grandfather do it once. Only his way worked."

He nodded. "Is that who built this coop?"

"No. My great-grandfather built the stone coop. My grandfather built the pen."

"It's unique. I'll give him that." He glanced at the structure.

"It goes perfectly with Snow White's cabin, and I think it's beautiful."

He arched a brow. "Snow White's cabin?"

"That's what I call it. My great-grandmother loved fairy tales, so my great-grandfather renovated the original cabin to look like the house from the story."

His gaze turned serious again. "That's actually really sweet. I'd like to see it sometime. But right now I want to get this pen fixed up before you lose your chickens."

"Chickend—"

"Yeah, what's up with *that*? Is everything in your life a game? A fantasy? A fairy tale?" he asked.

"Aren't you judgmental?"

"Sorry. Just grounded in reality." He turned a hot gaze on her as he crouched by the hole in the pen. "And I don't like being messed with."

"Oh, like you weren't messing with me in the bushes?" She crossed her arms, staring him down.

He rose to his full height, towering over her. "Just playing your game, sweetheart."

"Oh, really? *My* game? Because from the feel of things, you sure seemed to enjoy it."

His biceps twitched. "What's not to enjoy when I've got a gorgeous woman's body pressed against mine? You're playing with fire." His gaze dropped to her panties, and her insides sizzled. "Maybe this is how you get your men. Maybe you *like* fire."

"My *men*?" She laughed. "You have no idea who I am. Real men don't live up to the heroes I create. I wouldn't waste my time with them."

"Then why screw with my head?"

She was pretty sure he would not appreciate knowing it was the cure for her writer's block, so she said, "I wasn't screwing with you."

He stepped forward and hauled her against him. "Is this what you want? For me to take your panties off right here and have my way with you?"

The challenge in his eyes drove his point home, but she knew he wouldn't do anything without her consent. He might have serious eyes that wreaked havoc with her girly parts, but they were honest eyes.

She schooled her expression, hoping to reclaim the upper hand. The problem was, being in his arms felt *really* good, and she'd seen, and felt, a flash of something sad and hauntingly familiar in him when he'd released her like a hot potato. She had a feeling his gruffness wasn't caused by her teasing, despite what he claimed. But she wasn't as good with emotional situations in person as she was on paper, where she could rewrite a scene dozens of times until it bled or wept or lusted off the page. It didn't help that she was afraid to stop the ruse and lose her muse, and equally afraid not to, because she wanted to know what she'd said or done to cause the sadness she'd seen in him. Her game had just become real.

He released her a little too roughly and said, "I didn't think so."

Chapter Four

BEAU SPENT THE morning fixing the chicken pen, and as long as he was down there, he cleaned out the coop, which looked like it hadn't been cleaned for a month. Every time he caught sight of that damn brown chicken, guilt and anger stacked up inside him. It was like the guilt gods had it in for him. Even almost two thousand miles from home he couldn't escape his memories. The discomfort of his past battled once again with whatever the hell was going on between him and Charlotte. That was another situation he wasn't sure he was ready to deal with. She definitely turned him on, even if she was frustrating as hell.

After fixing the pen, he changed the bulb in Charlotte's office while she was in the shower. Then he patched the drywall in the suite upstairs that had been damaged the weekend of Josh's wedding and put an oil-based primer over the lipstick in the bathroom where the girls had written on the walls. Those must have been some potent marijuana brownies, or they'd consumed massive amounts of alcohol, for them to have caused such havoc. More than likely it wasn't the chemicals but rather a case of women letting loose and having a little too much fun. He tackled a few of the smaller items on his list, then set to work on the kitchen. Charlotte had told him she had house-keepers come in once a month to clean the inn top to bottom, but some of the cabinets had leaves and claw marks inside. He'd heard from his cousins that raccoons had been nesting in the kitchen. He wanted to do a complete inspection of the inn and make sure there were no critters partying in clever places and no way for them to get in.

He doubted Charlotte would even notice if they had. Did she ever check after the cleaning crew to make sure they'd done their jobs? From what he'd seen, she never left her damn office except to gather eggs in the morning.

In her *underwear*.

Heat streaked through him as images of her dancing seared through his mind. She was so damn sexy in those rubber boots and panties. He would have liked to have taken her in his arms right there in the grass, with the sun beating down on them and those woodsy eyes gazing up at him.

The sound of the front door opening jerked him from his fantasy. He wiped his hands on a rag and peered out of the kitchen. A linebacker-sized man wearing a cowboy hat and carrying two grocery bags in each arm and another in each hand was heading for the stairs.

"Hey," Beau said, stopping him before he went any farther.

"Hi. You must be the guy who's fixing up the inn. I'm Cutter. I'd shake your hand, but..." He glanced at the bags and smirked. "Girl's got me pretty loaded down."

"I'm Beau. Nice to meet you. Thanks for reminding me. I need to make a trip to the grocery store."

"That won't be necessary. Charlotte hooked you up. I've got steaks, chicken, fish, and all sorts of food for you. Not everyone can live on protein bars."

Beau ran an assessing eye over him. "You work for Charlotte?"

Cutter scoffed. "Don't we all?" He winked. "But I really work at the Woodlands Dude Ranch."

"You work for Wes? I'm his cousin."

"Small world. Have you seen Wes and Callie's little girl, Belle? She's so damn cute. Makes me almost want one of my own."

"Yeah, she's a cutie."

"Well, I'd better get downstairs. Can't leave my girl hanging. She needs her fix, if you know what I mean."

Cutter winked again, grating on Beau's nerves, right along with his outright claim of Charlotte being *his* girl.

"She's in her office."

"Yeah, I know where to find her. Gotta get in and get out. It's ladies' night around town."

"Really? Charlotte'll like that. Seems like she needs to get out a bit more."

Cutter smirked. "It'll be a cold day in hell before Charlotte gives up writing time for anything, much less a bar. Have a good one."

Beau watched him descend the stairs. He seemed like a nice enough guy, if Beau could ignore the fact that the asshole was looking forward to ladies' night without his *girl*. Beau's hands curled into fists. There was no way in hell he'd let Charlotte get hurt by him. He made another addition on his Things to Talk to Charlotte About list. Right under *security*, he mentally scribbled, *cheating assholes*. Then he shoved that sucker to the top of the list and went back to work, trying to ignore the fact that he felt protective of her in ways that he shouldn't.

A little more than an hour later, he headed downstairs to

make sure Charlotte was still alive, and to shower. The woman was really married to that keyboard. As he approached her door, he heard her giggle, and it brought a smile to his lips.

Until he realized he hadn't seen Cowboy leave.

When he stalked into his suite, he saw the handcuffs hanging on his headboard and made a mental note to cut the damn things off.

CHARLOTTE'S OFFICE WAS too dark. She had never noticed that before Mr. Hot and Serious came along, but after hours of writing and then catching up with Cutter, it was suddenly all she could think about. Maybe that was because her muse bank was empty and needed a refill. Beau had been less than generous with his shirtless self today. She'd seen him carrying supplies up from the workshop only *once*. They needed to talk about security, all right. She needed security cameras so she could get an eyeful of inspiration anytime she *needed* it.

Or *wanted* it.

Great. Now I sound as creepy as a stalker.

She stood up and stretched, telling herself she was merely looking for inspiration, but even thinking about Beau made her pulse quicken. She'd talked through a few potential scenes with Cutter, which usually put her in a fantastic mood, but she had absolutely no idea what should happen next in her book, and her mind kept revisiting that flash of sadness she'd seen in Beau's eyes. She'd been so sidetracked by it, she'd even written a similar scene into her story. Her editor was probably going to make her take it out, because erotic romance was driven by sex more than tender emotions, but she wasn't going to worry about that now. At least she was writing again. She was going to Port Hudson, New York, to meet with her editor at the end of the Mad Prix awards weekend, and she had promised to send the first third of the manuscript the week before. She'd already delayed the meeting once, and now she was down to the wire.

She needed to stop worrying about what she'd seen in Beau's eyes and get back to the ruse so she could get some inspiration and keep writing. But even the thought of toying with him felt wrong.

She walked by the light switch and swatted at it. "Stupid light." The lights came on, and she stilled. "Holy crap. You fixed it?" She flicked the switch on and off, delighted with the discovery. She couldn't stop smiling as she went into her kitchen to unpack the groceries. She and Cutter had come up with a system that didn't interrupt her writing process. He separated the frozen and refrigerated items into separate bags and put the bags in the fridge and freezer for her to sort later, and he left the pantry items in bags on the counter.

There were no bags on the counter. She opened the refrigerator and found the contents neatly unpacked and organized. Surprised, she opened the freezer and found more of the same. Cutter wasn't the kind of guy to forget to bring food *or* to go to the trouble of putting the groceries away. She'd met him when she was researching dude ranches for a book, and they'd hit it off right away. When he'd found out she sometimes went days eating nothing but eggs from the chickens, so she wouldn't have to give up writing time to drive down the mountain, he'd offered to bring her groceries. He was a lifesaver, like the big brother she'd never had.

Beau must have unpacked the groceries. She went upstairs

to find him.

She stood in the middle of the first floor and called out, "Beau?" Answered with silence, she weaved in and out of the study and dining room calling after him, and finally went into the main kitchen.

She ran her hands over the sparkling counters and along the front of the cabinet doors, several of which were no longer hanging from their hinges like loose teeth. *Beau's been a busy boy.* She never used the main kitchen. It was too big and reminded her that she was alone. She didn't really like cooking anyway. She'd much rather be writing than worrying about bake times and ingredients.

She looked through the glass terrace door and saw Beau standing by the stone barbecue, flipping a steak. Her heart rate kicked up, and she told herself to calm down as she drank in every inch of him, from his damp hair to the more relaxed look on his face and his kissable lips as he tipped his beer up to them. Boy had Cutter given her a hard time when she'd asked him to bring beer and wine coolers. *Just admit it; you're into the guy.* She'd denied it vehemently and would have sworn on it if he'd made her, because Cutter has been all over her for years about living such a solitary life. She liked her life, and she'd tried giving men a chance, but a relationship wasn't in the cards for her.

Beau glanced over. His chocolate eyes locked on hers, then slid down her body. Tingles skated up her limbs and skied down to her core, plowing to a scorching halt low in her belly. He lifted his chin. God, she loved that casual, manly acknowledgment. He pointed to the grill and lifted his brows. Then he pointed to her. She was aware of every move he made, but her eyes never left his. The sadness was still there, simmering beneath the I'm-just-a-serious-guy mask she now saw so clearly, and she wondered how she'd missed it before.

She must have been staring at him for too long, because he held his hand palm-up and turned away. She inhaled a ragged breath, a little nervous about having noticed so much about him. It was easier when she could just be her sassy masked self. But she'd never been able to ignore another person's pain, and Beau was doing all sorts of things that weren't on the repair list. She could no sooner ignore his emotions than she could ignore her need to write.

She stepped outside, and the brisk evening air swept over her midriff, reminding her she'd left her button-down shirt hanging over the chair in her office and was wearing only a black tank top and cutoffs. Okay, maybe Beau's heated gaze should have tipped her off, but she hadn't been thinking about clothes when she'd seen him through the door.

A heavenly aroma surrounded her. It had been so long since she'd smelled anything this delicious, hunger like she'd never felt before trampled the lust he'd stirred.

"I'll pay big bucks for a piece of whatever you're making," she said as she joined him by the barbecue.

The evening breeze picked up his fresh, musky scent, obliterating any thoughts of food. What did he do, bathe in Potent Male body wash? And why did he seem so much bigger every time she saw him?

She grabbed his beer from his hand and took a gulp.

He chuckled. "Would you like me to get you a beer from the fridge?"

"No, thanks. I hate beer. But my mouth was dry." He was watching her so intently her mouth went dry again. Oh man, what was wrong with her? She downed the rest of his beer without thinking.

"I see it's a love-hate relationship." His gaze lightened with the tease. He stepped closer, sucking up all the oxygen as he took the empty bottle from her.

"Sorry. I'll get you another."

He was already two steps ahead of her. As soon as he walked inside, she filled her lungs with air. *Yup.* He was definitely an oxygen thief.

He came out with two beers and set one on the table. "That's for the next time you're parched."

"Thanks."

"Why do you have beer in your fridge if you don't drink...?" He winced and said, "I'm an idiot. *Cutter.* Sorry. I should have thought about him. I'll replace his beers."

"No. They were meant for you."

The edge of his mouth twitched. "Really?"

"Yes. I normally drink wine coolers, but your beer actually tasted good. I think I'll have that beer after all." Pulling herself together, she grabbed the other bottle and took a sip. "*Ew.* This one doesn't taste so good." She swapped it with the one in his hand and took a sip of his. He was looking at her like she was ridiculous. "I swear this one tastes better."

"Seriously?" he asked.

She shrugged. "Who knows what goes on with chemicals, right? The kitchen looks amazing, by the way. You didn't have to do all that work. Thank you."

"It didn't take long." He gazed out over the lake, his expression serious again.

She peeked at the grill as if she knew something about cooking. Beside two steaks were tinfoil bundles with steam seeping out from where he'd cinched the sides together. "This smells delicious. Do you have enough to share?"

"Half's got your name on it."

"Thank you. I almost never cook, although I can make a mean pancake. If you're lucky, maybe I'll make you some one day. My motto is, if it can't be eaten raw, straight out of the wrapper, heated up on a hot plate, or microwaved, it's not worth the trouble."

"Pancakes," he said softly. "What do you do with the eggs you collect if you don't eat them?"

"I eat them. I just stick them in the microwave." Ignoring his disapproving look, she hiked herself up and sat on the railing.

"Whoa." He swept his arm behind her. "Careful. I tightened up those balusters, but they're not made for sitting on."

She looked at the railings, trying to ignore the heat of his hand blazing through the back of her shirt, and said, "Seems to be okay."

He shook his head and kept his arm around her, a firm barrier between life and death.

"Why are you so serious?" She patted the railing beside her. "Climb up."

"No thanks."

"Come on," she urged. "When's the last time you did something just for the sake of enjoying it?"

"I'm cooking because I enjoy it."

"I have a feeling you're cooking because you need to fuel your body to get through tomorrow."

He drank his beer without answering. She didn't like being shut out, even if they'd only just met.

"So, tell me…" She waited until he looked at her. When she had his attention, she asked, "Why did your relatives send you out here instead of just wrangling Rex or one of your other cousins who live in Colorado to help me out? If they wanted to pay for the repairs so badly, they could have even hired a local handyman."

"Probably because it's not about *paying*. They care about you, Charlotte, and they want to make sure the job is done right. Rex runs a ranch; he's not a builder. And my other cousins in the area aren't either. This is what I do for a living. Also, my cousins all have families and can't put in the time here."

"You don't?"

"I have a family, but not one of my own. No wife and kids."

"Why not?"

He sipped his beer, clearly not interested in answering.

"Come on," she urged. "No long-term girlfriend? No pretty little filly hoping for a ring?"

He looked at her with the same serious expression. "You ask a lot of questions."

She sipped her beer, and his hand pressed more firmly against her back. "Afraid I'll fall?"

He didn't answer, but his lips tipped up in another almost-smile.

She wrapped her fingers around his arm, and his muscles flexed against her palm. She couldn't resist trying to earn a real smile. "If I fall, I'm taking you with me."

"Think you're strong enough to take me with you?"

"Think you're strong enough to keep me from doing it?" she challenged.

He drank his beer, staring out at the setting sun, his hand still firmly in place.

Well, there was one way to get his attention. A little flirtation might even get him to open up. If nothing else, she'd get more fodder for her story. She ran her fingers lightly over his muscles, enjoying the darkening of his eyes so much, she trailed her fingers along his shoulder and neck, all the way to his jaw. His scruff was short and remarkably soft, in direct contrast to his hard jaw beneath it.

"Charlotte..."

His warning was clear, but she didn't care. "What? Are you afraid of a little human contact?" She liked the way he looked at her, like she was someone who could get under his skin. But she hated the way he quickly swept it under the carpet, his expression turning to granite.

"Hardly," he ground out. "Are there any more cowboys dropping by that I should know about?"

"Cowboys?"

He gave her a slant-eyed stare. "Mountain men?"

"Cutter?" Laughter burst from her lips, and she lost her balance. "Beau!" She clung to his arms as he hauled her off the rail.

"I've got you," he said, holding her against him tightly as he searched her eyes. "You okay?"

"Yes," came out breathless. "Thanks."

He held her a beat longer. Long enough for her to feel the heat of his gaze burrowing into her and to think about the way his thumb was moving in a slow rhythm on her arm. It felt like something had shifted, like maybe he was feeling this new connection, too.

He released her abruptly and stepped over to the grill.

Had she imagined the intimate way he'd touched her? The way he'd looked at her? Because his eyes were now trained on the steaks. He grabbed two plates she hadn't noticed earlier and moved the tinfoil bundles away from the flames. His jaw was clenched again. It must hurt to carry around that much tension. She watched as he piled steaks, vegetables, and sliced potatoes onto the plates, all flecked with spices. It smelled so scrumptious she might have moaned.

He handed her a plate, shoved a hand into the pocket of his cargo pants, and withdrew a fork and knife for each of them. "We should talk about security."

"Security?" She set her plate on the table, and he took the seat across from her. He was a master at changing subjects, but how could he ignore the heat between them?

"Yes. I'm pretty sure your boyfriend wouldn't appreciate you traipsing around in your panties or leaving all the doors unlocked. And that's another thing. I should be aware if you've got more guys coming up, so I know who to expect and who I need to worry about." He stabbed his fork into the steak and cut off a hunk, then shoved it in his mouth.

"Boyfriend?"

"Grocery boy, whatever." He stabbed another piece of meat.

She stifled a laugh. "Cutter is one of my closest friends."

Beau arched a brow, his expression still serious. "Do you try to sleep with all the guys who work for you?"

Her jaw dropped open. "First of all, I don't sleep with Cutter, and second of all, what the hell?" *Hell* came out sounding equally amused and irritated.

"I'm just saying that I should be aware if there are going to be men coming in and out of this place, so I don't accidentally kill one." He speared another hunk of meat.

"Oh, so now you're killing my *fictional* boyfriends? Because that's the only type I have. I'll try to keep them in line."

He gave her a deadpan look.

"You need to lighten up," she said, pointing her fork at him.

"Maybe if you were a little less *light*, you'd see the trouble with traipsing around in your underwear."

She liked his overly protective nature, even if it was confusing, given that he kept pulling away from her. It had been a long time since anyone had worried about her like that.

She ate a piece of steak, closing her eyes and savoring the flavor as it melted in her mouth and exploded over her taste buds with near-orgasmic perfection. "Mm."

"And doing *that*." He pushed to his feet and sucked down his beer.

Her eyes flew open. "What?"

He waved his beer at her. "That whole close-your-eyes-make-those-noises thing."

"Oh," she said as innocently as she could muster. "You mean this?" She slowly placed a piece of meat on her tongue, closed her eyes, and made the most sensual, erotic sounds she could.

"*Fuuuck.*" He drew the word out so long she had to suppress a giggle.

She made what she hoped was a dramatic, seductive show of licking her lips as she went to him. This was research at its best. His jaw tensed as she stepped closer and dragged her finger down the front of his shirt. She liked doing that to him. Not only did his body tense up, but it warmed beneath her fingers, and his eyes took on a greediness that she had a hard time looking away from.

"You mean *that*? Because I like the way it makes you sweat." She brushed against him like a cat in heat, getting lost in the intensity of his stare and the heaviness of his breathing. "I like seeing you grind your teeth and feeling your body get all revved up, like a champagne bottle ready to explode."

She lifted his beer from his hand and took a long, slow drink before setting it beside the grill. Feeling even bolder, she touched the center of his strong chin and sighed. "It's a shame you refuse to uncork all that energy, because I can only imagine the sheer power and raw passion behind all those corded muscles."

She sauntered away.

She hadn't taken two steps before Beau grabbed her, hauling her into his arms and smothering her lips with his, giving her no time to think. His tongue snaked into her mouth. He tasted of lust, fire, and the unique flavor of *Beau*. His hand pressed against her back, their bodies pulsing and grinding. His other hand pushed into her hair, and he cupped the back of her head as he intensified the kiss. She was right there with him, grasping his shoulders, his head, his neck, wanting to touch all of him at once. She was his willing captive as he explored her mouth and shifted his weight, wedging his leg between hers. She stumbled back into something unforgiving. *The railing.* He'd buffered the blow with his hand on her back, and *Lord.* That he could think about protecting her when he was turning her brain to mush and her body to liquid heat was even more of a turn-on. He kissed her harder, more demanding. This wasn't the kiss of a lover. This kiss had *grit* and *fervor*. Gone was the ruse of research, replaced with reckless desire, as Beau reclaimed the upper hand, kissing her breathless. It wasn't enough. When he eased his efforts, she amped up hers, not ready for their connection to end. She wanted his grit, his fervor, his *passion*, but he tore his mouth away, leaving her noodle-legged and fuzzy-brained.

An arrogant smile formed on his lips as he picked up his beer and said, "That loose enough for you, shortcake?"

Chapter Five

BEAU WOKE WITH the sun the next morning, hot, bothered, and feeling guilty as hell after another fitful night's sleep filled with erotic fantasies of Charlotte and nightmares of Duncan Raz. In his dreams, he'd stripped off Charlotte's clothes and quickly lost himself in her sweet, sexy sassiness. Until Duncan appeared like a villain in black, a stark reminder that the last person to deserve someone like Charlotte was Beau. He took a cold shower and headed down the hall for coffee. The lights were on in Charlotte's office, and he heard her fingers flying across the keyboard.

"You're up early," he said as he came to her side. Several newly empty Twix wrappers had joined the other chaos on her desk.

She held up one finger, then finished what she was writing and saved her work before tipping her face up sleepily. Dark crescents underscored her half-closed eyes, and she was wearing the same slinky outfit she'd had on last night. "Hi."

"Have you been writing all night?" After their kisses, which had left him hard as stone, she'd run inside, claiming she had to write, leaving him hot, bothered, and alone with his tangled thoughts. He'd wrapped up her dinner and put it in her fridge, and then he'd pounded out his frustrations by handling a few more repairs. She was still writing when he'd turned in just before midnight.

"Mm-hm." She reached for a bottle of water.

"Wouldn't your mind be fresher if you got some rest?"

She shrugged as she drank, her eyelids fluttering closed. They blinked open as if she were startled. "I've got to write when my muse speaks." She yawned and said, "I should get the eggs."

He put a hand on her shoulder, and her soft, warm skin hit a note of familiarity. "I was heading out for a walk anyway. I've got it. You need to rest."

"Rest is for the weak," she said halfheartedly. "Do you walk every morning?"

"When I can. Your property is too gorgeous not to enjoy."

She glanced out the window. "Yeah, I guess. Thanks for getting the eggs. There's a basket under the sink in my kitchen."

She *guessed*? He had a feeling she'd never gone too far past the chicken coop.

As he headed for the door, she said, "Hey, can you grab me a protein bar while you're in there?"

"You shouldn't put that processed crap in your body. How about I make you an omelet when I get back inside?"

She held up one finger, yawning as she set her water bottle on the desk. "You don't have to go to that trouble. My body thrives on processed crap."

He gritted his teeth. "Well, not today it doesn't. I'm making you a real breakfast."

She was stubborn as sin and so ridiculously comfortable with short-changing herself. He wanted to take care of her as she should be taking care of herself. Okay, maybe not in the same way, but that's how he rationalized the burgeoning, unfamiliar feelings messing with his head as he made coffee and then headed out for his morning walk.

Beau drank his coffee as he walked around the lake. He couldn't imagine a more beautiful location, and he had no idea how Charlotte resisted the call of nature. And what was she doing to herself, pulling an all-nighter? For all he knew, she did it often, out here alone with no one to remind her that there was a world outside her office and that her health mattered.

He set his empty mug on the front porch and went to collect the eggs, thinking about following Charlotte into the woods the previous day. He felt himself grinning, baffled by the way she made him *feel*. Not just the way she turned him on, because she was the sexiest woman he'd ever met, in a chaotic, ten-directions-at-once kind of way. But it had been a long damn time since he'd wanted to protect anyone outside his family, and he liked it that way. No ties meant no chances for heartbreak, or for hurting others.

When he reached the bushes where he'd first had her in his arms, his body flooded with heat. *Jesus. She's not even here and she turns me on.*

He pushed through the bushes, glad to see her chickens pecking around inside the pen. Bandit would have had a field day chasing chickens. *Chickendales.* Charlotte's voice rang through his mind as he collected the eggs and cleaned out the nesting boxes. Who named their chickens after actors and male dancers?

The brown chicken stepped into the coop and stared at Beau.

"Don't look at me like that. You're only a chicken," he said to Duncan, who scampered back into the pen. He'd have to find another name for the damn thing. Either that, or Duncan would become *dinner*. His gut twisted with the memory of Charlotte's frantic expression and the fear in her beautiful eyes when she'd realized the chickens had gotten loose. He had a feeling she'd love them even if they didn't provide eggs.

He stood outside the pen and glared at Duncan. "You're one lucky bird that that incredible woman loves you."

When he got back to the inn, he washed the eggs and his mug, then stopped in Charlotte's office to see what she liked in her omelets. She was fast asleep at her desk, her head resting on her outstretched arm beside her keyboard.

He crouched beside her and said, "Charlotte?" She didn't flinch. "Char?"

Aw hell. He scooped her into his arms, and she nuzzled against him, resting her cheek against his chest. She smelled sweetly feminine and felt good and right in his arms. Like she was made for the cradle his body created.

Why the hell was he noticing that? *I'm here to work, not to play research games.*

He carried her into her suite, struck again by how wrong her furnishings were, all bland creams and dark browns. The heavy curtains looked like all the others throughout the inn, cheerless and uninteresting. Charlotte was anything but bland, cheerless, or uninteresting.

He slowed at the threshold to her bedroom, feeling as though he were looking at the very heart of her. Deep-piled white throw rugs covered the old hardwood floors. An ornate canopy bed, with only half the frame erected, was layered in fluffy white and pink blankets. A fancy white and gold chest sat at the foot of the bed, the price tag hanging from the latch like a forgotten child. A matching dresser decorated the far wall, and beside it, a dark mirror rested against the side, looking out of place among the lighter hues. Two pink armchairs and a white sofa with frilly pillows created a nook by a stone fireplace. Several colored notebooks lay on the floor beside an unopened box of holiday lights, and in the corner of the room was a pile of unsheathed pillow forms. Two sets of French doors sat wide open to the yard. A single white sheer hung on one of the doors, blowing in the breeze.

He carried Charlotte to the bed, trying to calm the frustration inside him. How could she leave her bedroom doors wide open for anyone to walk in? Not to mention animals. He made a mental note to search every inch of her room to insure there were no critters hanging around.

He pulled back the blankets and found a romance novel and a leather journal on the sheets. He set them beside a lamp with no shade on a cardboard box she was using as a nightstand, and then he gently laid her on the sheets.

"Roman," she whispered, and curled up on her side.

Who the fuck is Roman? He glared at her despite the fact that she was fast asleep and wondered how many *non-boyfriend* boyfriends she had.

He covered her with a blanket and she sighed, snuggling in deeper. She looked peaceful beneath her pretty blankets. He caught himself staring and ground his teeth so hard they just might crack. He quietly closed the French doors. The lock was broken on one of them. *Great.* He locked the other door, nearly tripping over packages of curtains and pillow shams and a single curtain rod. *Job number two.*

He searched her bedroom for unwanted visitors and then glanced at Charlotte, noticing that the cardboard box beside the bed was actually a box containing a crystal chandelier. Upon closer inspection, he realized it had decorative *pink* crystals.

Christ. It's like a half-ass attempt at a fairy-tale bedroom.

He added dead bolts to the list of things he needed to pick up in town and went to fetch his tools.

CHARLOTTE BOLTED OUT of bed, wondering how the heck she'd gotten to her bedroom. She checked the time on her phone—*4:08.* Panic spread through her like wildfire at the missed hours of writing. She rushed through a shower, pulled on a pair of shorts and a tank top, and as she grabbed a sweater from her drawer, she realized her French doors were closed, and they had *curtains.* She looked around the room, taking in the string of holiday lights strung around the fireplace and the beautiful canopy on her bed! *Beau...*

She ran her fingers over the pretty pink and white canopy that had been sitting in a box forever. She'd started putting up the canopy frame when she'd first moved in years ago but had never gotten around to finishing. Like the curtains, she hadn't thought about them in ages. She pulled on her cardigan, realizing she still had absolutely no recollection of going to bed, and she connected the dots right back to surly, burly Beau.

She mulled over how warm, cozy, *and* nervous that made her feel as she went to get coffee. What had he thought about when she was in his arms, when he saw her bedroom? Did he only see her room through his contractor eyes, or did he stand beside her bed, looking at her as a man would a woman? Her lips tingled with the memories of their kisses. Was he thinking about them, too? Had he used her image to satisfy his unsated desires last night?

Okay, Char. Calm the heck down. He carried you to bed. No big deal.

She found a note from Beau beside the coffee machine. His handwriting was bold and capped, kind of like him. *Your chickens were all accounted for this morning. I wrapped up last night's dinner and put it in the fridge. You should lock your bedroom doors. Beau.*

"You're bossy even when you're not around," she mused.

She tugged open the fridge and found new eggs in the egg bowl beside last night's dinner. Before Beau arrived, she wasn't sure how she'd feel having someone else around all the time, but she liked being around him. He was intriguing, with his seriousness and hot-flash-inducing glances. He'd definitely helped with her writer's block, although it probably wasn't smart to have made her hero a contractor with a serious chip on his shoulder. If he ever read the book, he'd *know* he was her inspiration. The trouble was, Beau had also stirred emotions she'd safely locked away for a very long time, and she wasn't sure how to handle them.

After making coffee, she grabbed a protein bar and a Twix and went into her office. She tapped her keyboard, bringing her monitor to life. Her manuscript was still open on the screen, and another wave of panic engulfed her. Did he read it? Their kisses had made it into her story, followed by a detailed fantasy in her heroine's head. It had taken her two hours to get their kisses right, but *wow*. Every blazing second was worth reliving. Each time she'd revised the scene, she'd remembered something new—his scent, the way his whiskers had scratched the edges of her mouth, the feel of his fingers pressing into her skin, and the hard press of his arousal against her belly, hips, and thighs as he ground against her. She'd also recalled the little things she hadn't realized she'd noticed, like the heady noises of appreciation he'd made, the way his big hands had engulfed every spot they'd touched, and the devastating look in his eyes afterward. He'd acted cocky as hell, but she'd seen so much more in those serious eyes. She'd been unable to speak, had needed to pick it apart to try to understand it. She still didn't know exactly what she'd seen, but one thing was for sure. Beau Braden was hiding something in those heat-filled, sad-rimmed eyes, and she wanted to know what it was.

She grabbed her laptop and coffee and headed upstairs to find out. Music drifted down from the second floor. As she climbed the steps, she thought about how much she loved everything about the inn, from the sweeping staircases to the attention to detail that had been put into the building of it. Even though she rarely left her wing, when she did, she was surrounded by happy memories of her parents and grandparents. The only family she'd ever had.

Paint fumes and the song "Drunk on Your Love" sailed into the hall from the suite where Beau was working. She peeked into the room and saw him standing on the ladder, shirtless and beyond sexy, a toolbelt hanging low on his swaying hips. *Ha! Burly Beau likes to dance!*

She snuck in and sat against the wall on the opposite side of the room. *Inspiration Station.* She opened her laptop as quietly as she could and pulled up her manuscript. As he sang about touch and fire in her eyes—*yes,* she pretended he was singing *to her* with his raspy voice that beckoned all the emotions she'd felt last night—she wondered if *he* had woken up drunk on *her* love. Or rather, *lust.* Her stomach flip-flopped. She'd been flat-out drunk on him last night. It would be nice knowing she hadn't been alone in that feeling, but he was not an easy-to-read guy, and she wasn't looking for a man in her life anyway, so it didn't really matter if he was drunk on her, or just plain horny.

Everything *other than* last night's kisses had been about research. Pure, simple motivation. *That's my story, and I'm sticking with it.*

The song ended, and she held her breath, hoping he wouldn't turn around just yet. A scene was forming in her mind, and she wanted to flesh it out before she lost the thread. It was strange for her to come up with ideas around him, much less be able to bring them to life in the same room. She always wrote alone, and she preferred it that way. Or at least she always thought she had.

"Eyes on You," one of her favorite songs, came on the radio.

She pressed her lips together to keep from accidentally singing as Beau dipped his brush in the paint can that was resting on the ladder shelf. She was shocked that he knew every word to the song. His singing and dancing drove the rest of her scene. This was her favorite part of the process, when an idea sparked images so vibrant she became a part of them. Soon she was lost in her characters' world. She laughed when they did, warmed as they touched each other, heard the hero's deep voice and felt the fluttering in her heroine's chest just as she did.

Fingers snapped in front of her face, jolting her from her reverie.

Beau crossed his arms, glaring down at her. "Good *morning*, Sleeping Beauty," he said sarcastically. "How long have you been sitting there?"

She shrugged and couldn't resist doing a little fishing. "How long did you watch me sleep this morning?"

His jaw clenched.

She gasped, and that tummy flutter went full force again. "You *did* watch me sleep!" She saved her work and set her laptop down, then popped up to her feet.

"I never said that," he growled. He strode away and moved the ladder to another section of the wall.

She followed him. "You never said you didn't."

He set the paint can on the shelf and climbed the ladder. "Did you get some food?" he asked, ignoring her statement as he dipped the brush in the can.

"Yup. Thanks for collecting the eggs. And for hanging my curtains and my canopy. Oh! And the lights around the fireplace. That was really nice of you, although I have no idea how I slept through it all." She pulled the protein bar from her back pocket, tore it open, and took a bite. "Wait. I got distracted from your Peeping-Tom habit."

He continued painting. "Says the girl who sleeps with her doors wide open for all to see. How do you know you don't have a neighbor who watches you at night?"

"Because I own hundreds of acres. I have no neighbors."

He looked at her out of the corner of his eye. "You know what I mean. It's not safe. You need a watch dog. You could have all sorts of creatures in this place. Raccoons, squirrels. You're lucky a bear hasn't found you for breakfast."

"Who am I? Goldilocks?"

"I bet Goldilocks closes her doors."

"What is with you? You're not my father."

He dipped the paintbrush, his jaw rigid again. "How'd you end up out here all alone, anyway?"

"I assumed Hal or Josh filled you in on my life." Charlotte didn't mind talking about her personal life, but obviously Beau minded talking about his, and that gave her an idea. "What was that all about yesterday?"

"You really do need to get out more if you don't recognize a kiss as a kiss."

"Ha. Ha. Not *that*." She wanted to talk about the kiss, but not yet. "What happened at the chicken coop? You froze."

"I didn't freeze," he said tightly.

"You definitely froze." She leaned against the wall, watching his muscles flex as he carefully painted the trim, his jaw working double time. She'd hit a nerve. "I'll share if you share," she said hopefully.

He waggled his brows. "Like Show and Tell?"

"Sort of. I'll reveal some of my story if you share some of yours. Deal?"

He didn't respond, but she had a feeling he was thinking about it, so she pressed on. "I came here to grieve after losing my grandfather. He was the last of my family members, and I've been here ever since."

He stopped painting and looked at her empathetically. "I'm sorry. I didn't know that. I knew you inherited the inn, but I didn't realize you had no family."

"It's okay. I have friends. Well, besides Cutter, most of them don't live around here. But I have my LWW sisters. We're scattered all over now, but we're still close."

"What is that? Some sort of sorority?"

"Sort of. It's a group of friends from college. We all loved to write, so we rented a house together. One night after too many shots we decided it wasn't cool that sororities had names and we didn't. We each had dreams of writing professionally in one form or another, and we were pretty sure we wouldn't want to call ourselves the Bad Bitches Who Write when we were sixty years old, so we went with Ladies Who Write. Three of my friends founded LWW Enterprises. You might have heard of them. They do films, publishing, real estate, and a bunch of other things. I'm published under their erotic romance imprint." And no, she didn't get any special favors by being an LWW girl. Her editor was not pleased with her at the moment, due to her missing her first deadline.

"You realized your dream. That's cool, and impressive."

"Well, haven't you?" She took a bite of her protein bar, watching his face grow serious again. Josh and Hal Braden had told her that he was incredibly successful, and they'd warned her that it might take a while before he'd have time to come out and do the repairs on the inn. She'd been so grateful that they were making arrangements for the repairs to be tended to, she hadn't minded the delay. Although she had been curious about why they'd suggested Beau do the work when he lived so far away.

"Sure."

She groaned. "Come on, Beau! Give me more than that. Why did you agree to come out here? It's a heck of a long trip just to do some handyman work."

"Because my relatives asked me to. I travel a lot, and I like it that way." He climbed down, picked up the paint can, and moved the ladder farther down the wall.

"Why?"

"Because the world is too big to hole up in one place forever." He climbed the ladder and began painting again.

"Don't you ever want a family of your own?"

He scoffed. "Do you? I might travel a lot, but your life seems even more solitary than mine."

"I did, once upon a time," she admitted, and his eyes softened. "I grew up with parents who were madly in love. My father was always hugging and kissing my mom, whispering things. I used to want to know all their secrets, because whatever he whispered always made her happy. And my grandparents were the same way. But I lost my grandmother when I was twelve. I lost my parents when I was a senior in high school, and then it was just me and my grandfather. So, yes. I used to dream of finding Mr. Right and having a beautiful family. But then I started dating in college, and it wasn't anything like what I imagined. Everyone said it would get better, but the college-dating realm just sucked for me. Guys didn't want to connect. They wanted to fuck."

"Not all guys," he said, eyes trained on her.

"Well, the ones I went out with."

"So you gave up and became the girl who lives alone at the inn?"

She mulled over his question as she finished her protein bar. "When I came out here to grieve, I started writing. It wasn't a plan to stay here forever. It just happened." She pulled the Twix from her front pocket.

"Protein bars and Twix? It's a wonder how you make it through the day."

"A girl's gotta have her chocolate fix." She broke it in two and held half out for him. "You should try it. I bet it makes you smile."

"Chocolate *fix*," he said under his breath, and smiled.

That grin gave him a whole different look: rugged and mischievous instead of rugged and stern. She liked it.

"Thanks, shortcake." His fingers brushed over hers as he took the candy, lingering long enough for their eyes to connect, sparks to ignite, and for his expression to turn tense again.

As they ate the candy, she asked, "What about you?"

"I eat real food," he said, dodging the question.

"I'm going to get this out of you one way or another, so you might as well just give me something. Make it up if you have to. Just stop *backstory blocking* me."

He began painting again, the amusement she'd earned lingering on his very kissable lips.

"Beau! You are so frustrating."

"You're kind of cute when you're frustrated. I'm thinking about being even more frustrating."

She rolled her eyes. "*Kind of?* You sure kissed me like I was more than *kind of* anything."

"Damn, girl. You're either on a mission or not interested. There is no in between with you, is there?"

"I don't even know what that means. Stop changing the subject. What kind of guy were *you* in college?"

His serious expression returned. "Not the kind that you went out with."

Interesting. She stared up at him, waiting for more, but he had the strong, silent thing down pat. "So...?"

"I had a girlfriend through college. And now I don't. Okay?" The pain in his voice was inescapable.

Her heartstrings got a firm tug with that confession. Beau had to be at least thirty years old, and he was still pining for a college girlfriend? She wondered if the breakup was recent. "So, you loved and lost, and now you're not the dating kind?"

He finished painting the trim without answering, and she worried he might shut down completely. When he climbed down the ladder, she got a good look at his face, and the sadness she saw made her stomach hurt.

"Beau, I'm sorry—"

"Don't be," he interrupted. "You nailed it. I loved and lost, and I'm definitely *not* the dating kind."

Chapter Six

BEAU WAS RELIEVED when Charlotte stopped her inquisition and went back to writing, but when she returned to her office, she took the energy in the room with her. The music felt flat and eventually became white noise to the ghosts in his head. For the first time in years he actually *wanted* to connect with a woman beyond satisfying a sexual urge. That rattled him. It should have scared the hell out of him, but Charlotte was captivating in a complicated way, which for some strange reason made her even more fascinating. She had opened up to him, and he felt bad about shutting her down. As he worked through the afternoon, he couldn't stop thinking about the way she'd said he *backstory blocked* her. *Backstory blocked?* She really did live in a writer's world. Avoidance was his go-to tactic, but that wasn't the man he wanted to be around her. He didn't know why, and he didn't really care about the reasons. All he knew was that it felt wrong to cast darkness over her bright light, and he wanted to fix it.

He finished up for the day, stripped as the shower heated up, then stepped beneath the warm spray. His chin fell to his chest, and he let the warm water loosen the muscles in his back and neck. He heard the faint ringing of his cell phone in the bedroom. Zev had texted him earlier with the message, *Hey, bro. Jilly's worried about us. When will they back off?* Zev had been with Beau at the bar the night Tory was killed. Two days later Zev had broken up with his long-time girlfriend, Carly Dylan, who also happened to be Tory's best friend. He'd quit college and had taken off for the start of what he claimed was an *adventurous lifestyle*, chasing one treasure after the next. Beau knew better. Even though Beau spent months at a time in Pleasant Hill, he was never there this time of year. They were both running from that night. But ghosts were tricky. They hovered in the eyes of the living and the hearts of the guilty.

The bathroom door opened, jerking him from his thoughts.

"Oh my God, tell me about it," Charlotte said.

Beau pulled open the shower door wide enough to stick his head out, shocked to see her holding up her finger, indicating she needed a minute, as she listened to whoever was on the other end of *his* cell phone.

"I know." She wrote her name on the steam in the mirror as she said, "He's a little serious, but I'll break him of that. How's Aiyla?"

Aiyla was Beau's cousin Ty's wife. They'd both competed in the Mad Prix last year, and shortly after, Aiyla had been diagnosed with bone cancer and had undergone a partial leg amputation. Beau had renovated a house for them in Peaceful Harbor, where they now lived. But none of that explained why the sexy brunette was talking on *his* phone in *his* bathroom.

Charlotte listened for another second and drew a heart around her name on the mirror. "Good. Hug her for me. Hold on a sec. I'll give you to Beau."

She lowered the phone and said, "I found the key to the handcuffs! They were in my bathroom medicine cabinet. I have no idea how they got there, but at least they're off your headboard." She lifted the hem of her shirt, showing him the handcuffs hanging from a belt loop on her cutoffs. "Your phone rang when I was unhooking them, and I saw Ty's name. I hope you don't mind that I answered it."

"Don't any of the locks in this place work?" he asked as he took the phone.

Her eyes swept over the shower doors. "Oh, are you shy? Sorry. But don't worry. I can't really see anything through the frosted doors. Just a general outline." She tilted her head and squinted. "Um, maybe *shapes*, too."

"Jesus, shortcake. Get out of here before I pull your pretty little ass in here with me."

She hollered as she left the bathroom, "Hear that, Ty? He's already loosening up!"

"Shortcake?" Ty said as Beau put the phone to his ear.

"Bro, that woman is nuts. Like the good kind that you can't ignore," he said into the phone, and noticed he was smiling again. "She either makes me grit my teeth or smile. There is *no* middle ground."

"Let me get this straight. You've been there for what? A day or two, and you've already got her handcuffed to your bed?"

"*No*. She had a…Hell, Ty, you *know* her." Ty and Aiyla had spent time with Charlotte at last year's awards ceremony. "Why didn't you warn me about her sex dolls and her inability to lock doors? The woman has no sense of security, and I swear when she's not writing, her mind moves in ten directions at once."

"That's Char. She's a trip."

"She's a trip, all right. Did you know she was alone up here? That she has no family at all?"

"Yeah, I know," Ty said compassionately. "I'm glad you're

there with her for a little while. Will you be around for the awards ceremony?"

"I'll be here. I leave the following Thursday. Listen, I'm in the shower…"

"So I heard." Ty chuckled. "I also heard that you were planning on taking the offer for that reality show in L.A. I'm going to miss you, man. I was just calling to see if you could recommend someone to build a garage with a darkroom above it for us."

He'd really like to be the one to do the work, but that would take time he didn't have. "Sure. I'll hook you up with one of my buddies."

"Great. One more favor. Aiyla is flying out to meet me at the finish line. If you—"

"Say no more. I'll watch out for her. How's she getting here from the airport? You know I'd be happy to pick her up. Just give me a time and flight number."

"It's okay. She's thinking about connecting with a few of the other supporters and coming in as a group. She wanted to come out earlier, but my wife's calendar is busier than the president's. I'd really appreciate it if you could be there when she arrives at the inn, to make sure she's okay."

"You've got it, buddy." Beau knew how much Ty worried about her, despite the fact that Aiyla was one hell of a strong woman. After learning Charlotte was truly alone, Beau put her right up there at the top of the list of strong women he knew. "Listen, I've got to get out of this shower and buy some damn locks."

"Why? Afraid you don't measure up to a blow-up doll?"

Beau chuckled. "Catch you later, asshole."

As he toweled off, he saw Charlotte's name written in the

steam on the mirror, and just like that he was grinning again. He shouldn't be. He should be bothered that she'd come into his room unannounced, answered his phone, and pranced right into the bathroom. But that was Charlotte, and for whatever reason, he wanted to discover even more of her quirks.

CHARLOTTE OPENED ANOTHER Twix bar as she typed a text to her friend and LWW sister Aubrey Stewart. *I think I just committed a man faux pas.* She pressed send and opened another candy bar. Aubrey lived in Port Hudson, New York, Charlotte's hometown, and she ran the media division of LWW Enterprises, the company she'd founded with two of their LWW sisters, Presley Cabot and Libby Warren. Presley headed up the publishing department, and Libby ran the philanthropic efforts of what had become a multimillion-dollar empire. Charlotte loved all of her LWW sisters, of which there were many, but she was closest to Aubrey.

As usual, Aubrey responded right away, and Charlotte read her message. *With…? I'm assuming the man with the enormous ladder? Don't worry. Men don't notice mistakes.*

She had told Aubrey about using Beau for writing inspiration, but she hadn't yet told her about their steamy kisses. Her stomach tumbled as she typed her reply. *I walked in when he was taking a shower. I wasn't thinking! I was on the phone (his phone) with his cousin and just walked right in.* She sent the text, then quickly sent another that said, *GINORMOUS DISTRACTION.*

Her phone rang two seconds later, and Aubrey's name ap-

64

peared on the screen.

"Hey," Charlotte said in a hushed whisper.

"How ginormous? Are we talking garden-snake variety or python?"

"Like, all-I-can-think-about ginormous. It could have just looked that way because of the frosted shower doors, but..." She bit into the Twix bar.

"Where's the faux pas? Seeing his distraction? And why were you on *his* phone and not in the shower *with* him?"

"Oh my God. Slow down with the shower-with-him thing. I know his cousin and saw his name on the phone, so I picked it up. But *focus*, Aubrey, please! How am I going to look at him without thinking about *that*?"

"First, why are you whispering? You live in a mansion and he'd have to be right there to hear you. And second, I swear we should have forced you to have a sex life in college."

"Just tell me what to do because I have another problem I need advice on."

"Okay, for the python issue, just pretend he's one of your characters. You think about fictional men's body parts every day. Tell yourself he's not real."

"Um...I sort of can't do that."

Aubrey squealed. "Did my sweet sister screw the hot contractor? I'm so proud of you!"

"No! We kissed." She stole a glance at the door.

"Okay, good. That's a start."

"Aubrey!"

Aubrey laughed. "I can't help it. I don't want you to get hurt, but if you both want to fool around and you agree that it's only temporary, then why not have some fun? As long as you can keep your heart out of it, that is." She paused and then said,

"Actually, maybe that's not a great idea. Beyond research for your books and writing fiction, you have no hands-on experience with casual sex."

Charlotte's heart took a nosedive. She didn't want casual sex. Was that all it would be?

"Anyway, this is not a big deal. When you look at him, think of the kiss, not the cock."

"Kiss, not cock. Got it. That might work." She repeated it in her head. *Kiss, not cock, kiss, not cock.*

"I bet you'll get a great scene out of this. Talk about inspiration."

"You have no idea how great. I have an incredible scene, but I still have one thing to work out." She wanted to get a sense of what it felt like to have someone Beau's size lying on top of her, and while the dolls usually gave her enough of an idea to play with, this time they fell short. *In more ways than one.*

"Is that your other issue?"

"No. I just…I think I *like* him, and you know real men never measure up to the fictional men I create. Even if we did get together, he'd eventually be jealous of my writing schedule. It's a recipe for disaster."

"Uh-huh. How long are you going to live behind that farce?"

"Experience tells me it's not a farce."

"*Limited* experience, which really qualifies as more of a *whiff* of experience and shouldn't be the basis for anything real. I swear I'm going to send Becca down there to teach you a thing or two." Becca Nunnally, Aubrey's ever-efficient assistant, who also handled Charlotte's fan email and social media, was a fellow Boyer University graduate and a walking sexpot with a fierce attitude. From what Aubrey told Charlotte, beautiful, perkyboobed Becca turned down almost every guy who asked her out, but the ones she did go out with, she never saw twice.

"God you're a pain. Keep Becca there. I think she's got way more of a sex life than she lets on. I bet she's got men shackled in her basement. *Real men*, not blow-up dolls."

"Then you two should get along just fine."

Charlotte rolled her eyes even though Aubrey couldn't see her. "I'm *not* into that stuff. Focus, Aubrey. Let's say I do want to take things further with Beau." She *so* did, especially since he said he wasn't like the guys she'd gone out with in college. "As you've so kindly pointed out, I don't have much experience in the real-life-man department."

"That's hardly a problem, Char. You'll figure it out. You're the queen of steamy scenes. Just bring it into real life."

Charlotte glanced out the window. "When I'm doing research, it's easy to flirt, but it doesn't last. I lose my train of thought around him. You don't understand how compelling he is. He's sort of broody, but then he gets this little smile that makes my stomach flip, and I turn into a bumbling idiot. After we kissed, I was so nervous I basically ran away."

"Wow. You're really affected by this guy. You ran away? Charlotte Sterling, have I not taught you anything? For God's sake, your heroines would never run from a man. They'd tie him up, whip him good, and make him submit."

"Yeah, but that's not *me*." Although when she was unlocking the handcuffs from his bed, she couldn't stop imagining him lying beneath her, arms shackled, while she drove him out of his mind.

"I wish I were there to check him out and make sure he's not a prick. I want you to finally have a sex life, but I don't want you to get hurt. Especially since you've got this crazy notion that true love should be like a fairy tale. It's going to be hard enough for you to accept that even great guys can be assholes. I think it comes with the penis."

"He's not an asshole," she said protectively.

"Says the girl asking for advice about men. He must *really* be something special, because I've never been able to get you to see Cutter as anything more than a friend, and that is one smoking-hot, sweet-enough-to-eat cowboy—and I do mean gobble down all eight inches of the man. The way I see it, you have two choices. You can run away every time things heat up, or you can pull up your big-girl panties, stand as strong as I know you are, and see where it goes."

Charlotte wanted to do that more than anything. But she was nervous.

"Who knows, Char. You might enjoy letting him pull those big-girl panties down."

"I'm pretty sure I will. *Would!* Would."

Aubrey cracked up.

"But I think he's hiding something."

"You just told me he's not a jerk!" Aubrey snapped. "See? You need me there."

"Not that kind of *something*. He doesn't say much, but in his silence, I hear…something sad. Maybe it's just loneliness. I don't know. But something is there that he's not sharing, and I don't feel like it's a jerky thing."

"Hold on, chickadee. You know his relatives. Just make a phone call. Do a little research."

She mulled over the idea of asking Hal Braden. Josh's father had known her parents, and he had gotten married at the inn. She'd known him forever, and he always watched out for her. It took only a minute for her to realize that wasn't what she wanted to do. "I don't want to go behind his back. I want him to share whatever it is because he wants to. *Ugh.* I don't know what I want. All I know is that I like him, and when he's around, this buzz of electricity sizzles between us." She fingered the handcuffs, which were still attached to her shorts, and dug the key out of her pocket. "Maybe I'm just nervous because I saw him naked and my brain sped down an erotic path paved with shower sex and handcuffs."

"That's an option. *Sex* it out of him. But maybe skip the handcuffs until you're sure he's as good a guy as you think he is."

They talked for a few more minutes, and before hanging up, Aubrey said, "Remember, *kiss, not cock.*"

"Kiss, not cock. Got it." She ended the call just as Beau came through her doorway wearing a tight black T-shirt and jeans that hugged his ginormous distraction. *Kiss, not cock. Kiss, not cock.*

"Can you break away for a bit and come with me into town?"

Her sex-starved brain zeroed in on *come with me.* She forced her eyes up to his as he walked toward her, but flashes of him in the shower came rushing back. She saw droplets of water streaming down his shoulders and chest, the outline of his body parts branded into her mind. This was not good. She was *not* a weak-kneed type of woman, but she was one hundred percent certain that if she stood up, her knees would fail her.

She unlocked the handcuffs to keep from staring, and they slipped from her hand. *Ugh!* Why was she all thumbs around him? She crouched to pick them up, and his *distraction* was *right there.* "Kiss, not cock," she mumbled to herself.

"What was that?"

She shot up to her feet and slammed the cuffs and key on her desk. "A line from my book," came out faster than a bullet. "Why are you going to town?"

"You need to pick out a medallion to go on the ceiling for your chandelier, and you need new locks on several doors around the inn."

"My *chandelier?*"

He exhaled, like she was messing with him. "The one in the box by your bed?"

"I forgot I had that light. How the heck did you even notice it?"

"Very little gets by me." He held her gaze, making her feel like he could see right through her. "And don't ask me to pick out the medallion. I've worked with enough women to know that anything I pick out will be wrong. Besides, you need a nightstand, too. And locking screen doors for your bedroom."

"I'm not that picky, and I don't need locks. I've lived here for years and no one has ever bothered me." *Except you. You bother me in ways I'd rather not think about.*

"Are you going to stare at me like I confuse you all evening, or come with me?"

"I was just thinking of a scene for my book, not staring at you." He didn't look like he was buying it. "I can't go to town. I need to figure out this scene so I can write."

"Great. I'll help you work out your scene, and then you can come with me into town." He glanced at the blow-up dolls on her couch. "Good to see you have female dolls, too."

"That's Amanda Seyfried and Tom Hardy."

"How do you choose…? Never mind." He rubbed the back of his neck. "Why don't we work out your scene together?"

"Us?" *Shit.* That's exactly what she needed *and* wanted. So why did she feel like she was about to swallow her tongue?

"Why not? Man, woman, *breathing*. Surely it'll be better than looking at dolls."

"No." She tried to walk around him, and he blocked her way with a teasing—and sexy-as-sin—look in his eyes.

"Are you the same girl who straddled a handcuffed blow-up doll? The same woman who unabashedly walked into the bathroom while I was in the shower?" He leaned in, his thigh brushing hers. "What's the matter, shortcake? Isn't this how you do your research with me? I seem to recall you saying I was better than a blow-up doll. Or don't you like it when someone else takes control? When the tables are turned?"

She pushed past him with a groan, and he chuckled. "Fine! I was trying to give *you* an out because you get all closed off when I get near you."

He clenched his jaw, his eyes suddenly serious. "I know I don't open up easily. You shouldn't take it personally. It's just easier when we're challenging each other."

"Yeah, no kidding," she agreed, a little relieved that he was having trouble, too. "Come on. Let's get this over with."

He cocked a grin. "Okay, where do you need me?"

She looked up at the ceiling, thinking of all the naughty places she needed his attention, and felt her cheeks burn.

"Look at that," he said in a low voice. "The erotic romance writer turned fifty shades of red."

She glared at him, then began pacing, trying to figure out where to start.

"Oh, come on. Don't be upset. It's cute when you blush."

"Uh-huh," she said sarcastically. "I know it's ridiculous that I blush around you." She set her hands on her hips, trying to focus on the scene structure. "Do me a favor. Don't talk for a minute. You're too distracting."

He took a step toward her, and she held her palm out. "Stop. Don't move. I need to get into my characters' heads."

"Should I call you Amanda?" he asked with a cocky grin.

"You know what? That's a great idea. Call me Shayna—"

"And you can call me *Roman*." He crossed his arms, glowering at her. "Another grocery boy?"

Her jaw dropped open. "Did you read my manuscript?"

"No. You called me Roman when I carried you to bed this morning."

"Oh my gosh. Really? That's so embarrassing." She covered her mouth, but she couldn't stop her laughter from coming out. "I swear I'll be the old lady in the nursing home talking about all these men, and they'll think I'm a slut. Roman is the hero in my story."

"That's better than a grocery boy," he teased. "And it's kind of cool that you get so caught up in your work. Passion for what you do is a good thing."

"Well, it's my life. *Literally*. Let's get this over with." She was nervous, but she'd look lame if she turned him down. Plus, she'd never know what it would feel like to have a man his size lying on top of her. *Him*. To have *him* lying on top of her. She didn't want anyone else to be in that position.

Great. Now she was thinking about all his body parts pressing down on her. *Kiss, not cock. Kiss, not cock.* That did *not* help. Now she was thinking about kissing his cock.

She tossed the dolls off the couch and grabbed Beau's arm, positioning him by the couch. Her hero was supposed to wrap his arms around the heroine's waist from behind, and when he kissed her neck, she'd turn, and they'd stumble to the couch kissing as he stripped away her clothes. She and Beau would

simply *pretend*, but then he'd lay her on the couch and she'd feel
what Shayna would feel as Roman came down over her. She
could do this.

"We need to..." She glanced at the couch, wondering if she
should just ask him to lie on top of her, but that felt too
mechanical. She worried it wouldn't feel the same as if they
pretended to do a little foreplay.

"Here's the setup," she finally said, hoping she didn't sound
too nervous. "It's after your shower. I mean, *Roman's* shower, so
he's naked." *Kiss, not cock*, she reminded herself. *I'm just a writer
creating a scene. It's not really Beau. He's Roman.* "Shayna is
painting in her studio, and you come in and put your arms
around her from behind."

He moved behind her, and his arms circled her waist, covering her entire belly. His forearms brushed against her breasts,
and she felt her nipples pebble with delight. *Sweet Jesus, please
don't let me embarrass myself.*

"Like this?" he asked in a rough whisper.

"Yeah," she said a little shakily. "And then you kiss her
neck, and she's still painting." She pretended to paint and
closed her eyes as his warm lips touched her skin. That was *not*
pretend, and it felt oh so good.

"How's this?" He pressed a kiss just below her ear.

"Good," she whispered. Each kiss was firmer, lasted longer
than the previous one. She tried to distance her thoughts
enough to pick apart the sensations, but she was already lost in
the feel of his hard chest against her back, his muscular arms
belted across her, and anticipation pulsing inside her with every
touch of his lips. "And her shoulder. Kiss my shoulder..."

His mouth trailed over her skin, and she melted against
him. His hold on her tightened, and she felt his arousal pressing

into her. *God you feel good. I want to turn around and kiss you. Oh yes, lick my shoulder like that. Mm. That's good.* She pressed her lips together to keep her thoughts from floating out.

"Like this?" He placed openmouthed kisses along her shoulder. "Better?"

"The best" slipped out soft and lusty. Her knees buckled, and Beau splayed his hand over her belly, his fingers brushing the waist of her shorts. Heat rushed through her core, and she imagined turning in his arms and climbing him like a mountain, wrapping her legs around his shoulders, and that incredible mouth of his—

"What's next?" he rasped.

He kissed her jaw, her earlobe, down her neck to her shoulder, working his way over every spec of exposed flesh. Every mind-numbing kiss sent a pulse of heat between her legs.

"Hey, shortcake?" he said in a low voice between scorching-hot kisses. He sealed his mouth over her shoulder and sucked. "What's next?"

Next? An orgasm if she wasn't careful.

She pushed from his arms, gulping in air, and headed for her desk. "That's a wrap. Get out of here. I have to write."

"No way, shortcake." He grabbed her arm and hauled her toward the door. "Town. *Now.*"

Chapter Seven

BEAU HAD NO freaking idea what he was doing. He hadn't intended to ask Charlotte to go into town with him. He'd only wanted to show her he wasn't a dick because he'd shut her down before, but one look at her had done him in. Going to town *alone* was the exact opposite of what he wanted. And what the hell kind of scene working out was that? *Holy fuck.* Now he was stuck driving to town with a hard-on that refused to deflate because Charlotte's scent filled the cab of the truck and her long legs were propped up on the dashboard, her knee-high fringed black boots bouncing to the music as she plucked away at her laptop. She'd complained the whole way to the truck about not being able to afford the time away from writing. He'd finally given in and retrieved the damn laptop. She hadn't spoken a word since.

It was a long ride down the mountain, and after half an hour of silence, he said, "Can I ask you a question?"

"Mm-hm." *Type, type, type.*

"How do you work out scenes with those dolls? They can't hold you or kiss you." *Or touch you the way I want to.*

Her fingers stilled and her cheeks flushed, as if she could read his thoughts. "I use them for positioning. I can usually get my head into theirs once I see how the mechanics work."

"Get your head into theirs?"

"Well, not *theirs*, but my characters'. You know, sort of *pretend* to be them, feel what they would feel if they were real. I don't usually have anyone to work out scenes with, except Cutter every few weeks when he brings groceries."

Beau gripped the steering wheel tighter at the thought of Cutter's hands on her. He told himself he was just watching out for her, but it was bullshit. It had been forever since he'd felt anything even close to jealousy, but he recognized the unexpected emotion just the same.

"I thought you and Cutter were only friends," he said tensely.

"We are. He's great at positioning, though."

He stared at the road as they sped toward town, gritting his teeth in an effort to keep his thoughts from coming out. But it was no use. They barreled out anyway. "You and I have very different definitions of the word *friends*."

She began typing again. "We do?"

"Mm-hm." *I don't kiss women I want to only be friends with.* He shoved that thought down deep and said, "Don't take this wrong, but wouldn't it be easier to watch porn?"

"Oh God. Have you ever *really* watched porn, other than when you need something to jerk off to?"

"Jesus, Charlotte." He'd just found the perfect boner killer—talking to Charlotte about jerking off to porn.

"What? It's not like it's a secret that people jerk off to porn."

"Yeah, well, I don't. So why don't you clue me in as to why dolls are better than porn?"

She leaned back in her seat, still looking at him. "Porn is cold and unemotional. To be honest, I have no idea how it turns anyone on. I mean, where is the love? The romance? The foreplay that makes your heart flutter? How about tender whispers or rough demands underscored by intimacy, not heightened by camera angles?"

"Not all people want or need emotional connections to get turned on," he said, although he'd never been one of those people. As much as he didn't want emotional connections, he'd always needed them to truly enjoy sex. Needless to say, he hadn't enjoyed sex in a very long time.

She gazed out the passenger window. "I know they don't," she said a little sadly. "You asked why I don't use porn for motivation. That's why. I can place the dolls however I need them to make sure the mechanics work—on the stairs, the bed, the counters."

He imagined making love to Charlotte in each of those places.

"And then I mentally put myself in their place, imagining a man's hands on me, or his mouth. I close my eyes and picture myself as the heroine. A redhead, brunette, blonde, buxom or flat chested, small waisted or curvy, until we become one."

She closed her laptop and absently touched her neck. He wanted to touch her neck. To feel her pulse fluttering against his tongue again.

"Then I picture my hero, from his face all the way down to his feet, moving through each body part until I can feel him breathing with me. Until my flesh goes hot because I feel his skin heating up, and I imagine the romantic things he'd whisper, the feel of his body pressed to mine, the sounds he'd earn by touching me, or kissing me, and the sounds he'd make."

Holy hell, he was hard again.

She turned toward him. Her skin was flushed, and in a sated

voice, as if she'd just experienced something wonderful, she said, "*That's* why I don't watch porn and why I'm totally fine up here by myself without having to deal with the dating world. I want what my parents and grandparents had, where relationships and intimacy mean something, and I don't really believe that kind of love exists anymore."

Beau knew that type of love existed. He'd had it once, and when he'd lost it, he'd been pretty sure he'd lost the ability to feel that way ever again. Charlotte made him feel again, and it bothered him that she would lock herself away because she thought she could never have it.

"It exists," he said. "You shouldn't give up hope. I think my parents have the type of relationship you're describing."

"Really?" Her eyes lit up, pushing all his buttons. She set her laptop on the floor.

"Yes. I'm sure of it. They met at a wedding at Hilltop Vineyards in Pleasant Hill when they were in college. My mother's family owns the winery, and she was there during the wedding, which my father was attending as a guest. The way my father tells the story, it was love at first sight, but my mother says it was lust at first sight and turned to love after my father refused to let her get away."

"I love that." She tucked her legs onto the seat and propped her elbow on the center console, looking adorable with her chin resting on her palm. "Tell me more. Do you know how he won her over? Did your mom play hard to get for a reason, or just because it was fun? Or maybe she didn't play hard to get at all, and he just thought she was because she was careful? What did their families think? Do they still hold hands and kiss all the time? I love the idea of holding hands and kissing. When they fight, can you tell they still love each other? That it hurts to fight, but they have to do it to clear the air?"

She asked so many questions, and Beau had a feeling those questions were who she was at her very core, part of her quirkiness, part of what made him *feel* again. *Happy* was the emotion of the moment, though she put him through a roller coaster of emotions every time they were together. "You want to know about their *fights*?"

"Yes, probably more than the rest. I think that's how you know true love. My mom was feisty but careful—"

"Like you." Beau glanced at her, catching her eye, and he realized he wanted to know about her parents, too, and in what ways she was like them.

"I'm a lot like she was," Charlotte said thoughtfully. "But I think I have a lot of my dad in me, too. He was a passionate man in his beliefs about everything from business to how they raised me. My parents didn't fight often, but when they did, I remember thinking about how much they hated it. Sometimes couples fight and you want to hide or save one of them from the other. It wasn't ever like that with them. Even if they told me to leave the room to give them privacy, I'd sit right outside listening, because their voices were my safe haven. They were always saying things like, 'I'm sorry you feel that way, but...' and 'Damn it, Patricia! I love you, but you're wrong about this.' They had this mutual respect *for* their love, and it seems like couples don't have that anymore."

Her eyes misted, but she didn't look away. Beau couldn't help reaching over and putting his hand on hers, squeezing it reassuringly.

"I remember thinking if that ever changed, I would be lost."

"And then you lost them," he said gently, his chest constricting with the harsh reality.

She blinked her eyes dry and nodded. "Their plane went down overseas…"

Her voice trailed off and she looked away, blinking repetitively. He wanted to gather her in his arms, but just as he moved to do so, she drew in a loud breath and faced him again, her expression solemn, eyes drier.

"After they were killed, I came to live with my grandfather. I was lost for a while, but he didn't let me get too far gone. We're not supposed to be talking about *me*. You changed the subject. Or I guess I did. We seem to do that a lot. Tell me about your parents and why you think they have what mine did."

He had a feeling she tried not to think about how much she missed her parents, and knowing they were killed explained even more. He was the king of bottling up his feelings. He knew how hard it was and how sadness and guilt and other dark emotions could eat away at a person. He didn't want that for her, but he knew better than to push a person who was hurting.

"Okay," he said, "but if you want to talk about your family, I'm a pretty good listener."

"Thank you. I appreciate it," she said. "Now, *please* tell me about your parents. Is your father as nice as Hal? Is he super serious like you? I want to know all about his pursuit of your mother. And I want to know all about your mom, too. I bet she was pursuing him in her own way, because love is like that. You can't turn away from it."

He kept his eyes trained on the road, not wanting to think too much about the truth in her words. "Hal's a rancher, and my father is an engineer, so you're talking about two different personalities. But my father is a good guy, maybe a little quieter than Hal, a little more serious. He's nice, but firm. He pushed us hard, taught us to be part of our community, to treat people well, respect ourselves, and all that. Pretty standard fare for parenting, I suppose. From what my cousins have told me, the apple doesn't fall far from the Braden familial tree. My mom was the same way when we were growing up, but she has a playful side, and she brings that side out in everyone, including my father."

"And the good stuff?" she urged as he turned onto the main road. "Their love story?"

As they drove toward town he told her about his father writing love letters to his mother while they were apart and sending her flowers, showing up unannounced for surprise dates. Charlotte listened with bated breath, asking a million questions. Every so often she'd ask if she could use something he said in a story, or she'd say it gave her a great idea and she'd open her laptop and type for a few minutes.

When he was done, he realized he'd been talking for more than twenty-five minutes.

Charlotte sat back with an awestruck expression. "Wow, that's beautiful. I think my favorite part of their story was when he showed up with a bicycle built for two, a picnic, and flowers. That's so romantic."

"I never thought this much about my parents' relationship. To me, they're just Mom and Dad. They love each other, and they love us. I guess I've always taken it for granted that they always would."

"That's why you're not a romance writer and I am. I love fairy tales and happy endings."

"Hey, I never said I didn't like a *happy ending*." He slid her a seductively playful look.

"You should read my books," she said as she set her laptop down again. "They have both kinds of happy endings in them."

"Thanks, but I prefer to experience happy endings, not read about them." Her cheeks flushed so bright, he had to grin, and went for a safer subject. "I thought people were addicted to their phones, but not you. You're addicted to that laptop."

"Addicted to *writing*, not my laptop. How else will I get my *happy* on?" she said cheerfully.

"By living life. Leaving your office every once in a while. Talking to real people."

"I talk to real people. I'm talking to you, and I have friends I talk to." She leaned his way again, her beautiful eyes locking on him. "Let's get back to you. You said you loved and lost. Was your love like your parents', instant and unstoppable? What changed to make you two break up?"

A wave of apprehension washed through him.

"We've probably had enough love talk for today," he said as ranches and pastures gave way to the narrower streets of Weston, and he turned onto Main Street, which was built to replicate the Wild West, complete with dusty roads, horse posts, and old-fashioned storefronts. He concentrated on the road, trying to ignore the heat of her stare. "The hardware store is right down the road."

"It must have been a bad breakup. I'd say I don't mean to pry, but I do. You're obviously still hurting. Was it recent?"

He felt his walls going up again and remained silent as he turned into the parking lot. Damn it. He didn't want to shut her out, but talking about Tory wasn't easy. He cut the engine and met her inquisitive, compassionate, and too-fucking-beautiful eyes.

She placed her hand over his, as he'd done to her, and said, "I'm a good listener if you ever want to talk about it."

"We didn't break up. She was killed in an accident. It was a long time ago, and I don't like talking about it."

"Oh, Beau." She crawled right up onto the console and embraced him. "I'm so sorry. That's heartbreaking. No wonder you don't want to talk about it."

He was struck dumb for a minute, soaking in her comfort. She'd lost her entire family, and here she was, trying to soothe his decade-old wound. Struggling against the desire to stay right there, he put his arms around her in a quick hug. But she didn't move away when he lowered his arms. She sighed and continued holding him, her face buried in his neck, her warm breath pushing away the discomfort of having revealed something so private.

She felt *too* good, *too* right. He needed to get a grip on his emotions or the next few weeks would be hell. He needed space, but he also wasn't ready to drive back up the mountain and go their separate ways.

"Thanks, shortcake, but *uh*, how about if we get your medallion, buy the locks we need, and then maybe we can grab some dinner while we're down here."

"Okay," she said with a heavy sigh.

She made no move to separate herself from him, and those sighs made him want to stay right there. What kind of magical powers did she have that she'd opened doors he'd long ago nailed shut?

"C'mon, shortcake," he said before he gave in to his emotions.

She lifted her head from his chest, her gaze moving over his face. "Why do you call me shortcake?"

"You're a tiny gal and you're sweet as sugar when you're not talking about porn. What else am I going to call you?"

"Charlotte?" She wrinkled her nose, looking adorable as

hell.

"There are millions of Charlottes in the world, but I have a feeling there's only one *you*. Now, how about we get going before we end up researching truck scenes?"

Her neck blushed, and it spread up her cheeks. Damn, that was hot, and cute, and *not* doing anything to make him want to get out of the truck.

"Going!" she said. She pushed his door open and crawled over him.

He slapped her ass on her way out, and she glared at him.

"Who climbs over the driver to get out?" He stepped out of the truck. "You're like Tinker Bell, flitting about without a care in the world."

"I was already halfway there," she said as they walked toward the entrance to the hardware store. "More importantly, if you call me shortcake, what am I going to call you?"

"I'm sure you'll think of something," he mumbled, putting a hand on her back and guiding her out of the middle of the sidewalk as they passed a group of people.

"Let's get the locks first," Beau suggested when they entered the hardware store. "I have a feeling the medallion might take a while."

"Okay, but if you insist on buying a lock for my bedroom doors, then I need a color-coded key so I don't mix it up with all the others." She strode determinedly down the aisle in front of them. The *bathroom* aisle.

He took her hand and led her toward the other end of the store. "This way, shortcake."

"How do you know? You live a million miles from here."

"Guy radar." He pointed up at the signs hanging from the ceiling at the end of each aisle.

"Short girls don't look up."

There were about a dozen dirty jokes on the tip of his tongue. He wasn't going to touch that with a ten-foot pole, lest he end up sporting his own flagpole. "Great, then you probably won't care what your medallion looks like after all."

They found the locks, and Beau picked out one for the French door in her bedroom and the others he needed.

"Where do we get colored keys?"

"The locksmith. How often will you use that door instead of the front door?"

She shrugged. "I use that door in the mornings when I collect eggs, but I leave it open, so I don't really need a key."

"Yeah, about that. If you want to leave the doors open, we need to put up a security screen door that locks and has steel grates, so you don't end up with raccoons or other unwanted *visitors* partying at your inn."

"You worry too much about people breaking in."

"Maybe you don't worry enough. Let's pick up screen doors, and after we get the medallion and pay for these, we'll circle back to the locksmith and get colored keys."

"Pink, please."

"Of course." *As if there were any other choice.*

"Look, it's Hal!" Charlotte pointed across the store. At six foot six, with thick hair that was more silver than black, Hal Braden was a hard man to miss. Charlotte grabbed Beau's hand, dragging him with her as she made a beeline for Hal. She dropped Beau's hand and wrapped her arms around Hal. "I've missed you!"

"Hello, darlin'." Hal hugged her tight, and Charlotte seemed to sink into him. Hal was in his early seventies, but he still worked on his ranch on a daily basis, which kept him in shape. He was thick chested and thick hearted. Hal was still desperately in love with his late wife, Adriana, who passed away years ago, leaving Hal with a broken heart and six children to raise.

"What a fun coincidence, seeing you here." Charlotte gazed up at Hal with so much love in her eyes, Beau could feel how much he meant to her. "Thank you for sending Beau to fix the inn," she said, stepping out of the confines of his embrace. "He's doing a great job."

"I knew he would." Hal opened his arms and nodded at Beau, motioning with his hands for Beau to step into his embrace, which he did.

"How's it going, Hal?" After Tory was killed, Hal had offered Beau an open invitation to stay with him while he found his footing, but Beau had needed to fly solo. He'd thought he needed to fly solo forever, but Charlotte was making him question that decision.

"All is well over at the Braden ranch," Hal assured him. "I'm heading out of town to visit Hugh and Brianna. I miss those grandbabies somethin' awful. I appreciate you coming out to fix up the inn. Charlotte's parents were very special people. They'd like knowing she was being well cared for."

"Why does everyone think I need looking after? Burly Beau here wants to put locks on my doors," Charlotte said with a hint of annoyance, but the appreciative glimmer in her eyes outweighed her snarkiness.

"You know why, darlin'. Family knows no boundaries. Everyone needs looking after. Even your man, Beau. It's good to see you out and about. Your mama wouldn't have wanted you to disappear from the rest of the world. She'd want you to create your own fairy tale." Hal looked at Beau and said, "I knew you were exactly what she needed." He patted Beau on the shoulder. "Give your family my love, and you keep watching out for our girl. She's stubborn, but the best of them always are."

As he walked away, Charlotte said, "I love him so much."

"He's the best." Beau took her by the arm and said, "This way, shortcake. You have more shopping to do."

He had thought picking out the medallion might be a trying process, but it took Charlotte almost an hour to pick out the doors. Most of that time was spent trying to decide on the color, but the decorative scrolls also played a major role in her decision. He'd never known choosing between brown, black, or white could be so time-consuming. She finally chose the most elaborately decorated white security screen doors he'd ever seen, and then she turned those hopeful doe eyes on him and asked him to paint the scrolls pink. How could he say no to that? But now he realized choosing the medallion would rival the time it took to choose the doors. They'd been staring at the display for thirty minutes, and Charlotte still had a displeased look in her beautiful eyes.

"What's wrong with this one?" Beau pointed to an intricately decorated medallion that would go perfectly around her chandelier. "I can paint it pink."

She looked thoughtfully at the display. "They're all round or square. They feel unoriginal. When I'm lying in bed, I don't want to see something boring, or feel like I could be in *anyone's* bedroom. I want to see glittery stars or…"

"Something magical." Why hadn't he thought of that? Charlotte created entire worlds for a living. Of course she'd want something unique, and on top of that, she seemed to have a not-so-secret affinity for fairy tales and fantasy-level relationships.

Her eyes lit up. "Yes! Exactly!" She threw her hands up toward the ceiling, as if relieved someone *finally* understood her.

Beau took her hand and walked out of the aisle.

"Where are we going now?" She hurried to keep pace.

"The lumber department."

"What is it with men and wood?"

He grinned.

"Ohmygod. *Beau!* Really, why the lumber department?"

He was suddenly acutely aware of the feel of her hand in his, and when had she wrapped her other hand around his forearm? She'd probably done it in an effort to keep up by using his momentum. "You want magical, and there's only one way to achieve that. I'm making the medallion for you."

She squealed and threw herself at him when he was midstride, nearly sending them both to the floor. He caught her around the waist and lifted her off the ground to keep from plowing her down.

"Damn, girl. I nearly trampled you."

Wide, happy eyes gazed back at him as she said, "Thank you."

"For what? Dragging you out of your office to pick out things you don't want?"

"*Yes*, because what we want isn't always what we need."

"That's funny," he said as he set her feet on the floor, but she didn't drop her arms from around his neck, and man, was he glad she didn't. The happiness shimmering in her eyes changed in the space of a breath to something rich and seductive. "I was just thinking that, for the first time in forever, what I want might be exactly what I need."

AS THEY WERE paying for their purchases at the hardware store, Beau suggested they hit the furniture store to get Charlotte a nightstand, but she didn't want to do any more shopping. She just wanted to be with him and talk about something other than the inn or work. A little while later they were seated at a table on the crowded patio of the Wicked Spur, a restaurant that had been recommended by the cashier at the hardware store. Twinkling blue lights dangled from tall umbrellas above each table. It might have given the place a romantic feel, if not for the vibrant yellow and green lights outlining fake palm trees scattered around the patio. Then there was the gorgeous view of the parking lot and vending machines. The band was the Spur's saving grace. The guys looked like the members of ZZ Top, but they sang upbeat country songs like they were heaven sent.

Charlotte watched Beau as he read the menu with the same concentration he'd used as he'd inspected each piece of wood he'd bought, as if he were checking a fine diamond for clarity. Did he do everything that discerningly?

"Are you going to pick out something from the menu, or just stare at me?" Beau asked without looking at her.

"What are you having?"

He lowered the menu, and she saw a new contentment on his face. His jaw wasn't clenched, and his eyes were softly serious, not quite as guarded. He looked at her for so long, she half expected him not to respond. He was good at not answering her questions. The back of his truck was loaded up with wood, molding, doors, paint, and other supplies, but he hadn't given her a single clue about what type of medallion he was going to make.

"Did you even look at the menu?" He cocked a brow, and the almost-smile she'd come to appreciate appeared on his handsome face.

"Mm-hm." It wasn't a complete lie. She had *looked* at it. She was just too busy looking at *him* to think about food. She was learning to read him, figuring out when to back off and when she could push. Beau was complicated. She couldn't figure out how close he was to his family, because he'd received texts from two of his brothers, and she'd noticed that he hadn't responded to either. But then he'd received a call from his sister, Jillian, and he'd not only answered right away, but his happy expression had lingered after the call, when he'd told Charlotte that Jillian talked about as fast as she did. She'd learned other things, too, like how seriously he took his word. Not only from the things he'd said and done since they'd met, but by the fact that she was now the proud owner of two pink keys. The salesman had told them he was out of pink, and Beau had insisted he go into the back and see if they have more. With a huff and a grumble, the guy had begrudgingly carried out Beau's request, and sure enough, he'd returned with a box of pink keys.

"And what did you decide to get?" he asked, bringing her mind back to their conversation.

"I don't know. There are too many choices." She hoped that was true, but his snicker indicated she'd missed the mark.

He leaned forward as if he were sharing a secret, and a tease rose in his eyes. "It must be hard for you to go to restaurants that don't serve candy or microwavable meals."

"You think you're so funny." She enjoyed this teasing side of him. "I eat real food."

"Mm-hm. A bite of steak doesn't count."

The waiter arrived with their drinks before she could respond. He had a baby face that contradicted his broad shoulders and muscular arms. Beau eyed his cowboy hat, and she stifled a giggle.

"Sorry the drinks took so long. The bar is slammed tonight," the waiter said as he set a glass in front of Charlotte. "One strawberry daiquiri with extra whipped cream." He set down Beau's glass. "And one beer. Have you decided on dinner?"

Charlotte picked up the menu. "You go first. I need a sec."

"I'll have the covered wagon," Beau said. "Hold the onions."

"Good choice. You must be hungry," the waiter said.

Charlotte scanned the menu and found the covered wagon. *A half-pound burger with the works. Perfect.* "I'll have the same with extra fries and a side of pickles."

"A woman who's not afraid to eat. Nice," the waiter said as he collected the menus.

As he walked away, Beau arched a brow. "Your stomach isn't going to know what hit it."

"My stomach will be fine." She sipped her drink. "*Mm.* This is so good. You have to try it." She moved to the seat beside him and pushed her drink in front of him.

"No thanks."

"I bet you only drink big-man drinks, right? Beer? Scotch? Whiskey? Just taste it. Come on. I'll taste yours." She grabbed his beer and took a sip. "Your turn."

He took a sip and made a face. "It's like drinking candy."

"I know. *So* good!" She took another drink. "I like this cheesy place. The music is good, and the lights are pretty, even if we are looking at a parking lot." That earned a genuine smile.

"You look younger when you smile."

"Do I look old when I don't?" He took a drink of his beer, no doubt to wash down the sugary goodness of her daiquiri.

"No, but I still like to see your smile." She looked at the people sitting at nearby tables, and her writer brain immediately began weaving stories for each of them. She wondered why she couldn't weave a backstory for Beau. She'd tried, but she kept coming up empty. "I bet you had a dog growing up."

"Why is that?"

"Because you seem like a dog guy. Rough and tumble, serious but caring. I don't know. You know how people say dogs are loyal and protective? That's how you come across."

He took a long pull of his beer, watching her as intently as she was watching him. "We had a dog. Or rather, I had a dog. Shadow. He was a German shepherd, and he was a great dog. He lived a long life. We had to put him down when he was twelve."

"Did you cry?" She tried to imagine him crying but couldn't.

"No. I missed him, but I went for a ten-mile run." He shrugged, and she could see that was how he dealt with things. He bottled everything up.

"Did you get another dog?"

He shook his head. "Not right away. I didn't want to replace him. Then a few years ago I was renovating a house, and this dog showed up. Darn thing followed me everywhere." His expression brightened as he spoke. "I tried to find his owner, but nobody claimed him. So I brought him home, and after a week I realized the dog was a thief. He stole everything from keys and socks to *books*. Nothing is off-limits for my guy."

She melted a little at *my guy*. "Where is he now?"

"Bandit? My parents are watching him while I'm here. I miss him, though. He's usually with me." He took another drink and said, "Do you always study people?"

"I don't often see people. But I do love finding mannerisms and things to use in my writing."

"Can I ask you something else?"

"Go for it." She plucked the strawberry garnish from her drink and bit into it, swaying to the music.

"Where did you live before moving here?"

"I grew up in Port Hudson and went to college there, but I spent summers at the inn with my grandparents, and every winter break with my parents and my mom's father in a small village in France, where she was from. After we lost my grandmother, I started spending winter breaks with my grandfather instead of going to France because I didn't want him to be lonely, and then I visited my other grandfather over spring break until he passed away. When we lost my grandmother, my grandfather closed the inn, opening only for certain events. After my parents were killed, we sold the house in Port Hudson, and I came to live here. And after my grandfather died, I inherited the inn and everything he owned."

"You have suffered so much loss. That must have been difficult, leaving your friends, your school, and going to live in an inn that was no longer open?"

The waiter brought their meals, giving Charlotte a chance to wrap her head around the fact that Beau genuinely wanted to know about her background. Most people shied away from the details, focusing on what she'd inherited instead of what she'd lost and how her life had changed.

The burgers were enormous. "There is no way you can eat that," Beau challenged.

"Watch me." She picked up the burger and took a huge bite.

"Can I get you anything else?" the waiter asked.

Beau chuckled at her chipmunk cheeks and said, "I think we're good, thanks."

After the waiter left, Beau waited for her to swallow and said, "You don't have to eat it all."

"*Yes*, I do." Charlotte took another big bite.

"Have it your way." He ate a fry. "If I'm getting too personal with my questions, just tell me to back off."

"What if I don't want you to back off?" she asked, surprising herself. His eyes went hot, and she gulped her drink. She waved at his food and said, "Eat your burger." *So I can think.*

His tongue swept over his lips, making it even harder for her to focus. She knew how those lips tasted, how they felt warm and insistent…

Oh boy…

She looked down at her food to avoid falling into him again.

"We don't have to talk about it," he said, reminding her that he was still waiting for an answer.

"I don't mind talking about it. It was hard leaving my friends and my home. My best friend Aubrey's family offered to let me stay with them, but I needed to be with my grandfather. I was just so sad. As I mentioned, I was a senior in high school. My parents had guided me through life, and suddenly…" Her throat constricted.

Beau put his hand on hers. "It's okay. We don't have to talk about it."

"I'm okay. It's just hard to say it aloud sometimes. I wanted to sort of hole up and hide, but my grandfather wouldn't let me wallow. He told me, 'Sometimes you've got to let the pain sink deep into your bones until it aches so badly you think you'll shatter. Only then can you truly move on.' He was a wise man, and he saved me from myself. Every day we went for walks and talked about my grandmother and my parents. We talked about *life* and we talked about death, the good times and the bad. And when I say talked about it, I mean we bitched and we celebrated, and sometimes we just walked in silence. That was good, too, because reflecting on things can be as good as laughing and crying, as long as you don't get mired down in the sadness. But my grandfather was always there to help me find my way back to the surface. And we weren't always alone at the inn. My grandfather had a staff that included a chef, groundskeepers, housekeepers, and he opened the inn for a handful of events, including the awards ceremony for the Mad Prix every summer."

"You were lucky to have him, and don't worry, I'll have the work done by the weekend of the ceremony."

"Oh, um, okay." She paused to take a bite, toying with the idea of coming up with *more* work for him to do to keep him around longer. But she knew how silly that was. He had a life to get back to, and she had writing to do.

"I'm trying to imagine what it's like for you to host the awards ceremony. You might actually have to leave your office."

"You act like I never leave my office, but look around you. No laptop. No desk."

"Being out looks good on you," he said, and bit into his burger.

"Thanks. *Talking* looks good on you." They ate in silence for a few minutes, listening to the music.

"How do you pick what events you open the inn for?"

"It's pretty easy for me. I opened for Josh's wedding because

Hal had gotten married there, so I knew it was important to Josh. And my parents were the original coordinators of the Mad Prix. The awards have always been hosted at the inn, and I grew up attending them. The staff has been doing it for so many years, they really don't need me around. In fact, I pretty much just pop out to welcome them, make an appearance during the ceremony, and other than that, I can hole up in my office and know it'll all be carried out smoothly."

"Sounds like you've got a good team to make it happen. My brother Graham is competing this year."

"That's awesome. Three Bradens in the race? He and your cousins Ty and Sam can duke it out for first place." Sam was one of Ty's older brothers. He hadn't raced last year, but he had in previous years.

"Actually, Sam won't make it this year. His wife, Faith, is pregnant with their first child, and she's having a hard time with morning sickness."

"Oh, that's a shame, but how exciting to have a baby!"

"They're elated."

They ate in comfortable silence, broken only by the music from the band and the din of the other diners. Not for the first time Charlotte noticed how different she felt being away from the inn, surrounded by life and activity. She noticed everything: the fragrances of colognes and perfumes, the aromas of various foods, and even the scents of nature and cars carried in the air. She felt lighter, away from the pressure of her deadlines, and rejuvenated, filling up her well with the sights and sounds of others. She was glad Beau had dragged her out, even if she needed to write. He seemed a little different, too, although he had that sharp look in his eyes again, like he was overthinking something.

"Go ahead," she said as she plucked a fry from her plate. "Ask me whatever it is that you're thinking about before it burns a hole in your brain."

"Am I that transparent?"

"Not usually," she said honestly. "But I'm learning to read your wrinkled brow."

"You are, are you? Well, you caught me. I'm just wondering where you were living when you lost your grandfather." He finished his beer and stole one of her fries.

She knew that for him to continue asking questions had to mean he was letting his guard down a little more. "I was still in Port Hudson. My grandparents didn't have my father until my grandmother was in her thirties, and my parents didn't have me until later in life, too. By my senior year in college, my grandfather was pretty much bed bound. He had a full-time nurse, but a nurse isn't family. I knew how lonely he was, so I tried to come back as often as I could. He watched my graduation ceremony on Skype. After graduation, I wanted to come back, but he told me I needed to stay there and start my life. I had interned at *Port Hudson News*, writing articles and doing whatever they needed, and they offered me a position. A few weeks later my grandfather passed away. I honestly believe my grandfather waited to die until I was settled, only I never felt settled away from my family. I know that's weird, but it's true."

"You came back alone?"

"No. My girlfriends, my LWW sisters, Aubrey, Presley, and Libby, and a few of the others came back with me, but after a week I asked them to leave. I needed to deal with it in my own way, and I couldn't just leave the Chickendales, or give them away. I know they're just chickens, but my grandfather and I raised them together."

Beau reached for her hand again. "They're your family."

She nodded, floored that he understood and wasn't mocking her. "Exactly. It was just me and them. I took the same walks my grandfather and I had, remembering the stories he'd told me about his relationship with my grandmother. I didn't want to lose those memories, so I began journaling. Before I knew it, it was winter, and I had written their love story. My friends were pressuring me to come back to Port Hudson, so I told them about what I'd written to prove that I wasn't withering away up there on the mountain. They were knee deep in launching LWW Enterprises and they wanted me to join them and work hand in hand with Presley on the publishing side. But I'm not a corporate business person."

"You may not be a corporate business person, but I think you could succeed at anything you tried, given what you've gone through and what you've accomplished."

"Thank you. It means a lot to me to hear that. When I turned them down, Presley wanted to read the story and possibly publish it, but I didn't give it to her. It was too personal to put out there like that. I mean, it's an amazing love story. You'd think my grandparents were childhood sweethearts, but they weren't. They didn't even meet until my grandmother was almost thirty years old, which was an old lady in her day. She was supposed to marry her best friend, but he was killed in the war. She thought she'd never love again, and then a few years later she met my grandfather on a train, and she fell in love. She used to say that the heart is like a garden. If all the elements are right, it can breathe life into a wilting soul."

He was studying her face so intently, she wondered if he thought she'd made it up.

"Sounds like they were very lucky," he said. "If you don't

mind me asking, how did you go from writing a personal love story to *erotic* romance? They seem a world apart."

"Hey, don't let the genre fool you. The difference between erotic romance and contemporary is what drives the story. In contemporary, it's love, like my grandparents' story. In erotic romance the story is driven by sex, but they're still love stories. They're just edgier. No-holds-barred, so to speak. People have sex all the time, and some people have kinky sex. That's part of life. I'm proud to say that my characters always find their forever loves, even though they take a darker, hypersexualized path to find it."

His low chuckle gave her goose bumps. "Okay, I get that. Your books are emotional. But why the switch in genres?"

"I got into it on a dare, believe it or not. I'm happiest when I'm writing, and being here makes me feel close to my family. I didn't want to go back to Port Hudson. The girls were teasing me about my nonexistent sex life, and one thing led to another, and they dared me to write something erotic. To *live vicariously* since I refused to pick up guys at places like this." She waved her hand. "By late spring I had finished my first manuscript. I fell in love with the excitement and pace of the genre so much, I continued the series and became Presley's first client. She heads up the publishing division, and she's an amazing writer. We spent a few months working out the pacing and creating a series around the story. I have an assistant who handles my social media, but I keep a pulse on what fans are saying. Their love of my alpha characters and the worlds I create make me want to write *more* in the genre, not less. That's why the writer's block I've had ever since starting this second series feels like it came out of nowhere. I'm glad it's lifting." A silent message of understanding passed between them.

"Me too. But erotic romance seems a world away from the

type of love you described growing up around."

"It is, which is probably another reason why I love it so much. It's not something I ever want or will have, so it's all new and challenging for me. Writing about contemporary romance would just remind me of what I don't have."

He held her gaze for a long moment, like he was trying to figure her out, and then he said, "You're incredibly strong, the way you worked through your grief and turned your passion into a career."

"Thank you."

"But don't you get lonely up there all alone?"

The intimate question took her by surprise. Each of his questions were personal, but this felt even more so, and she needed a moment to think about how, and if, she wanted to answer it. He was watching her intently, like he didn't want to miss a word of her response, which made her worry about her response even more.

"You are full of questions tonight. Do you mind if I ask how you worked through your grief?"

He sat back and grabbed another fry. She knew he wasn't going to answer. She could feel it in her bones, and she wanted to push him to open up, as he'd started to in the truck. But she recognized the armor of grief. Beau might come across as fierce and unbreakable, but she had a feeling that beneath that armor was a fragile heart still encased in his lost love. She didn't want to break that encasement, but she wanted to help him heal and to coax his heart back to life, because by not answering, he was telling her more than words ever could. He either hadn't dealt with his grief or there was more to the story.

Giving him time to think and holding on to a shred of hope that he might surprise her by responding, she took a bite of her burger and turned her attention to the band. They were barely visible beyond the crowded dance floor. Charlotte couldn't remember the last time she'd danced with a man. She ate the last of her burger and caught Beau staring at her, which sent her pulse sprinting. How did he do that by just looking at her?

He was focused on her mouth, which made her even more nervous. Was he going to kiss her? She chewed faster, trying to swallow, but she'd taken too big a bite.

"Come here." He slid a hand around the back of her neck, drawing her closer.

Oh God! Swallow, swallow, swallow! Oh no, she'd taste like burger, but there was no time for a drink. He leaned in, and she closed her eyes, preparing for the kiss. Something brushed over the corner of her mouth.

"There," he said softly. "Just a little sauce."

Her eyes flew open, mortification consuming her. She'd been ready for a kiss and he'd just been cleaning up her messy eating? *Guess I don't have to worry about burger breath after all.* Was it possible to mourn something she'd never had? She'd thought they were connecting, that he was asking all those questions because he was interested in her. Maybe she had been on the mountain too long.

He set a napkin on the table and said, "I have no idea how you fit that big burger in your little body."

Her dinner must have been infused with lust, or maybe just opening up to Beau had caused it, because she wanted much more than that burger in her body. She needed to get her mind out of the gutter.

He finished his beer and licked his lips. "I have a feeling there aren't many challenges you can't win."

I challenge myself not to desire Beau Braden.

"Oh, I can think of one."

Chapter Eight

"I NEED TO dance off this burger." Charlotte pushed to her feet in her slinky little cutoffs and grabbed Beau's hand, trying to pull him up with her.

He didn't budge. Resisting Charlotte while she ate was hard enough, but resisting her while she shared her memories had pushed him to the limit, nearly shredding his resolve to keep his physical distance. He'd wanted to be closer to her, to hold her while she spoke. He'd wanted to soothe her pain, and more than that, he wanted to share his own past with her. Last night's kisses had come tumbling back, reminding him of how right she'd felt in his arms, how their mouths were made for each other. Those new, powerful feelings made him feel even more connected to her. He was hanging on to his control by a thread, and if she were in his arms, that thread would snap faster than a twig under his boot.

"I'm not opposed to dancing by myself," she said sassily. "But I thought it might embarrass you." She swayed her hips, scanning their surroundings. "Cutter!"

She waved toward the parking lot, where Cutter and Chip Shelton were strutting toward the patio. Chip was Beau's cousin Wes's business partner at the Woodlands. He was a great guy, but like Cutter, he was single, and friend or no friend, Beau saw both cowboy-hatted men as competition.

"Cutter will dance with me," she said happily.

The thought of Cutter's hands on Charlotte made Beau's blood boil. How could any man be close to her without wanting more? Beau pushed to his feet as they approached and slipped an arm around her waist. "*I'll* dance with you."

"I do *not* believe my eyes," Cutter said with a grin. "Charlotte Sterling has left the inn. I feel like we need a billboard to commemorate the moment."

Chip's shaggy blond hair brushed his collar. "Hey, Beau. Cutter mentioned you were in town. How's it going?"

"Great. It's good to see you." Beau reluctantly released Charlotte long enough to return Chip's embrace. "Do you know Charlotte?" He snaked his arm possessively around her again, meeting Cutter's curious gaze with a confident one of his own.

"Sure do." Chip crossed his arms and said, "What I don't know is how you got her to come down the mountain. More book research?"

"I met Chip and Cutter a few months after I moved here," Charlotte explained. "The hero in my first novel was a cowboy, and I called up to the Woodlands and picked their brains."

"That's when she swindled me into being her grocery delivery boy. We invited her to stay at the ranch and immerse herself in the experience, but she claimed she couldn't afford the time away from writing." Cutter's gaze skirted over the nearby tables, lingering on a group of women.

That's it, man. Look away.

It probably made Beau a prick for being glad she hadn't accepted their invitation.

"They took me on a FaceTime tour of the ranch and answered my endless questions for weeks," Charlotte explained.

"It was painful," Cutter said with a playful grin. "She's like a pain-in-the-ass sister you can't turn down."

"You can say that again," Chip agreed.

"Well, now I know where I stand with you two. At least Beau doesn't think I'm a pain in the ass." She slipped her arm around his waist, beaming up at him. "And he's going to dance with me!"

"She's already got you wrapped around her little finger, huh?"

If he had his way, he'd end up wrapped around more than just her little finger. Ignoring their question, because it was none of their damn business, he said, "Good to see you guys. We'll catch you later."

He held Charlotte close as they weaved around tables and dancing couples. The song ended just as he gathered her in his arms. "Shit."

"Gee, and I thought you agreed to dance only to keep me from dancing with Cutter." She put her arms around his neck as the next song came on.

"I don't get how those guys can look at you and not want to be with you." There was no way he was letting her out of his arms.

"I don't exactly put out a flirtatious vibe."

Was she insane? Everything she did made him want her more. "It's not about how flirtatious you are. It's your very essence, the energy you radiate. And don't fool yourself, shortcake. Everything you do is alluring." He glanced at Cutter, checking out every woman in the place. "They aren't looking for someone like you, and that makes me one hell of a lucky guy. And make no mistake, I feel nothing brotherly toward you."

Her eyes darkened, and she said, "Good," in a sultry whisper.

The band began playing another song. Unfortunately, it was a fast one, and Charlotte's arms rose above her head, her shoulders and hips swaying seductively to the beat. Their body heat ignited as he met every swing of her hips with a bump and grind of his own, thanking the stars above that he'd been born with rhythm. She danced over to his side, dragging her fingers across his shoulders and swaying her hips as her fingers trailed down his arm. He captured her hand in his and twirled her into his body, guiding her arms around his neck.

"Oh, you're *good*," she said with a lustful look in her eyes that nearly killed him.

"You have no idea how good, sexy girl."

He put his hand on her lower back and wedged his leg between hers, holding her there as he rocked his hips and chest, moving slower than the music demanded. Her eyes flamed as she fell into sync, moving fluidly with him. He slid his hand down her back, pressing on her ass until she pulsed her hips in time with his, and their mutual challenge scorched and morphed into something wicked and wild. The dance floor was crowded, but all he saw, all he felt was sweet, sexy Charlotte and the inferno between them as their bodies moved in perfect harmony. He took her hands in his, drawing them over her head. Without missing a beat, she moved against him, riding his thigh. His body flamed, but it was his heart that was swimming from the look of longing in her eyes.

He held her arms up as her breasts brushed against him, driving him out of his fucking mind. Her lips were parted, her eyes boring into his, as he ran his hands from wrist to shoulder, then pushed his fingers into her hair. Angling her face beneath his, he brushed his lips over hers, catching the hitch in her breath. She smelled like sin and sweet salvation. His teeth grazed her neck, a spot he couldn't wait to devour. He trailed the backs of his fingers along the sides of her breasts and down her ribs. They were perfectly in tune with each other, and he was so damn turned on, he clutched her hips, grinding against her. Her eyes turned hungrier as he lowered his cheek to hers and brought their torsos together, slowing his pace and swaying sensually.

Her hips pressed temptingly against his rock-hard cock. He dipped her over his arm. Her long dark hair *whoosh*ed around her, and as he brought her upright, her arms circled his neck. Passion brimmed in her eyes.

Beau didn't know how many songs they danced to, or when the crowd thinned, but when he became aware of the band packing up, he and Charlotte were still wound together like mating snakes. He was completely and utterly lost in her. Neither one of them said a word. He wasn't even sure he could. He felt more alive than he could ever remember feeling, and it was all because of Charlotte. He didn't care that they were standing on the dance floor or that they were surrounded by dozens of people. He captured her mouth in a torturously intense kiss. Spirals of ecstasy whipped through him, hot and urgent, as he took the kiss deeper. But it wasn't enough. He needed to devour her. He fisted his hands in her hair, earning a hungry moan, which snapped his brain into gear.

He didn't want to embarrass her or make her regret being out with him. He tore his mouth away, grabbed her hand, and strode to their table. He dug out his wallet with one hand, holding her tight with the other, and tossed two hundred bucks on the table.

"Beau," she said breathlessly.

Her eyes told him it was a plea for more, but he had to be sure. He didn't want to fuck this up. He hauled her closer. "Tell me. Stop? Go?"

"Go!"

He dragged her out the gate and recaptured her lips, more demanding this time. She pressed her whole body into his and he lifted her into his arms. Her legs circled his middle, and she grabbed his head with both hands, holding it like a vise as they ate at each other's mouths. Their tongues tangled as they stumbled around his truck and out of sight. He backed her up against the cold metal, using it for leverage to free his hands to explore her body. He sealed his mouth over her neck, and she arched forward, giving him better access and pressing her breasts against his palms.

"Fuck, Char," he ground out, realizing this couldn't go anywhere, even in the dark parking lot. He needed more of her, and he'd never make it all the way up the mountain.

"Truck," she panted out.

He reclaimed her mouth as he opened the door and set her on the seat, unwilling to break their connection. She clung to him, pulling him in as she leaned back. Why the hell hadn't he rented an old truck with a bench seat? He drew back with a series of frantic kisses, trying to remember if there was a hotel nearby, but his mind was a nest of erotic fantasies, and Charlotte was front and center in every one.

"We've gotta get out of here."

"Drive someplace," she said urgently. "Hurry!"

Hell yes.

Minutes later they were on the road, heading out of town. He had one hand on her thigh, his fingertips teasing beneath the fringe of her shorts. She kissed his upper arm, nipping and licking and driving him out of his mind. She lifted her hips, wiggling until his fingers pushed beneath her panties. She put her hand on his, her eyes drilling into him as she pressed his fingers into her slickness. She moaned and sank her teeth into his arm. He pulled off the road into a dark parking lot and drove to the far end, out of sight from the road.

She began crawling across the console before he even cut the engine. He reclined his seat as she straddled him, and they feasted on each other's mouths. He pushed his hands beneath her shirt, groaning at the feel of lace and her warm flesh. He was *starving* for her. He managed to sweep her beneath him in the confined space. Her wild hair spilled over the seat, and her eyes shimmered with desire as he pulled his shirt over his head and tossed it to the passenger seat.

Her hands roamed all over his chest, face, and arms. Moonlight dusted in through the windows, giving away a hint of shyness in her eyes despite her openly groping him.

"God, you're gorgeous," he growled as he lowered his mouth to hers, kissing her slow and sensually, like he'd been wanting to do since…Hell, if he were honest with himself, she'd made his gut go funky the very first time he'd set eyes on her.

"I've been dying to do that," he said between heart-thrumming kisses.

He kissed and sucked his way down her neck, earning one plea after another. He pushed up her shirt, revealing the swell of her breasts straining against pink lace. He glanced up, catching an innocent expression that made his heart squeeze.

"Don't stop," she begged.

He pressed a kiss to her ribs as he unhooked the front clasp of her bra and pushed the material to the sides. He lifted his gaze to hers as he cupped one beautiful breast and pressed a kiss to her nipple. Her eyes widened, and her hips rocked up, making his cock throb. She moaned and writhed, bowing up beneath him as he dragged his tongue around her nipple and placed openmouthed kisses all over her breasts, except where he knew she wanted it most. He ground his hard length against her center, wishing there were enough room to bury his face between her legs. He wanted to bring her more pleasure than she'd ever imagined. To show her that real life—*he*—was a million times better than any fictional world, or hero, she could create. The cab of a truck was not where he had envisioned making love to Charlotte, and certainly not their first time, but he could at least take them both where they desperately needed to go. To see and feel her come apart for him—for them— would be enough to tide them over. As he kissed and tasted, teasing and taunting, he tried to mentally work out a position where he could pleasure her thoroughly.

"Beau, *please...*"

The ache in her voice sent him into motion. He lowered his mouth over her nipple as he shifted to his side, sucking and grazing his teeth over the taut peak, earning a stream of sinful pleas. He unbuttoned her shorts and pushed his hand beneath her damp panties. Heat slid through him like lava as he dipped into her tight, slick haven. She gasped, and he crashed his mouth to hers, wanting to capture her pleas, to feel the passion moving through her as he furtively sought—*and found*—the spot that would make her toes curl. A shudder rumbled through her, and she grabbed his wrist, rocking her hips. Long, surren- dering moans sailed from her lungs into his as he played over her pleasure points. She clutched his arms, whimpering as her body trembled and shook. He lowered his mouth to her breast again, sucking hard as she cried out his name. Her inner muscles clamped down, pulsing tight and perfect around his fingers. His cock swelled painfully behind his zipper, desperate to get in on the action.

As she came down from the peak, he kissed her harder, rougher, needing to feel her come apart for him again. She moved with him, fucking his fingers, until she tore her mouth away and "Beau!" sailed from her lips like a celebration.

He took her in another fierce kiss and felt her tugging at the button of his jeans. His cock throbbed at the thought of her delicate fingers or her hot mouth wrapped around it. If she took hold of him, there would be no slowing down, no waiting for a more appropriate time or place to make love to her. She pushed her fingers into the waist of his briefs, brushing over the swollen head.

He groaned and grabbed her hand. "Not here. Not like this. I can wait."

"But—"

Her words were drowned out by a loud and repeated *thud* on the window. He turned, sheltering Charlotte with his body as a bright light shone over them.

"Police. I need you to step out of the car."

Are you fucking kidding me?

"Ohmygod!" Charlotte scrambled to button her shorts.

He pressed his lips to hers as calmly as he could. "Don't worry, shortcake. They can't see us." He hooked her bra, righted her shirt, and buttoned her shorts.

"You don't know what they can see!"

"Tinted windows. They saw nothing. Just act normal."

She gave him a deadpan look as they sat up.

He reached over and tucked her hair behind her ear. "If you weren't so damn irresistible…" he said with a smile, hoping to earn one from her. But she looked petrified. He wrapped his arms around her and kissed her temple. "I'm sorry, Char. I haven't made out in a truck since…" *Holy shit. Do not go there.* "I'll handle it, and I won't ever put you in this position again."

Another bang on the window had him opening the door. He pulled on his shirt and stepped out of the truck, meeting the serious eyes of a policewoman. "Evening, Officer."

She shone the flashlight in his eyes, then swept it over his shoulder at Charlotte, who ducked her head, her cheeks flaming red. "Charlotte Sterling? Is that you?"

Charlotte's head snapped up. She stared at the policewoman, her lips curving up in that shy smile that made him want to wrap her in his arms and protect her, so different from the sassy smile that challenged him at every turn. "Hey, Heather."

Heather?

"You okay?" Heather shone the light at Beau again, openly assessing him. "Is this *date* consensual?"

Charlotte put her hand on his shoulder, as if she sensed he was about to snap.

Beau tried—and failed—to bite back his anger. "Yes, it's consensual!"

"Yes," Charlotte assured her. "Sorry. This is my friend Beau."

"Something wrong with the rooms at the inn?" Heather asked with a hint of amusement in her eyes.

We were too fucking hot and bothered to wait. "No, ma'am." He went for levity. "We just got carried away doing a little research for her books."

Charlotte stifled a giggle. "Yes, exactly."

"Okay, well, how about you get *carried away* somewhere other than on private property." Heather raked her eyes down Beau's body and turned off the flashlight. "I can't wait to read *this* book."

Charlotte climbed over the console to the passenger seat and said, "In my version, the policewoman might as well carry a bucket of ice water instead of a flashlight."

Chapter Nine

CHARLOTTE PACED HER bedroom the next morning, berating herself for how awkward things had been after she and Beau had arrived back at the inn. He'd been a perfect gentleman on the way home, holding her hand and apologizing a hundred times for putting her in an uncomfortable position, as if she hadn't had a hand in the idea. Hadn't she lifted and wiggled until he'd taken the hint and *finally* touched her? When they'd come downstairs, she'd once again gotten flustered and nervous as a girl of eighteen, and she'd fled. She was an idiot. She had a sexy beast in the other room who happened to also be a great listener and who was slowly opening up to her. And here she was, a nervous, hot-and-bothered wreck.

Maybe she should take a few pages from her heroines' playbooks. *They have all the moves and the greatest lines.* She walked into the bathroom and stared at herself in the mirror. Her hair was a mess from his hands in it last night. Her Superman shirt was two sizes too small, stopping just above her belly button, but the matching panties still fit. It was one of her favorite sleeping outfits because it was soft as butter and made her feel like she was strong even when she wasn't. She'd had it since she was eighteen, and she didn't care that the seams were frayed and there was a tear at the hem of the shirt. Last night she'd needed every pick-me-up she could find. Including two Twix bars.

She frowned at her reflection. She looked more like she was going to a sleepover with her girlfriends than like a seductress.

"I can do this," she mumbled to herself, and stalked determinedly into her bedroom. She rummaged through her drawers, tossing out lace thongs, push-up bras, and corsets she wore when she was trying to get in the mood to write BDSM scenes. She planted her hands on her hips and surveyed the chaos at her feet. *Black, red, or nude?*

Black said *fuck me*, red said *hard and rough*. She had no idea what nude said. She sank down to the edge of her bed.

She wasn't about *fucking* or *faking*. *Being with Beau* wasn't about fucking or faking. That was what she wrote, but not who she was or what she wanted. *I like who I am, and I think he does, too.*

She liked being with Beau, talking to him, *dancing* with him. Oh, how the man could dance! He was definitely *large and in charge*, but there was a tenderness about him. Or maybe that wasn't the right word. *I'm a romance writer and I can't even script my own love life.*

A memory of her mother tiptoed through her mind. Charlotte had been in eighth grade. The other girls had started wearing makeup, but Charlotte didn't like how she looked with eyeliner and blush, and she'd wanted to fit in. Her mother had come into her room and found her crying. She'd wiped the eyeliner from beneath Charlotte's eyes with a tissue and said, *You're perfect just as you are, ma chéri.* Charlotte pressed her hand to her stomach, remembering the way it had knotted up as she'd told her mother that boys wouldn't like her if she didn't look as pretty as the other girls. Her mother had brushed

Charlotte's hair over her shoulder and said, *Do you see how your papa looks at me when I'm sick? When I'm tired? When we dress fancy and go out? The boys who matter will look at you that way, too.*

Even all these years after losing them, Charlotte could still picture her father gazing adoringly at her mother with compassion and love so palpable she could have drowned in it. Her mother was right.

She didn't need lingerie. She needed to talk to Beau and get her feelings out in the open. No games, no research.

She pushed to her feet and strode out of her bedroom and straight out the door of her suite. Her stomach tumbled as she entered the hall, making a beeline for Beau's room while begging herself not to chicken out. She reached for his doorknob—and hesitated.

If it's locked, I'll turn around and keep my feelings to myself.

She closed her eyes and grabbed the knob, leaving the decision in fate's hands. It turned, and her eyes flew open. Her pulse went crazy as she pushed the door open and said, "Beau—"

His bed was empty. The sounds of the shower gave away his location. The door was ajar, and she stood before it, remembering what she'd seen the last time she'd barged in. It had been much easier when she'd been distracted by Ty's phone call and not on a mission to lay her heart in his hands. Her heart had led her to write her grandparents' story, which had led to the career she loved. Her heart had begged her to stay at the inn, which had eventually led Beau right to her front door.

Her heart had yet to lead her astray.

She inhaled deeply, hoping Beau would treat her heart as carefully as it deserved. She closed her eyes and drew her shoulders back, silently asking herself if she was one hundred percent sure about allowing herself to be so vulnerable with a man she barely knew—even though she was pretty sure he was equally vulnerable.

It took only a second for her choice to become clear—and she walked into the bathroom. As Beau yanked open the shower door, the warning in his eyes instantly morphed to desire.

"Charlotte." His gaze blazed down her body, turning all her nerves into live wires.

"You didn't lock your door," she said shakily.

A wicked, and also somehow intimate, smile lifted his lips. "There's nobody here I want to keep out of my bedroom."

He leaned his forearm on the shower door, and it slid open, revealing his powerful thigh and half of his ripped abs, stopping just to the left of his biggest distraction. Only it was no longer his biggest distraction. His eyes, his loving, hurting heart, and his compassionate nature were.

"Oh" was all she could manage. Lust simmered inside her as she drank in his nakedness. She couldn't take her eyes off him or force the words she'd come to say. She was swimming in memories of being in his arms, kissing his magnificent mouth, feeling his passion. She lowered her eyes, trying to muster the courage to speak.

"Was there another phone call?" he asked in a low, gravelly voice that scorched over her skin.

"No."

She swallowed hard, and when she met his gaze, she saw the look she'd always dreamed of. It sent her stomach into a tempestuous dance. Taking another leap of faith, she took off her shirt. Beau's muscles corded tight. For the first time in her life, words *truly* failed her. Even in her mind she couldn't string two together. But as she shimmied out of her underwear and stepped toward his outstretched hand, she knew there was nothing she could say to make this moment more perfect.

He gathered her in his arms and closed the shower door, holding her against him as warm water rained down on them. His slick, hard body felt safe and alluring.

"Charlotte—" He breathed her name like he was marveling at a gift, then brushed his lips over hers.

"Sorry about last night," they said in unison.

"Don't," he said, and cradled her face between his hands, looking at her like she was all he'd ever wanted.

Only she knew that wasn't true. His heart, or at least part of it, still belonged to someone else, but maybe she was all he'd ever wanted *since...*

"You're perfect." Honesty blazed in his eyes and his voice. "I shouldn't have allowed us to go so far in the parking lot."

"I wanted to. I wanted *you*. But after we got home I was a fumbling idiot, and I ran away."

"You were nervous and adorable, and I haven't stopped thinking about you for even a second. And now you're here with me, beautiful and *naked*." The warmest smile she'd ever seen appeared on his handsome face, and he said, "I love that you don't respect personal boundaries."

Her laugh was silenced by the sweet press of his lips.

"Charlotte, you know I'm not here to stay," he said between tender kisses.

"I know. I don't care." It wasn't exactly true, but it wasn't a lie, either. Given the choice of having this connection with Beau or forever missing out on him, she couldn't choose anything else. "I want you."

He kissed her again, rougher, more possessive.

"Wait," she said. "I haven't been with a man in forever."

"It's been a long time since I've been with a woman, too. I've never been a player, and..." His eyes grew serious again. "In case you're worried, you should know I'm clean."

Relief and appreciation swept through her. She'd been too caught up in them to worry about that, but he'd done the worrying for both of them.

"We don't have to do anything," he said. "Just let me kiss you."

The sincerity in his voice only made her want him more. She went up on her toes as his mouth covered hers, the warm shower spray seeping into their kisses like secrets. His entire body embraced her like he never wanted to let go. She loved his strength, his *possession*, the sinful, guttural noises he made as his hands slid over her skin.

"Touch me," she pleaded.

His eyes blazed into hers. She went up on her toes, and he met her halfway in a kiss that sang through her veins. It was slow and tender, and then his beautiful mouth was on her jaw, her neck, and *good Lord*, her breasts, sending her up on her toes again. *God*, he was good with his mouth. A river of desire raged inside her with every graze of his teeth, every hard suck. She leaned back against the cold, wet tile in an effort to keep her wobbly knees from failing her. He *possessed* every spot he touched as he moved down her body, kissing her belly, her hips. His hand moved between her legs, and like a laser to its target, he found the magical spot that shot bolts of lightning through her core. He rose, still driving her wild with his hand, and took her in a rough kiss. Lust surged through her. She clutched at his hair, his shoulders, his biceps, lost in a world of fiery sensations. He tore his mouth away, panting as he spread her thighs.

"I need more of you." He dropped to his knees and sealed

his mouth over her needy sex.

"*Oh*, Beau—"

She gasped in sweet agony as he expertly took her to the clouds. Quivering and quaking, she clawed at the wall to keep from melting down the drain. His hot tongue plunged in and out of her, and then he trapped her clit between his teeth, using his fingers to send her soaring again. She cried out, her voice echoing off the walls as he worked his magic over and over again until she collapsed into his arms. Before she recovered, his mouth was on hers, the taste of her arousal clinging to his tongue. He kissed her roughly, reigniting the inferno inside her. She'd been starved for him all night, had lain awake thinking about reciprocating the pleasures he'd given her. She'd dreamed about having his hard shaft in her hands, loving him with her mouth. And now, as his cock pressed temptingly against her belly, she reached between them.

"Char," he said in a heated whisper, and grabbed her wrist. "I can wait."

"I can't," she said, and pushed him against the tile as she kissed her way down his body, slowing to enjoy the feel of his pecs flexing against her mouth, the expansion of his abs with his heavy breaths.

He tasted clean, hot, and sweet, like a man made just for her. She felt his eyes on her, watching as she tasted and nipped and built up courage. She didn't want to rush as she explored his body. Each time she touched her lips to his hot flesh, his erection twitched against her, and she liked that too much to hurry past it. He tangled his hands in her hair, and she glanced up. Her knees weakened with the hungry and appreciative look in his eyes. She hadn't even known that was possible, and it made her feel bolder, more aggressive. When she reached his hips, she slid her hands to his ass. Heat spiked inside her at the confidence she'd mustered, the desires he'd unleashed in her. She wrapped her hand around his hard length, holding his gaze as she swirled her tongue around the broad head. His chin fell to his chest with a *hiss*, spurring her on. She lowered her mouth over his shaft, and he groaned. His hips bucked forward so hard she gagged and pulled back.

"Fuck," he ground out, and caressed her jaw. "I'm sorry."

"This is much easier on paper," she said, feeling foolish.

"What?"

Gulp. She glanced up at his confused expression, and then she looked at his big, beautiful cock and said, "My heroines *never* choke. They make it seem easy and sexy, but this is *way* different. They're all open throats and 'give it to me harder.' But you're *huge*, and I haven't done this in…Let's not go there."

"*Huge*, huh? That's something coming from a woman who creates body parts to her liking. Come up here."

He helped her to her feet, taking her in a series of slow, intoxicating kisses, until he'd obliterated her embarrassment.

"You don't have to do anything," he said reassuringly. "I just like being close to you."

"Oh no. I'm going to do this, and I'm going to blow you away…"

He chuckled, and she realized her pun.

"Man, I like you, shortcake." He kissed her again, smiling against her lips. "You already blow me away."

"You ain't seen nothing yet," she said sassily, and dropped to her knees, determined to give him the best blow job he'd ever had.

Or at least not to choke.

She closed her eyes, pushing away all thoughts, and concentrated on the hot hardness in her hands and the emotions sprouting inside her. As she slicked her tongue from base to tip, even those thoughts fell away. She licked and sucked, cradling his balls as she took him in her mouth. He moaned as she found her rhythm, working him with her hand and mouth. The shower rained down on her as he gently grabbed her head. She felt restraint in his grip and continued her efforts, wanting to shatter his control. The longer she pleasured him, the more confident and comfortable she became, learning to relax her throat and tease him in ways that made him shake and groan. She took him to the back of her throat, withdrawing so slowly, his fingers fisted in her hair, causing a sting of pain and pleasure. She worked him up until she could tell he was holding on by a thread. Then she concentrated on the wide crown, taking him to the back of her throat.

"Jesus," he ground out.

She drew back and gazed up at her big, strong man. His jaw was clenched, his eyes a torrent of control and desire. "Don't hold back," she pleaded. "I'm good now. I want more. I want everything you have to give."

His brows knitted again, his gaze torturous. "I don't want to hurt you."

"You won't. I know you won't."

She guided his shaft into her mouth and grabbed his hips, readying for his powerful thrusts, but he pumped slow and steady, going deeper with each thrust. She moved with him, and when he stopped short of her throat, she pushed, taking him all the way to the root. His fists tightened in her hair as they quickened their pace. Flames licked at her skin, taking her higher as tension mounted in his thighs. She wanted his hands on her, wanted him inside her, taking her like he was fucking her mouth, but she wasn't about to stop. She was so turned on, she knew if she touched herself she'd come in seconds, but she wanted to come by *his* hand—or mouth, or deliciously perfect cock—and she wanted *him* to come for *her*.

"Charlotte," he warned, trying to pull out of her mouth.

She held him tighter, refusing to release him until he was free from *all* his barriers. Each thrust became more precise, more powerful, and when warm jets of his arousal hit the back of her throat, he ground out her name, his hips pulsing in fast, hard jerks. She stayed with him, waves of ecstasy throbbing inside her as the last of his climax rocked through him. When she finally set him free, he lifted her to her feet, and she melted against him, boneless, sated, and so full of *them* she couldn't speak.

"What have you done to me, shortcake? I've never come so hard or felt so much." He framed her face as he'd done earlier, but this time he caressed her jaw. "Did I hurt you?"

She shook her head, drunk on him and dizzy with desire. He must have seen passion bubbling out of her pores, because he took her in another penetrating kiss as his hands and mouth worked their magic again, sending her spiraling into ecstasy and catching her when she finally, *blissfully*, floated back down to earth.

He kissed her tenderly, and then he lovingly bathed her, placing gentle kisses along her body as he went.

Afterward, he wrapped her in a towel and gathered her close. "I know you have to write, and I have work to do, but I don't want this feeling to end. Spend the morning with me. Show me Snow White's cabin. Take me on the walk you used to take with your grandfather."

Even in her euphoric state, her knee-jerk reaction was to say she needed to write. It was so strong, she had to visualize pushing it away and putting it under lock and key in order to move past it. That scared her as much as it fascinated her, because nothing had ever made her happier than she felt at that very moment.

"What do you say, Char? Just a few hours?"

"I'd love that," she said.

Just as the panic of falling farther behind on her deadline creeped in, he kissed her, pushing it away once again.

BEAU HAD BEEN with Tory so long, he couldn't remember a time when he hadn't been in love with her, and in the years since, not only hadn't he felt anything for another woman, but he hadn't thought he was capable of it. He knew life could change in an instant, but he'd never imagined it changing for the better.

After collecting the eggs, they made omelets—or rather, he made them and she watched like he was creating art. Beau realized how much he'd missed having someone special in his life. He noticed other things about himself, too, like how interested he was in what Charlotte had to say and how the more he learned about her, the deeper he wanted to dig. After breakfast, as they walked hand in hand through the woods on the trails she'd once walked with her grandfather, she shared stories about her family, holding his rapt attention.

"My grandfather used to sing the whole way down to the barn. Did I mention that he had the worst singing voice ever? It was awful, which is probably why I can't carry a tune across the street. But I always loved listening to him sing, and he didn't care if he was off-key. I loved that about him, that he could be happy even with his weaknesses."

The longing in her voice was inescapable, and Beau's desire to explore *all* of her emotions made his chest feel fuller, bringing a level of happiness he'd thought he'd never feel again. Just as he acknowledged it, guilt piled on like dirty laundry.

"Because it wasn't a weakness to him," he said to distract himself from the guilt. "It was only seen as a weakness by others. Your grandfather sounds like he was a strong man, which makes sense since you're so strong."

"Thanks. He definitely taught me to be strong." She pointed through the trees, looking radiant in her sexy, colorful sundress. "We're almost there. That's the tip of our barn. When I was growing up in Port Hudson, I had the most beautiful horse named Winter. My parents took me to a rescue ranch to pick her out when I was six, and I fell in love with her the second I saw her. She was eighteen, and dusty white with one big brown eye. She'd lost the other when she was a foal. My parents tried to get me to take a younger horse, but I knew she was meant to be mine. We brought her with us when we came for the summers, and I used to ride her everywhere. My father also loved to ride, and at the time my grandparents had a horse named Princess."

Beau pushed a branch out of their way. "What happened to the horses?"

She ducked under the branch and walked down the hill toward a thicket of trees blocking the view of the barn. "Winter died when I was sixteen, and the year after my grandmother died, we lost Princess. But they left us with great memories," she said cheerily.

She pulled him through a gap in the trees to a clearing. A babbling brook snaked along the left side, and a small rustic barn with a steep-pitched roof lay just ahead. The brook had several rocky-ledged waterfalls, which were clearly man-made, adding a mystical feel to the beautiful setting. Vibrant wildflowers poked out between long blades of unkempt grass. Beau was struck with a vision of Charlotte as a young girl playing in the grass, dreaming up fairy-tale worlds as her horse grazed nearby.

"Gosh, I haven't been down here in years," she said as they headed for the barn. "It looks smaller than I remember."

"Years? You do realize you live on your own little slice of paradise, right?"

"Yes, and I know I don't appreciate it as much as I should, but stories do not write themselves. And I guess life has gotten in the way of my walks."

"We need to fix that," he said, noting the damage to the peak of the roof, the missing shingles, and a few rotted boards he could fix while he was there. "How long has it been since you've ridden?"

"Since Winter died."

He lifted the iron drop-bar latch on the barn door. "There are no locks?"

"There's nothing to steal," she said with a sassy grin as he pulled open the door.

The musty smell of old wood, hay, and years gone by assaulted them.

Charlotte stepped inside and closed her eyes, inhaling deeply. "I love this smell. I miss it."

The peaceful look on her face gave him that tight feeling in his chest again. Beau pressed a kiss to her lips as she opened her eyes. "It'll smell even better if we clean it and air it out. This is the difference between the real world and the fictional one you live in."

"Oh, I don't know. I'm pretty good at conveying things on the page." She walked down the center aisle of the dusty barn, peering into each stall. She lifted an old leather harness from a wooden hook on the wall and sniffed it. "The smell never really goes away."

She set it back on the hook and walked toward him.

He gathered her in his arms and kissed her. "I don't think your sweet scent will ever go away, either."

"Beau…" she said a little shyly.

He touched his lips to hers, loving the way she could be brazen one minute and tentative the next. "It's true. I came here expecting to be completely focused on work and nothing else. And then there you were, crawling on top of a handcuffed blow-up doll. I haven't been able to think straight since."

"You've had the opposite effect on me. I had writer's block so badly I could barely string sentences together, and now it's like you've opened a vein."

"I'm not sure how I feel about you using me for research," he teased.

"I'm not using you for research. Or at least, not anymore."

He chuckled. "Maybe we both need a dose of real life while I'm here."

His cell phone rang, and he begrudgingly pulled it from his pocket. Nick's name flashed on the screen, and his chest constricted. Goddamn it. He didn't need his brother checking up on him. He sent the call to voicemail, his walls creeping up around him again.

"Aren't you going to answer that?" she asked.

"No," he said as he headed out the door. "Let's go see the

cabin."

She hurried after him. "I can give you privacy if you want to call whoever it is back."

"It's just my brother Nick. I know what he wants."

"And I take it you don't want to talk about whatever it is?" She laced her fingers with his and stopped walking. "Beau, last night you said two of your brothers had texted and I noticed that you didn't reply to them either. I'm sorry for being nosy, but is something going on between you and your family?"

He clenched his jaw, scanning the tree line for the trail, and headed toward a gap in the trees. "Do we follow that path to the cabin?"

"Yes, but…" She sighed, hurrying to keep up.

He felt bad for being short with her and stopped walking. "I'm sorry. There's some stuff going on back home that I'd rather not think about."

"Maybe talking about it will help."

"It won't. Look, I like hanging out with you, and I don't want the ugliness of that situation to ruin the little time we have together."

"*Hanging out?*" The hurt in her eyes cut right through him. "Is that what you call this after what we've done together? Because I *hang out* with Cutter, and I'd never let him do those things to me!" She stalked away.

"Goddamn it." He caught up to her and stepped into her path so she had no choice but to hear him out. "I'm sorry. That's *not* what I meant. I'm upset, okay? I'm angry, confused, and not thinking clearly, but it has nothing to do with you. I like being with you, and I haven't felt like this, or been this close to anyone, in a very long time. I just don't want my life to fuck it up."

"Your *life*? Don't worry, Beau. You're doing a good job of messing it up all on your own. I realize we barely know each other, but it still hurts to be shut out." She crossed her arms and shifted her eyes away.

He wrapped her in his arms, hating himself because she was right. She had no idea of the noose he'd worn like a bow tie for so long it had become a part of him. He kissed the top of her head and said, "I'm sorry, Charlotte. I'm pretty messed up this time of year. Or maybe always, but especially now. I don't want to hurt you or lay my crappy past on you."

She gazed up at him, sunlight reflecting in her serious eyes. "I laid my crappy past on you, and you didn't run from it."

"Charlotte," he said softly. "I don't think I could run from you if you were holding a gun to my head. You've found parts of me that I thought had died a long time ago. I'm sorry for snapping and for shutting you out. You don't deserve either, but it's hard for me to control it when it comes to this. Please don't push it right now, okay?"

"I'd like to agree, but it would be a lie." She shrugged apologetically. "I take it this is about the girlfriend you lost?"

He turned around, wondering if he should have walked away before they'd ever kissed, because when he looked into her eyes, it was impossible to remain steadfast in his resolve to keep his distance.

She walked around him until he was staring directly over her head to avoid falling back into her beautiful eyes. She jumped so her eyes met his and said, "Beau!" She jumped again. "Please"—*jump!*—"talk"—*jump!*—"to"—*jump!*—"me."

He couldn't help but haul her against him. "Where did you come from?"

"From two people who were madly in love," she answered.

"And from what you told me, so did you. We've both lost people we loved. If anyone understands what you've gone through, it's me. I think it might help to talk about your feelings, to honor them instead of letting them choke the life out of you every time you think about her."

He felt like a fish on a hook. Every time he tried to swim away, one look at Charlotte reeled him back in. Except that analogy didn't work at all. A fish would die if it were caught, and he had a feeling Charlotte was the only thing that could breathe life back into him.

She wound her arms around his waist and kissed his sternum. "Just think about it. That's all I ask."

"That's *all*, huh?"

She held up her finger and thumb and mouthed, *Just a little bit.*

"You drive me crazy, shortcake."

"Maybe you need a little crazy in your life."

Chapter Ten

"KEEP YOUR EYES closed," Charlotte said as she led Beau down a stone path lined by rough-hewn tree stumps, which were connected with long branches like velvet rope stanchions. They stood before the Tudor-style home her great-grandfather had renovated to look just like Snow White's cabin. The chocolate-colored A-line roofs sloped nearly to the ground, dipping where roofs shouldn't dip, as if they'd melted in the sun. Between the taller peaks were two small dormers, and just below, another drippy roof sheltered a bay window beside the arched barnwood front door. A crooked stone anchored the right side to the rocky patio.

"Okay," she said, excited to share one of her favorite places with Beau, hoping it might ease the sting of whatever was eating away at him. "Open your eyes."

His eyes opened, but they didn't find the house. They landed on her, and the emotions in them made her stomach tumble. Beau didn't say a word. He simply kissed her forehead, the tip of her nose, her cheeks. She melted a little more with each touch of his lips, and when he cradled her face the way she'd come to anticipate, she held her breath, hoping he wasn't going to tell her they'd made a mistake.

"I have had my eyes closed for so many years; it's going to take some time for me to adjust to your beautiful, bright light. But I see you, Charlotte, and I want to see more of you. I also want you to see more of me, but it'll take time."

Forget melting at his kisses. His words, expressed with such sincerity, turned her to a swoony puddle of goo. She went up on her toes, meeting him in a dreamy kiss full of hope and unspoken promises. His thumbs caressed her cheeks as their lips parted, and a new smile she'd never seen before softened his features.

"I came out here to fix up your place. I had no idea *I* might be on the agenda."

"Neither did I. I don't want to fix you," she said honestly. "I just want to know you."

He lowered his lips to hers in a slow, drugging kiss. Then he glanced down at the oddly shaped maroon, forest green, and peach slabs of rock and cobblestones bound together with thick white concrete beneath their feet and said, "Have we entered Fairy Tale Land?"

"I know I have," she said breathlessly. The amusement in his eyes brought her back to reality. "Sorry. It's not my fault that your kisses give me the best kind of high."

He touched his lips to hers. "Yours too, shortcake." He glanced at the house. "Are we about to be greeted by seven whistling dwarfs?" He took her hand and headed for the door. "This house is phenomenal."

"It is amazing, isn't it?"

"I've never seen anything like it." His gaze swept over the roofs. "Actually, I take that back. I've seen roofs that slope like this, but usually on houses that are in complete disrepair, not purposefully built. Please tell me you lock *these* doors."

She reached into a nearly invisible pocket in her dress and withdrew a blue-and-yellow polka-dot key. "Voilà!" She handed it to him.

"Polka dots." He chuckled. "We're going to clean out that barn and lock it up, too," he said as he unlocked the door.

She loved his enthusiasm, but though she was having a great time this morning, the voice in the back of her head reminded her of her deadline. "I don't have time to clean out a barn. I have a book to write."

He pocketed the key, giving her a get-serious look. "By *we* I meant *me*. You'll sit your pretty little ass down by the brook and type away on your laptop."

"Oh, will I?" She knew she would. He was her inspiration for this story, and more importantly, she wanted to be with him. "Don't you have enough work to do around here? You're only here for another few weeks." Her stomach sank as she said it. She finally felt something real, something good enough for her to be standing outside instead of sitting at her keyboard. She hated that their time together was ticking away.

His brows knitted, and she wondered if he was thinking the same thing. As if he didn't want to think about it either, he shifted his gaze away and said, "I'll make the time. I don't like the idea of your family's legacy rotting away or being left open to God knows what."

"Bears and other creatures, right?" she teased, pushing thoughts of his leaving away. "Maybe we should buy a *security door* for the barn."

"You need that security door," he said.

"Who are you, the evil witch Gothel?"

"Who?"

She rolled her eyes. "Gothel is the witch who locked Rapunzel in the tower."

He swept her into his arms and said, "Trust me, shortcake. I have no interest in locking you in a tower. I want to get you *out* of that inn so you can experience life. With your laptop, of course." He gave her a chaste kiss. "Although, having you shackled to my bed? Now, that might be fun."

Her mind raced at the prospect as he turned the knob and pushed the door open. The scents of cedar and love filled her as they stepped inside.

His gaze swept over the hand-sculpted stucco and stone walls, none of which were straight. He ran his hand along the carved wooden cap on the half wall separating the living room from the cozy eating area and looked up at the exposed-beam ceilings, saying, "Wow. Your great-grandfather did this? This is amazing. Did he hand-carve all the beams?"

"With his own two hands. The beams, these wood caps on the half walls. He made every arched door, and he purposely made them all different sizes and widths, and he made the intricate iron hinges, too. I wish I had known him." She took his hand, leading him through an archway carved into a giant tree trunk to the kitchen. Pine cabinets with elaborately carved doors were built into the uneven walls on one side of the room. On the other side sat an old-fashioned iron stove, begging for a teakettle. Its flue wound up behind it and disappeared into a stone wall in which a rounded brick oven was built, bringing back a wealth of warm memories.

"When I was little, my grandmother made pizza in the brick oven. I've never tasted anything so good, except maybe the steak you made the other night."

"I bet you have great memories of this place. No wonder you like fairy tales." He marveled at her great-grandfather's handiwork. "Charlotte, this attention to detail is insane. Nothing is plumb, and the ceilings look like frosting. I love how he made it wavy to fit the storybook home. And these pine cabinets? Look at the way each door is arched and a different size than the next. He must have worked endlessly to achieve this. This wasn't just a renovation. This is a masterpiece." He crouched to inspect three small arched openings between the countertop and the cabinets above.

"Aren't those nooks cool? My grandfather said his father made *everything*. He even made the steps from trees on the property." She pointed out of the kitchen to the stairs that disappeared behind the tree-trunk archway.

"*Cool* doesn't even come close to what he's done here. Look at this. Every step is a different size and shape." Beau crouched and ran his hands over the wood. "They're smooth as butter. Can we go up?"

"Yes, but be careful. One step is missing." Excited that he loved the house as much as she did, she hurried upstairs, slowing to step over the missing tread.

"I can fix that. I also noticed some things that needed fixing downstairs, chips in the stucco, a broken tile in the kitchen floor, and we should probably repoint the fireplaces, too."

"We?" she teased, although she kind of wanted to make the time and be part of fixing up the house. She hadn't been down here for so long, she missed it. She felt happier just being here. "You're making a big list for yourself. I don't think your relatives meant for you to do all this extra work, but I'm happy to pay you to do it."

"The list they gave me was short and easy. Having my hands on this would be a joy."

Beau remarked on every room, every view, every minute

detail. The master bedroom boasted a stone fireplace that looked as though it had fallen into place like rocks after a landslide. Two uneven hand-carved mantels made it seem even more off-balance. The walls were angled in on both sides, like an A-frame with a flat ceiling in between. Two big picture windows offered magnificent views of the property.

Beau inspected the fancy chandelier. "Is this where you got the idea to use a chandelier in your bedroom?"

"Yes. I love the way everything is so fairy tale-ish here. When I was young, I would sketch out plans for suites at the inn, creating a fairy-tale theme. I must have drawn dozens of ideas, and my grandfather would make a really big deal out of each one."

"Do you still have them?"

"No. I gave them all to him. It was kind of our thing. It started when I was little, with my crayon drawings. As I got older, they became more detailed. I even sent a few from college, because I knew how much they would brighten his day."

"That's sweet. I'm sure they did. Have you thought about redoing the inn now that you're here?"

"Oh, right. Like hand over a chunk of my inheritance and then have to manage the process and lose all my writing time? No way. Unfortunately, this is not a fairy tale where I can click the heels of my ruby slippers and *poof* it would be done and someone else could run it while I write."

They went back downstairs, and she took him through the rest of the first floor before locking up and heading back to the inn. Pine needles and leaves crunched beneath their feet, and the scent of forest and *Beau* hung in the air. It was nice, spending time with him, sharing her memories, and walking the path she'd enjoyed so many times with her grandfather.

"When I first came back to the inn, I thought if I ever decided to stay for good, I'd fix up the cabin, maybe get another horse, and go riding like I used to. And then I got sucked into writing erotic romance, and I wanted to use the study in the inn as an office because it has those great windows and a view of the lake. But I couldn't do it. All those dark walls and furniture stifled my creativity. The view didn't even matter."

The trail narrowed, and Beau put his hand on her back, allowing her to walk ahead of him. "Is that why you write in your office? Because it's brighter?"

"I know what you're thinking. How can a girl who doesn't even use lights half the time care about dark furniture, right?"

"It might have crossed my mind," he said as the trail widened again, and he fell into step beside her. "But I'm more curious about the rest of it. You've been here for several years and you're still living in the inn, and you have no horse. What happened?"

"I don't know. I got lost in my writing and never looked back. When I'm writing, I don't think of all this." She waved her hand. "I can honestly say that I've never felt like I was missing out on a thing. But today, being with you, and going into the barn and the cabin, has reminded me of all the things I'd dreamed of."

"Then maybe it's a good thing I came into your life, because a woman like you should not spend all her time indoors, and a house like that should not go to waste. We'll get it fixed up so you can stay in it."

"Beau, the way you're adding things to your list, you'll be stuck here forever. Not that I'm complaining." She worried that sounded too big for where they were together and said, "You're great for my writing."

"For your *writing?*" He wrapped his arms around her and nipped at her neck.

"Among other things," she said sassily.

His eyes smoldered. "About those *other things…*"

His lips touched hers, soft as a whisper. She wound her arms around his neck, trying to capture his mouth, but he continued the torturous teasing, brushing his lips over hers and then pulling back.

"*Beau,*" she pleaded as his lips swept over hers again.

"I could tease you all day long just to hear you say my name like that."

She had the urge to say his name like that over and over just to see how he'd react, but they'd been out for most of the morning, and she would never get her word count in if she didn't get started.

"No, you can't," she said as firmly as she could muster. "I have to get back to the inn and write, or I'll be writing all night, so if you want to kiss me, you better do it qui—"

His mouth came greedily down over hers, kissing her so deeply she felt it sweeping through her, lifting her up. She clung to him as their lips parted, her senses reeling.

"Maybe you can use that for inspiration." He took her hand and led her out of the woods.

"Inspiration," she said absently. She tipped her chin up toward the sun, basking in their beautiful morning.

Beau took her other hand in his and said, "I want to know more about your dreams, and what others you've let drift away."

She looked at him for a long moment, trying to piece together the changes she saw in him since this morning. He was warmer, more talkative. *Invested.* Her mind took that thought and wove it into more. But it was just another fairy tale. Their relationship had an expiration date, so she said, "You know how sometimes you dream about things and they just don't fit into your life?"

"It's been so long since I dreamed, I'm not sure I even remember how."

"That's sad. I'll tell you what, since you're doing so much to help me fix up this place, I'm going to reteach you how to dream. *Tonight*," she said excitedly. They had three and a half weeks left, and she planned to enjoy every single minute of them. But in order to do that, she needed to get writing! "Eight o'clock. Meet me under the stars."

He waved toward the grounds. "Where exactly? That could be anywhere."

"Come out back. You'll know where to go," she said playfully. "Now I really have to get inside and write."

He hauled her into his arms, wickedness dancing in his gorgeous eyes. "You dressed in that sexy little outfit, and now you're trying to run away from me? You should have worn that oversized men's shirt I saw you in the other day."

"I only wear those when I write. They're my father's old shirts. Whenever I wasn't sure I could do something or I was struggling, he'd say"—she lowered her voice—"'Dig deep, sweetheart. You're a Sterling, and Sterlings never take things at surface value. Even ourselves.' His shirts remind me to put my best words forward."

"Aw, babe, I love knowing that about you, and that's the sweetest thing I've ever heard. But exactly what mood were you shooting for with this outfit?" He grabbed her ass. "Because it *definitely* put me in a certain mood."

Her insides heated up, and the feel of his hard body lit

sparks beneath her skin. But the meeting with her editor was fast approaching. She forced herself to wiggle out of his arms and walked backward toward the inn. "Eight o'clock," she said with an unstoppable grin. "Be there."

"I'll bring dinner!" he called after her.

"I'll be dessert." She turned and headed up the hill, humming and floating on cloud nine—until she realized what she'd said.

She spun around, and Beau was grinning like a sexy fool, which threw her off a little since there was nothing foolish about the man.

He threw his arms up and said, "You expect me to concentrate on work with *that* on my mind?"

"Maybe you can use it for inspiration!"

BEAU UNLOADED THE supplies they'd bought in town and installed the exterior security doors on Charlotte's bedroom, and as promised, he painted the decorative scrolls pink. He finished touching up the bedroom and bathroom on the second floor, and then he made sandwiches and brought one in to Charlotte, but she waved an empty protein bar wrapper, claiming she'd already eaten. The thank-you kisses made his efforts more than worthwhile. He spent the afternoon fixing loose slates on the patios and repairing balcony railings. When the sun finally dipped from the sky, he headed out to the terrace to get started on the medallion design for Charlotte's room before getting ready for their date. *Date?* The word felt funny rolling around in his mind, but thoughts of Charlotte made it feel ten types of good.

Beau called his cousin Josh on his way outside and caught him up to speed on the repairs.

"That's great, Beau. I really appreciate you taking care of all of that for us," Josh said. "I hear you and Char are getting along well."

"You heard? Oh right, we ran into Hal last night. I guess he mentioned it?"

"He didn't, actually, but you know Weston gossip travels fast." Josh and his wife were fashion designers, and since having their little girl, Abigail, a little more than a year ago, they split their time between living in New York and Colorado. "All it takes is one set of eyes to light the gossip trail on fire."

Shit. Had he heard about the run-in with the cop? "It wasn't what it…" He gazed out at the lake, imagining Josh's amused dark eyes as Beau tried to come up with a cover story. "Okay, yeah. It was exactly what it looked like. But isn't that some kind of breach of ethics or something for the cop?"

"Cop?" Josh said with interest. "I want to hear *that* story. Max and Treat were on their way home and saw you guys making out in a restaurant parking lot."

"Damn it. I must have lost my mind to expose her like that."

"The whole town probably knows by now. You know how the girls talk, and they adore Charlotte. They're pulling for the two of you. In fact, they're probably placing bets or planning your wedding."

"*Man*, this sucks." The last thing he wanted was for Charlotte to become the talk of the town. "Listen, I need a favor."

"I don't possess the power to erase memories, dude. Sorry."

"That's too bad, because it'd be a shame to embarrass Charlotte."

"Embarrass her? The woman was making penis pancakes for a scene in her book when we arrived for our wedding. I doubt anything can make her blush."

Beau shook his head, chuckling and taking pleasure in knowing exactly how to make her blush. He and Josh talked for a few more minutes, and after their call, Beau sat at the table and began designing Charlotte's medallion. A few minutes later, a hollow *thud* interrupted his thoughts. He glanced around him as another *thud* sounded. He got up to check out the source of the sound and peered over the railing. Something flew off a balcony and landed on the grass with another *thud*.

What the hell?

Sheets sailed through the air, floating silently to the grass below. Beau stared at the mess of linens and bundles tied together with rope and ribbons spread across the lawn. More linens flew from the balcony, and then Charlotte's head and upper body appeared. Her hair curtained her face as she looked down at the mess. She disappeared again, and Beau felt himself smiling, wondering what she was up to.

He leaned his hip against the railing, thinking about her. If there was one thing he'd figured out, it was that unless she was dragged out of her office, she left it only to collect eggs or work out scenes. He waited for a blow-up doll to come soaring off the balcony.

As he stood pondering the complex woman who was awakening parts of him he wasn't sure were safe to unearth, she appeared on the lawn. She was bent over in her pretty little sundress, tugging a cardboard box in the direction of the woods. She huffed out a breath, flipped her hair over one shoulder, and began plucking the sheets from the grass and tossing them onto the box. She lifted a tied bundle and put it on top of the linens. Leaving the other linens behind, she grabbed the edge of the box with both hands and tugged it backward across the grass. She stopped every few seconds to wipe her brow or set her hands on her hips and survey the land behind her. Then she gave the box a hard *yank* and flopped onto her butt.

Beau opened his mouth to ask if she needed help, but she lay back, eyes closed, arms spread out to her sides. A peaceful expression appeared on her beautiful face. He was dying to know what was going on in that creative mind of hers. She looked too happy to interrupt. A few minutes later she pushed to her feet and began the tug-wipe-hands-on-hips process again. This was far too entertaining to miss, and Beau settled in for the show.

A few box-tugging minutes later, he heard a distant ringing. Charlotte shoved the bundle to the ground, threw the linens over her shoulders like she was digging for gold, and tore open the box. She withdrew her phone and popped up to her feet, heading in the direction of the lake. She spun in a circle, walked a few feet, then veered off in another direction. Her melodic laughter was music to his ears, and Beau went back to drawing.

Later, as he showered and prepared dinner, visions of Charlotte were still dancing in his head.

Chapter Eleven

AFTER FINDING CHARLOTTE'S suite empty, Beau headed out back with dinner, which he carried in the basket Charlotte used to collect eggs. The gray-blue sky lit his way as he crossed the yard toward glittering lights in the distance. As he neared the lake, serenaded by chirps and animals skittering through leaves, scents of damp earth and pine rose to greet him. It was so peaceful, all sky and mountains, without the noise of the city that never seemed to quiet back home. Even though Pleasant Hill was a fairly small town, it was still a town, full of busy, close-knit people who thought everyone's pain should be felt by all. The serenity and solitude of being on the mountain called to Beau on a visceral level. His gut knotted with the reality that in a few weeks he was set to move to Los Angeles and take on hosting a reality show that would allow him to travel all over the map. The perfect job for a guy who never wanted to put down roots. But it didn't come without issues. The show would bring him into the limelight. Beau was a private man, and that attention wasn't appealing in the least. But it was the tradeoff for being far away from Pleasant Hill and all the sad eyes that knew he was to blame for Tory's death.

As he neared the woods, he came across several garden stakes protruding from the ground. Sparkling fairies, butterflies, and flowers dangled from the stakes, leading him into the woods. He neared the lights he'd seen from the inn, and a web of linens came into focus. Sheets were knotted at the corners, strung up by ropes and suspended in the air. The ropes were tied to branches and tree trunks at odd angles and varying heights, creating peaks and valleys. It wasn't a tent, or even a canopy. The design was haphazard, with strings of tiny white lights hanging unevenly around it, like raindrops that had lit up wherever they'd fallen. It reminded him of Charlotte's attempt at decorating her bedroom, and he was blown away knowing she'd gone to all of this trouble for him. A worn, frayed blanket was spread on the ground and covered with several nearly flat, colorful pillows. Bundles of wildflowers tied with pretty ribbons were placed all around the blanket. The cardboard box he'd seen her lugging across the grass sat empty a few feet away.

Charlotte appeared from behind a tree, holding a bundle of flowers and looking angelic in a gauzy white dress that brushed the tops of her bare feet. White rope crisscrossed over her ribs like some sort of sexy toga. Thin strips of leather snaked along her wrist and forearm. She came closer and twirled. Her dress floated around her legs, and Beau realized the rope around her middle was an extension of the spaghetti straps resting on her sleek shoulders, holding the dress up with a simple bow in the back. One tug was all it would take...

"You found it!" she said excitedly.

He still wasn't quite sure what *it* was, but that didn't matter. He'd found Charlotte, and the stars in her eyes lit him up in a way nothing, and no one, ever had. *Charlotte* was what made being here so enticing. He had a feeling they could be in the middle of a city and she'd still be all he saw.

"I sure did." He set the basket on the blanket and reached for her hand, pulling her in for a smooch. She tasted like mint and sunshine. "You look absolutely gorgeous. How is it possible that I missed you after we spent all morning together?"

"Because we're good for each other," she said sweetly.

"But I take you away from writing. That's got to annoy you."

She shook her head, drawing circles on his chest with her finger. "I like that you do, and you inspire so much creativity in me, I think you're good for my writing—and for my heart. See my smile?"

"Yes, I do." He kissed her again, wanting to soak her up like a sponge.

"Don't get too big of a head about it," she teased. She handed him the bouquet of flowers. "These are for you."

"They're beautiful, and it's been a really long time since I went out on a date, but isn't the guy supposed to bring the flowers?" He reached into the basket and withdrew the wildflowers he'd picked for her.

Happiness radiated off her. "Thank you!" She smelled them and said, "I haven't gotten flowers since my dad was alive. He sent them to me every year on my birthday. These are beautiful."

"As are these," he said, holding up the ones she'd given him.

"Those flowers aren't technically for our date. They're for your crash course in dreaming."

"My crash course, huh?" Like a bear drawn to honey, he kissed her again. "You've gone to a *lot* of trouble to help me. What is this fantastic...*layout*?"

She waved at the linens like she was presenting a grand prize. "*This* is how we're going to open your mind to dreaming again. Welcome to your *dreamscape*! It looked much better when my family made it, but it'll still work. I'll show you."

He had a feeling if anyone could make magic happen, it was her.

"Do you want to eat dinner first?" she asked.

Not unless you're on the menu. "Whatever you'd like."

"Let's eat and talk. I'm *starved*."

He waggled his brows. "I like a woman who's not afraid to eat."

"I found that out firsthand," she said softly, scarlet staining her cheeks.

"Hey." He tipped her chin up so he could see her eyes. "You totally blow me away. *You*, not just sex. You know that, right? And in the shower, you literally blew me away. Like, obliterated everything that has ever happened in my life before that moment."

"Shh. You're embarrassing me."

He kissed her again, keeping her close. "Sexy and adorable is a killer combination."

They sat on the blanket, and he opened a wine cooler from the basket and handed it to her, grabbing a beer for himself.

"I know you have an affinity for food that's quick and you can eat with your hands," he said as he removed the lids from each dish and set them on the blanket.

She giggled.

"You have the dirtiest mind." He slipped a hand around her shoulders, drawing her closer, and said, "I like your mind, babe, all of it."

"And I like your...*mind*...too," she said haughtily. "And your cooking skills. This smells delicious. What's on the stick? I love anything on a stick."

"Don't get me started," he teased. "Grilled lemon chicken with peppers and potatoes."

She took a bite. "*Mm.* You missed your calling. You should have been a chef."

"You have been locked up here for too long. I'm going to take you out to a real restaurant and show you what fine food tastes like."

"Maybe after I finish my book in a month or so. I usually take a week or so off between books."

"A whole week, huh? You're as bad as I am."

The sounds of the leaves brushing in the breeze created a symphony as they ate. Just as he reveled in their closeness, reality crashed in. He'd be gone when she was done writing her book.

"The other day you said you travel a lot," she said, pulling him from the distressing thought, "but I thought Josh said you worked in Pleasant Hill."

"That's where my contracting business is based, but I take on projects all over the East Coast."

"What kind of projects? Like this one?"

"Not usually. I buy, renovate, and flip properties, and if the opportunity is right, I'll take on a design-build project. If the inn were mine, I'd renovate every room, make this your dream property. But that's all about to change. I'm taking a job in Los Angeles as the host of a new reality show, *Shack to Chic*. I'll have a new project in a new location every six to twelve weeks."

"Seriously? I'm sitting here with a soon-to-be famous actor?"

"A reality show host is hardly an actor. I'll just be me doing my job but working for a network."

"That's exciting! It's hard to imagine you in front of a camera, because you seem so private, but you must want that, right?

Or you wouldn't be taking it."

"I am private. It'll be a change, but I think it'll be a good one." Or at least he was trying to convince himself of it. "I won't have to think about where I'm going next." *Or carry the guilt that comes with escaping.*

"That sounds fun, especially if they give you creative freedom. I would hate to write by committee, and I'd imagine it's the same with what you do. Luckily, my editor gives me a lot of leeway with my books. If she told me how to write, I'd go bonkers. I can be a little stubborn. Gosh, you must be over the moon."

"I wouldn't say over the moon. It'll take some getting used to." He hadn't worked for anyone other than directly for his clients for so long, he wasn't sure how he'd handle being an employee, and being in the public's eye would definitely get on his nerves. But if it could alleviate some of the guilt he carried, it'd be worth it.

"And what about Bandit? Will you take him?"

"Absolutely. Once I sign the papers and get settled in, he'll be with me no matter where I go. I wanted to bring him here, but since he's moving with me to L.A., my mom asked if she could keep him while I'm gone. He's as spoiled as a grandchild would be. We tease my mom and say he's her granddog."

Silence was a breeding ground for havoc in a guilty man's brain, but as they ate in comfortable silence, Beau realized that since he'd met Charlotte, silence was no longer an enemy. Thoughts of her filled those moments, and that brought a new type of guilt, but it didn't last long. It was as if his brain didn't want him to forget the guilt he deserved, but his heart was now running the show, drowning out the other more often than not.

"Most of your family is in Pleasant Hill, right?" Charlotte

asked. "That's a long way from California."

"That's right." He'd gotten the opportunity because of his brother Nick's friendship with Maddox Silver, who was business partners with Nick's friend Jace. Maddox was well connected in the entertainment industry, and he'd hooked Beau up with the producers of the show. When he'd first told Beau about the opportunity, the distance from his hometown had been the driving factor for him to pursue it.

Charlotte set down the skewer she'd been nibbling on and picked up her wine cooler. "Can you tell me about them? About your family?"

"What do you want to know?"

She pulled her knees up to her chest and wrapped her arms around them. "Everything," she said a little dreamily.

"I've got a big family. That could take a long time."

"I don't mind. I miss my family," she said solemnly. "It'll be nice to hear about yours."

He wanted to fill up the loneliness he saw in her eyes. He moved the plates aside and said, "Come here." He put his arm around her, and she leaned her head on his shoulder. "I'm not sure where to start."

"What was it like to grow up with so many siblings?"

"It was loud *all* the time, and there was never any privacy."

"Did you share a bedroom?" she asked. "I always wanted to share a room with a sister."

"I shared one with Nick, who's a year younger than me. He was a pain in the ass when we were growing up, ornery as hell. But he's a good guy, still a pain, but he means well. He's a freestyle horse trainer. You'll like him; he's never without his cowboy hat." He narrowed his eyes and added, "Maybe you shouldn't like him *too* much."

She leaned into him, as if to say, *Don't be silly.*

"Jax and Jillian—*Jilly*—are twins, and opposites in most ways. Jax is totally chill, the type of guy that thinks before he speaks, while Jilly's a burgundy-haired tornado whirling through life. They're the most emotional of all my siblings, and they're both talented designers. Jax designs wedding dresses, and Jilly designs all sorts of clothing."

"She's the one you talked to on the phone. The one who made you smile?"

"You noticed?" Why did that make him feel so good?

"Hard not to," she said sweetly. "I like your smile."

He held her gaze, enjoying the way it heated up. "I like yours too, and yes, that was Jilly. She usually makes me smile. Like you."

"That's four of you. How about the other two?"

"Graham is the youngest. He's an engineer, like my father, but that's become a pastime for him. He's more of an investor these days. He travels a lot for work *and* pleasure. He's an adrenaline junkie, like Ty, but he's careful. He's hard to describe because he has two very distinct sides—the side that would walk a tightrope and the side that has to know everything is in order before he'll move forward. He and I have similar personalities—if you take away the adrenaline junkie part—but it wasn't always that way."

"Was he wild when he was younger?"

"No. I was. Zev is younger than Nick, older than Jax and Jilly. He and I used to raise hell. Graham has always had his head on straight."

"You mean there was a time when you weren't Mr. Clenched Jaw?"

He felt his walls going up again as they tiptoed around the

fire of his past. "Believe it or not, *yes*."

"Well, isn't that interesting?" A glimmer of mischief sparked in her eyes. "I want to hear all about it."

"How about we get to the Dreaming 101 course?" He started to push to his feet, needing space before his walls locked into place, but she grabbed his hand, keeping his arm around her.

"Don't go. Maybe you're right and we should switch gears."

She released his hand, and the desire to be near her over-powered his need for space. He knew Charlotte wasn't the type of woman who could share her heart without wanting his in return. He didn't know if he was capable of giving her what she deserved, but he sure as hell wanted to try.

He took her hand and said, "Thanks for being patient with me. I'd like to get there, Charlotte, but it's been so long, my gut instinct is to close the iron gates when the subject of my past comes up."

Her gaze softened. "I've been there. Remember? Let's get you dreaming again. That might help. Did you ever have big dreams of having things or going places? Accomplishing something outrageous?"

He knew what she was getting at, and he tried not to sound as uncomfortable as he felt. "Sure. A long time ago."

"Then we just need to open those gates that have gotten stuck closed." She reached for a bag from beneath the *dream-scape*. She sat cross-legged, facing him with the bag in her lap and excitement in her eyes.

He envied the way she wore her emotions on her sleeve and her ability to overcome so much and still have room in her heart for others.

"When I was seven years old and here for the summer, I kept having bad dreams," she said. "I don't remember why or what they were about, but my grandmother and my father said they could fix it. They gathered up sheets and blankets, pillows, and the stakes that led you in here with the fairies and sparkly butterflies and flowers. I remember watching them put it all together. Of course, theirs didn't look like a crazy person had done it."

"Yours doesn't either," he reassured her. "It's incredible."

"It's not, but thank you. I wish I'd paid more attention to how they did it. Theirs was the most magical thing I'd ever seen."

"I've never met anyone who believed in fairy tales or talked about things being magical the way you do."

"Because I grew up with grandparents who treated life like a fairy tale and parents who loved each other so much, everything about their love seemed magical."

"I understand where your fascination came from and why you cling to it so vehemently, and I hope that never changes. You're a very special, *rare* bird, Charlotte Sterling." He leaned forward and kissed her. "Thank you for letting me into your world. I think I needed this. I needed you."

"I told you that you needed crazy in your life."

Boy, did he ever. "So, tell me, do you believe in any one fairy tale in particular, or in everything magical or dreamy?"

"All fairy tales are dream worthy. Rapunzel dreamed of getting out of the tower, Cinderella dreamed of a better life, and Peter Pan, well, that one's all about dreams. And tonight is about your dreams. It was fun setting this up for you, even if I didn't do it perfectly." She gazed up at the web of lights and linens. "My father was an only child, and my grandparents made his entire life a fairy tale. The night I couldn't sleep, they sat me down on this very blanket and gave me one of these."

She withdrew a jar from the bag and handed it to him. Then she reached in again and gave him a blue notepad and a pen. She'd glued black lace around the middle of the jar, and she'd written *Bad Thoughts* in black marker on the glass.

"Bad thoughts?"

"I know it seems silly at our ages, but the idea is that you take the sad or angry thoughts that stop up your goodness, write them down, and put them in the jar."

She pulled another jar from the bag and handed it to him. This one was decorated with blue lace and silver glitter, and she'd written *To Dos* in blue ink. It was easy to imagine her as a hopeful little girl, believing everyone was good, because her family worked so hard to make it true for her. His parents had also worked hard to make sure he and his siblings were happy and safe, but not on a fairy-tale level. They were grounded in reality, teaching responsibility and making sure their six children knew that family always came first. More guilt piled on his shoulders with the thought of his parents doing so much for him, and here he was, about to move as far away as he could get.

Charlotte was watching him expectantly, and he shoved that guilt aside, unwilling to let it ruin their incredible evening.

"To dos?" he asked.

"Yes. The other thing that blocks us from dreaming is all the work we're thinking about while we're trying to sleep. It's amazing we can *ever* fall asleep with how busy our minds are."

"Especially yours," he said. "You've got all those heroes vying for your attention."

"Exactly." She pulled another jar from the bag. This one was labeled *Hopes and Dreams* with pink marker and was decorated with white glitter and pink lace. "I probably shouldn't have made yours pink, since you're a guy, but it's what we always did."

What had she put in her Hopes and Dreams jar when she was little? "I think I get the idea," he said. "What happens after I do this?"

"Then we lie down and hold hands, close our eyes, and…" Her brows knitted, and she looked so sweet, so earnest, he felt himself opening up to her even more. "I'm not sure, because I haven't had anyone to do this with as an adult. When I was younger, we would talk about our dreams until they felt so real we couldn't help but dream about them when we went to sleep."

She was too precious. She truly believed in this, and it made him want to believe, too. He set the jars aside and moved next to her, gathering her in his arms. "I think you were sent here just for me. You make me want to see things, good things, *possibilities*, the way you do."

"It's silly, I know," she said apologetically. "You don't have to pretend."

"Nothing about this is silly. It's thoughtful and imaginative. It's amazing, Charlotte. *You're* inspiring. And you're right. I don't have to pretend. For the first time in a decade, I don't *want* to pretend. I love the jars, and at some point I'm sure I'll use them. But I don't need them for this. I just needed *you*." He took her hand in his, fighting the constriction in his chest, and said, "If you're sure you want to hear it, I'd like to tell you about how I lost someone who was very special to me."

"YES," CHARLOTTE SAID without hesitation. "I want to

know whatever you're willing to share, and I promise not to ask too many questions or—"

He silenced her with a kiss, but not before she'd seen trepidation in his eyes.

"You can ask questions, and you might need to," he said. "It's going to be hard for me to talk about, but I think it might be hard for you to hear, too. If it's too much, just let me know."

"Okay, I will. A *decade*?" She could feel how big a step this was for him. She was nervous, too, because she knew how hard it had been to take those walks with her grandfather, to talk about her parents, to remember everything until it was etched in her bones.

He lowered his voice and said, "Almost a decade, and I haven't talked about it since it happened." He finished his beer and set the empty bottle in the basket. Then he pressed his hands to his thighs, his expression serious. "Actually, I didn't talk about it when it happened, either."

"Oh, Beau…" She put her hand on his, aching from the pain in his voice. "Before you came here, I didn't believe there was a man on earth I'd want to share my memories with. And all that stuff I told you on our walk, and the walk itself? No one else knows any of it. It's all too personal, and I know all of this—the jars, the dreamscape—is a little childish, but it was the only way I could think to try to help you. Thank you for trusting me."

"Charlotte, you are unlike anyone I have ever met. Your mind must run a million miles per hour, and you say exactly what you feel without hesitation. You handle blow-up dolls without embarrassment, but when I kiss you, you blush."

She felt her cheeks burn.

"I am attracted to everything about you, and whether things

are from your childhood or adulthood makes no difference. They're part of you, and that makes them special, not silly."

He pulled her closer, kissing her again. His lips were warm, his whiskers were rough, and she was happy and sad at once.

He brushed his thumb over her cheek and said, "Are you sure you want to hear what happened?"

"Yes. Kiss me again, and then tell me."

He slid his hand to the nape of her neck, taking her in a languid, intimate kiss, and then he kissed her again and again. His mouth was heavenly, and she couldn't suppress a moan from slipping out.

Keeping her close, he said, "If you keep making those noises, I'm going to keep kissing you."

"I want more kisses, but I don't think we'll stop there, and I want to understand your heart before I risk mine."

"If I were standing right now, your honesty would drop me to my knees."

"The fact that you're talking so openly would drop me to mine," she admitted.

He smiled, but it was tethered and told of his discomfort. "You have a strange effect on me, shortcake. I think we should go with it." He inhaled deeply, and then he said, "Her name was Tory Raznick. She was Zev's age, and in our neighborhood all the kids hung out together, so she was always around. She lived around the corner from my parents' house. You know how there's always one house with an endless stream of cookies and hamburgers and parents who all the other kids feel comfortable with? That was my house, my parents. I can't pinpoint when, or why, but one day she went from being my best friend's younger sister to the most beautiful girl in Pleasant Hill. At least to me. She was killed almost ten years ago."

She reached for his hand, his sadness bleeding out between them. "You were childhood sweethearts. I can't imagine how hard that must have been."

"I wasn't the greatest boyfriend. I partied all the time back then, but when I went off to college, I stayed true to her. And I loved her. I didn't know how *not* to love her. She was always there, and then"—he looked away, gritting his teeth—"she wasn't."

She wanted to crawl into his lap and hug him, but she was afraid it might be too invasive and make him feel too closed in. "I remember what that was like, wanting to pick up the phone to call my parents, expecting to see them walk through the door. No wonder this is such a difficult time of year for you. Is that why you won't answer your brothers' calls? Why you travel all the time? Because the memories are too much?" It made sense to her now.

"Yes. That's why I travel so often. And my brothers and I are close, but the reason they're calling is because the anniversary of her death is the weekend I leave for Los Angeles. They worry about me."

"If you miss her this time of year, that's understandable. They probably want to make sure you know you're not alone."

"I wish it was only that. I miss her, but she's gone, and I accepted that a long time ago. I'm not pining for her or waiting for someone to measure up to her. We were young, and who knows if we would have lasted, or if I would have driven her away with my partying. That's not what makes it so hard. It made it hard for a long time, but not anymore. Now it's everything else. Everyone loved her, not just me. She was a cheerleader in high school, and she always went out of her way to help other people, babysitting, volunteering. It wasn't just my loss or her family's loss. The whole community lost her."

"Oh, Beau. That's so sad. She sounds like an easy person to love. But don't you want to be around people who knew her? When I lost my parents, I needed to be around my grandfather because he knew them as well as I did."

He pinched the bridge of his nose, and when he met her gaze, his face was a mask of grief. "I can't face seeing everyone. I haven't seen her brother since the funeral, and I'm not sure I ever want to. He was one of my best friends, and when she died, it killed a piece of him, too." He inhaled deeply and said, "Duncan Raz was her brother."

"That's why you froze down by the Chickendales."

He nodded.

"Oh my gosh. I wish I had known. I'm so sorry."

"You have nothing to apologize for. He's a good-looking guy. You're a woman…"

"Not to make light of the situation, but he's not as hot as you, if that helps." That earned a partial smile.

"It does, but only because I want to be the guy you're fantasizing about."

Happiness floated through her despite their heavy discussion. "Well, you've got nothing to worry about there. Big, broody Beau has the starring role in each and every one of my fantasies, whether I'm awake or asleep. It's torturous." She leaned forward and pressed her lips to his. "I'm sorry you lost Tory, but if you've never talked about losing her, or spent time with the people who knew her best, then maybe doing so would help you find some closure."

"It wasn't just losing her," he said tightly. "It was how I lost her." He sat up straighter, fisting his hands, and looked away. The veins in his arms plumped like snakes.

"You don't have to tell me."

He turned, the hurt and longing in his eyes inescapable. "I want to. It's just…Charlotte, whatever you think of me right now is going to change, and I just want to remember this moment for a few seconds longer."

She felt guilty and selfish for the level of panic rising inside her. "Why will it change? I can't imagine that happening for any reason."

"I see disappointment and pain in the faces of everyone who knew her back home. I see anguish in *your* eyes because she died, and you didn't even know her."

"Because it's sad when anyone dies, Beau. But what you see in my eyes is for *you*. I can feel how much you hurt, and that makes me sad."

He pushed to his feet and paced. "Well, don't be sad for me," he said curtly.

She went to him and reached for his fisted hand. "I know what it feels like to lose the people you love. It will choke the life out of you if you don't let it out."

He stopped pacing and glared at her. She knew she should back off and give him space, but her grandfather hadn't allowed her to sink into the darkness, and Beau had already been mired in it for too long. She'd thought he'd hidden his feelings from her, but she'd been wrong. They were on his sleeve all along. She'd just been looking for the wrong ones. He could never be free until the noose around his neck was lifted.

"Whatever you feel guilty about or believe I'll hold against you can't be half as bad as you think. You're not in jail, so you obviously didn't kill her."

His fingers curled into a fist again, but she held tight.

"Charlotte, you have no idea."

She stepped closer, gazing into his tormented eyes, and said, "Then tell me. Unburden yourself to someone who wasn't there but who cares about you."

He looked out into the distance, up at the trees, at the dreamscape, and finally, he looked at her, anguish written in the tension and clouds in his eyes. "It's my fault she was in that fucking cab, okay?" he seethed. "It was Friday night and I was out partying with Zev. I never heard her texts. She wasn't supposed to come back until Sunday, but she flew home to surprise me. She texted me three times from the airport, and where was I? Drinking the fucking night away and talking about meaningless bullshit while she climbed into a cab. It was storming out. They hadn't gotten three miles from the airport before the cab skidded out of control, causing a three-car pileup. They were at the center of it. There was nothing left of the car but twisted metal."

Trying to make sense of his guilt, she said, "So she was in an accident in a cab while you were out?"

"Not just *out*." He jerked his hand away and paced. "Out *drinking* like a selfish kid without a care in the world."

"Ten years ago? You *were* a kid, Beau. That's what people right out of college do. They go out and party. They have fun and live their lives."

He held up his hand. "Don't do that, okay? Don't rationalize my inability to grow up. I know what I was back then, and I fucking hate that it took losing her to figure it out. But she died because of *me*, and everyone in that whole town knows it."

"Beau—"

He shook his head, looking defeated and furious at once. "I'm sorry, Charlotte. I shouldn't have gotten involved with you. It wasn't fair."

She went to him, and when he turned away, she moved with him, refusing to be deterred even by his glaring eyes. "So this is why you're so serious, why you live in the *real* world?"

He gave a curt nod. "Fantasies don't last."

"I understand why you feel that way, even if it breaks my heart to know it."

"It was a mess, Charlotte. Zev was going out with Tory's best friend, Carly, and they were so in love. I'm talking making-plans-to-marry-her love." He swallowed hard and said, "I turned myself around, buckled down and became responsible, even if I can't stay in Pleasant Hill for long stretches. But Zev? He took off and he's never looked back. We're lucky if he visits a few times a year for a couple days."

She felt on the verge of tears for the two of them, and for Tory and her best friend. But he trusted her enough to confess this to her, and she wasn't going to let him get away with giving up on having a happy life because of a mistake he'd made as a young man.

She hooked her fingers in his belt loop and said, "That's a lot of guilt to carry around, but I know a thing or two about carrying our fair share of burdens."

He looked at her finger curled around his belt loop, and a hint of humor rose in his eyes. "Do you think you can keep me here?"

"I don't think anyone can make you stay anywhere you don't want to be. I just wanted to be closer to you, but I thought you might swat my hand away if I tried to touch you." She tugged on his belt loop. "This is second best."

"Charlotte."

The warning in his voice wasn't strong, and she had a feeling he needed to hear what she had to say. "I'm going to tell you something that I've never told a soul. Not even Aubrey, who's my best friend in the whole world. When my grandfather died, I blamed myself. He was already brokenhearted when we lost my grandmother, and I was all he had left, and then I went away to college. I knew how lonely he'd be, even though we'd hired a nurse to live there with him. Nothing is the same as family. But he pushed for me to go—he knew how I wanted to write professionally—and he was right to do it. I needed to go to college, to be with people my own age and learn to stand on my own two feet. I needed to date and make mistakes. But after he died I realized how selfish it was of me to do it, regardless of what he wanted. Part of me knew he wouldn't last without me here."

Beau covered her hand with his. "Charlotte, you can't blame yourself."

"In my rational brain, I know that, but part of me will always carry that guilt, like a pebble under my foot that's always there, but hurts only when I put pressure on it. When I'm missing him or trying to work out a hero's personality and comparing everything they do to him. Of course, my relationship with my grandfather was nothing like I write, but I try to give my heroes some of his qualities, and I think keeping him alive, in a sense, helps my guilt. He loved us all so much. 'I love you' wasn't just three words he said. We *felt* his love in everything he did. I want my heroes to be like that. To love hard and forever, to show their emotions—even the awful ones. *I* want to be like that. The truth is, it was memories of my grandfather that pulled me through my grief over losing him. It didn't take away my guilt, but remembering our walks and how he gently forced me back into life by making me *feel* all the emotions that I wanted to hide from—or hide *under*—helped me put his death into perspective."

"I know a thing or two about hiding and running from emotions," Beau confessed. "It's easier not to feel."

A few days ago it would have taken courage to do what she did next, but now it felt natural to let her heart try to soothe his. She laced their fingers together and gazed up at the man she now understood so much better.

"I've never been in love," she said softly. "I can't pretend to know what that feels like. I know I said I understand what it feels like to lose someone you love, and I do. But I also realize it's different to lose a parent or grandparent than to lose someone who held your love in their hands and took a piece of it with them when they died. Someone whose face you probably see when you close your eyes and whose voice you might conjure when you need grounding."

His jaw tightened like a vise, and a lump formed in her throat.

"But, Beau, those are beautiful things that you should hold on to and experience as often as you want or need to. I think feeling those emotions—missing her, being angry at yourself if you need to—is a start. Only then can you forgive yourself for your mistake and really move on. You weren't driving the cab. You didn't cause the storm or the accident. You're a smart, big-hearted man. A *protector*. I have seen that even in the few days we've spent together. I get that you couldn't protect her, that you might even feel like you failed her, but you didn't *kill* her, just like I didn't kill my grandfather."

He didn't say a word, and the silence wrapped around them, binding them together, keeping them afloat in a sea of his confession and guilt.

"You said you never talked about Tory," she said softly.

"But now you are, and that's a start. Does it help at all? Because I'm a pretty good listener, and I will make the time every day you're here if you'd like to talk about her."

He lowered his forehead to hers and closed his eyes. "I have no idea if it helped." His eyes opened, brimming with too many emotions to separate. "All I know is that you're still here even after I told you it was my fault she's gone, and that's more than I could have hoped for."

"Because it's not your fault. I don't know why things happen, but I know that you going out with your brother didn't cause that cab to crash. And even though I think we were brought together for a reason, I wish with my whole being that you'd never lost her."

He slid his hand beneath her hair, holding the back of her neck the way she'd come to crave, his honest eyes pinning her in place. "I haven't felt anything good since that awful night. Until *you*, Char. When you're near me I feel alive, and when we're close, like we were this morning, I feel more than I ever have. I feel *whole*, and it's not fair to share my burden with you, but goddamn it, I want *you*. I want to be with you, and—"

She silenced his words with the eager press of her lips. He held her tighter, and she clung to his shoulders, reaching on tiptoes as he kissed her ravenously. His fingers tangled in her hair, guiding her mouth to the angle he craved, pouring his emotions into the kiss. She felt his anger, his confusion, his passion, and they both went a little wild, trying to fill a void within them. She wanted to heal his sadness, and in doing so, find the rest of the man who was making her want so much more than she ever had.

She tugged at his shirt. "*Off*," she pleaded.

He reached behind him with one hand and tore it over his

head. His mouth came down over hers urgently, sending her thoughts reeling as he crushed her to him. His chest pressed against her breasts, and his arousal ground against her belly as they made out with reckless abandon. They pawed and clawed at each other's bodies. He tugged her head back and sealed his teeth over her neck. Rivers of pleasure rushed through her.

"Charlotte," he panted out between mind-numbing assaults. "Need me to slow down?"

Their closeness was like a drug, and she wanted to overdose. Her heart took a perilous leap as she reached between them and tugged open the button on his pants.

"*Fuck*," he growled.

"Yes, *please*," she begged.

His eyes locked on hers, so wicked and wanting, she felt his desire slithering beneath her skin, winding around her like a python. He lowered his mouth to her shoulder, placing a series of tender kisses across it, slowing to suck and bite every few seconds, revving her up to spine-tingling proportions. Every graze of his teeth made her insides reach for him, and when his hand moved over the bow at her back that held her dress together, her body vibrated with anticipation. His rough hands coasted hot and greedy over her skin, like he was savoring the feel of her, pressing her tighter against him. But she needed more and pushed back. She lowered her mouth to his chest, curling her hands around his biceps. He smelled of musk and man, tasted of salty desire. She flicked her tongue over his nipple, feeling it pebble as a groan fell from his lips. He grabbed her head, holding her mouth where he wanted it. She was happy to comply, sucking and using her teeth on the sensitive nub, earning hungry moans and hard thrusts of his hips.

She wanted to feel his powerful body over hers, to be

marked by him from the inside out. When his hand met the bow on her back again, he stilled, and she gazed up at him. His eyes blazed into her, seeking approval.

"If you don't pull it, I will," she panted out.

"Good God, Charlotte—"

His mouth came devouringly down over hers, and he pulled the bow free. The rope loosened around her middle and slid off her shoulders as she succumbed to the forceful domination of his lips. Her dress slid down her body and puddled at her feet. Their bare chests collided, and his arms circled her. His hands flattened against her back, holding them so close nothing could come between them.

He tore his mouth away, still holding her captive, a world of emotions colliding in his eyes. She knew this was as different for him as it was new for her, and somehow she understood that he wanted her to know that, even if he couldn't say it.

"I know," she whispered, and the relief on his face made her belly flip.

He tugged off his boots and stripped bare. She'd touched him, tasted him, felt every inch of his hard body only hours earlier in the shower, and still she was shocked anew by his sheer beauty. He stepped closer and took her chin between his finger and thumb, pressing a kiss to her lips. Gone was the fury and confusion that had plagued him since the day they met, and she knew he truly *saw* her and wanted only her.

"Hi, beautiful." A genuine smile lifted his lips.

Her heart stumbled as he knelt before her and carefully slipped her panties down her legs, then kissed his way up her body. He took his time, his big hands running up her legs, his lips sending goose bumps chasing up her spine.

"I want to be so close to you," he whispered between tender

kisses, "you feel me wrapped around you in your dreams."

She had no idea how her wobbly legs carried her as he took her hand and led her to the blanket, but she was glad they did. As they lay down, she said, "It's been years."

"I know," he said, offering the same relief she'd given him.

She'd forgotten she'd already told him that. He gathered her in his arms, both of them lying on their sides, and he guided her leg over his hip, cupping her bottom. And then he kissed her. It wasn't the urgent kiss of fearful lovers worried they'd run out of time, or the easy kiss of familiarity. It wasn't a single kiss at all. These were smoldering kisses that seared through her veins, rousing passions she'd never known existed. He took her more forcefully, holding her tighter, breathing air *into* her, surpassing all the kisses she'd ever read or written. Her emotions soared, throbbing through her core, down her limbs, claiming every inch of her soul. Her nipples burned, her sex swelled, and just when she thought she couldn't take it anymore, he swept her beneath him, kissing her even more passionately. She disappeared into the velvety warmth of his mouth, the strong cocoon of his body, into a world like nothing she'd ever imagined. A safe, mystical universe of their own, where everything felt new and explosive.

When their lips parted, he rose onto his knees and dug a condom out of his wallet. She watched him as he sheathed himself, eyes locked on her, cock in hand. The image burned into her mind.

He came down over her, aligning their bodies. His big hands cradled her head, and he gazed deeply into her eyes. "I...*This*..." He closed his eyes for a moment, and when he opened them, his virility shone through. "I got the bad thoughts out. My to-do list is *not* on my mind. I want to skip right to my dreams, and I haven't dreamed in so long, I'm not sure these count, but I want more mornings like we shared, more nights like this. The talking as much as the closeness. I want more of you, Charlotte. You make me want to dream again."

"I want that, too. I never imagined real life could be better than the worlds I create, but I was so wrong."

Their mouths joined as their bodies came together, slow and careful. She felt her body stretching to accommodate him, aware of every inch as he entered her, until he was buried to the hilt. And she knew that just as he'd hoped, she'd feel his body embracing her, his thickness inside her, for days to come. Not because of his size or shape, but because he'd not only entered her body. He'd taken root in her heart.

Chapter Twelve

CHARLOTTE AWOKE TANGLED up in Beau. His hips cradled her bottom, his thighs pressed against the backs of hers, and his strong arms embraced her like he would protect her from the entire world if he had to. After last night she believed he'd try. They'd fallen asleep beneath the stars, their bodies intertwined, and they'd woken up a little while later and made love again before heading inside in the wee hours of the morning. It felt natural when he'd climbed into her bed beside her, not awkward as she'd thought it might. She didn't freak out or turn into a bumbling idiot. And when he pulled her close, lovingly holding her within the confines of his body, she'd felt as if she'd come home. Now she had the urge to turn around. She wanted to see his handsome face in a peaceful, resting state, as she'd witnessed last night, when they'd both been too sated and spent to move.

He nuzzled against her neck, his warm breath sending sexy memories skating through her. She wondered what he was thinking as his hands found hers and he held on tight. What was she supposed to say after a night like that? *Thanks for a good time? You were amazing?* He was *beyond* amazing. Not only because he'd loved her so thoroughly she felt like she was *his*, but because they'd connected in ways she'd only dreamed of. But *you were amazing* was about the cheesiest line ever. It would probably be too much if she said what she really felt. Did he feel the same intense connection she did? Like they'd free-fallen into something much bigger than *like*? This was so much easier in fiction. He'd probably run for the hills if she told him the truth. Wouldn't anyone after one night of great sex?

A pang of sadness hit her. *Was that all it was to him?*

He pressed his lips to her shoulder. "Thinking about word counts and blow-up dolls?"

"How can you think I'd have anything other than *you* on my mind after all we've shared?" She turned in his arms, reeled in deeper by the look in his eyes. It was as fierce and protective as it was sweet and tender. "I was thinking about how I can make the morning after sexy and seductive in my books but I can't think of a single quote-worthy thing to say to you beyond *thank you*."

He laughed, and she loved the way that happiness reached his eyes.

"It's not funny," she complained. "I want this moment to be unforgettable for you. I want you to remember our night when you're building a house on a hill or renovating a bedroom." She buried her face in his chest, realizing what she'd said. "See? I suck at this in real life."

He tipped her chin up, like he wanted her full attention, his smile still in place, and he said, "If anyone gets to say thank you it's me, because I've got a sassy, sexy-as-all-get-out sweetheart lying naked beside me after the most incredible, *unforgettable* night."

"Really?"

"Really. Stop worrying about being quote-worthy. I much

prefer the honest woman I've been spending time with. That's the person I'll think of as I build houses on hills or renovate bedrooms. You're the one I'll think of every time I walk through a field or the woods or see sparkling lights in the distance."

Every word made her fall a little harder for him.

He pressed his lips to hers. There was a welcoming in his kisses, a *belonging* that hadn't been there before, and she knew things were changing for him, too.

"I've been alone for a really long time. Even when I'm around people, I'm pretty much lost in my own thoughts. It's different when you're with me. I know you said you were behind on your manuscript, and I don't want to interfere with that. But it'd be nice if you were near me sometimes when I'm working, unless that screws up your mojo."

Oh boy. She could fall hard for this man, and that was dangerous given that he was only here for a short time. *Maybe I should have thought about that before our first kiss.* Like she would have been able to resist him? That definitely hadn't been an option. All the pieces of themselves that were bringing them together were too strong to ignore.

"Does it bother you that I spend so much time writing? When I was in college I interned at the local newspaper, and I was always researching or writing. The guys I went out with had a really hard time with that."

"I'm not a college kid. I don't need every second of your attention, and I'd have to be blind and deaf not to realize how writing fulfills you. I don't want to change that or screw you up while I'm here. It's enough for me to have you nearby. But I do have one favor to ask." He tucked her hair behind her ear and pulled her closer. "If you catch up on your manuscript by next Saturday afternoon and can manage a break, I'd like to monopolize a few hours of your time. I have a surprise for you, but it will mean leaving your computer. Not because I'm jealous of your writing time, but because I'd really like to do this for you."

"A surprise?" How had he come up with a surprise for her since last night? Or had he planned it before then? She wanted to say she didn't care how much time it would take away from anything else in her life. But her situation wasn't that simple. She had a deadline to meet.

"At least I hope it'll be a surprise," he said.

"I hate that I have to think about anything other than how much I want to be with you, but I promised to send my editor the first third of my manuscript a week from Tuesday, and we have a meeting in Port Hudson the following Monday, so I can't put it off. But if I knuckle down for the next few days, as long as I don't get writer's block, I know I can do it." She was excited to see her girlfriends while she was in New York, but she hated losing those two days with Beau.

"You know what? I *will* do it," she said confidently. "I'll make it happen. Thank you!"

She plastered her lips to his, both of them smiling as he swept her beneath him, grinning like he'd won the lottery.

"I really like you, Sterling."

"I'm not sure I believe you," she teased. "Maybe you should convince me."

He crushed his mouth to hers and then spent the next hour masterfully taking her up to the clouds and back again.

Afterward, as they lay catching their breath, their bodies glistening from their lovemaking, she said, "I'd like to put in a request for a repeat performance tonight, please, with an earlier wake-up call so I can be sure to make our date without missing out on another dose of my burly Beau."

He chuckled. "Then we need to get moving, check on the Chickendales, and fuel you up so you can whip out a few sexy chapters now that you have some inspiration."

She loved that he said *Chickendales*, but she loved her new *inspiration* even more.

He gave her a chaste kiss and stepped from the bed in all his naked glory. "Shower time."

She watched his fine ass as he crossed the room and disappeared into the bathroom. Basking in bliss and listening to the shower running, she buried her face in the pillow and squealed, kicking her legs from sheer happiness, and then she flopped onto her back, grinning like a fool.

"*That* was adorable."

She gasped, and he cracked up. "You were *watching* me?"

He strode toward her with his hand outstretched. "I wondered why you weren't joining me in the shower and came back to get you. I didn't mean to interrupt your little celebration."

"I was just…"

He cocked an amused brow. She couldn't think of a single thing to say to cover up the truth.

"Do you blame me?" she said. "It's not every day that I wake up to sweet 'n' sinful lovin'."

"Me either." He pulled her to her feet, his hot body growing hard against her. "But I think it's time we changed that."

Chapter Thirteen

CHARLOTTE STOOD IN front of her whiteboard the following Friday, trying to work out the next few scenes for her book, which she couldn't do without knowing where her characters were headed. She had always been a pantser, which was part of what had made her decide to have Becca handle her fan interactions. She was constantly taking notes on what they wanted and trying to fit in all their suggestions, but for a pantser, it was too confining. Plotting an entire story even without fan input made her feel hemmed in, and like a rebellious child, she would write in the opposite direction of anything she'd plotted. Three points in the story was all she usually needed to find her way, but there was nothing *usual* about the story she was writing. It had thrown her off from the start, first with writer's block and lately because the characters had veered toward contemporary love rather than erotic sex. She wanted her characters to take long walks and talk about life, or snuggle sometimes instead of getting down and dirty, but in erotic romance, the naughtiness fueled the emotions, not the other way around. She knew that had a lot to do with her burgeoning feelings for Beau.

Since their night under the stars, eight incredible days and seven passionate nights ago, she and Beau had found their rhythm as a couple. She never knew real life could be so incredible, and she definitely hadn't expected Beau to want to spend as much time together as they did. Their days began tangled up in each other's arms, followed by a steamy shower, a visit to the Chickendales, and a walk around the property. They explored a different trail every morning, brainstorming scenes for her books, talking about their lives, and more often than not, making out with the morning sun beating down on them. Charlotte looked forward to writing even more than ever. She'd followed his suggestion and had taken her laptop wherever he was working. The other day she wrote while sitting on a blanket in the sun while he'd sawed, sanded, and did a hundred other things in the workshop, stopping every so often to drop a kiss on her lips or cheek. It had done wonders for both of them, and he was opening up more every day. She loved being near him, watching him work. Sometimes she caught him staring at her, which reminded her of the way her father used to look at her mother, and the similarities sent her hopes soaring. But all their loveliness was playing out in her writing and causing issues. While life with Beau was more than she ever hoped for, her characters needed angst. They needed something that would tear them apart emotionally or test their love before their happily ever after. The problem was, she had no angsty notions inside her right now, other than the fact that Beau would soon be leaving. And that made her sad, not angsty like her story needed.

Her muse made her too happy. Even the thought of Beau made her all fluttery. She schooled her expression. *Stop being happy! I need angst!*

She was stuck.

And stuck was never good.

She tried to come up with a reason for her characters to have angst. At some point she and Beau would need to talk about where they went from here. She knew that the beautiful, a-little-less-tortured man would take a big part of her heart when he left. For now that conversation could wait because they still had time before he was due to leave, but she didn't have long before her manuscript deadline. If she didn't nail this scene and get a handle on where to take her characters next, she'd have to skip her date with Beau on Saturday—and that was *not* happening.

She had to break her characters out of contemporary love and kick their asses into erotic sex, no matter how much she was enjoying her own life. If she could give them angst, she could turn the fire into a scorching-hot erotic scene.

She needed dark-and-dirty inspiration.

She needed a *threesome*.

And silk ties.

And maybe hot wax. Or whips.

She went into her bedroom and changed into her leather and lace. Then she went to the room across the hall from her office and dug through her toy box. Armed with everything she needed, she headed upstairs to find Beau.

THE WHIR OF the saw vibrated in the old barn as Beau cut the last piece of wood for the medallion he'd designed for Charlotte's bedroom and set it aside with the others. He'd come up with what he hoped was the perfect design to bring together her love of all things happy and hopeful with a unique touch all his own. His mind traveled back to the morning when they'd made breakfast together. Or rather, Beau had made breakfast while Charlotte had tried to distract him with kisses and had asked a million questions about him and his childhood. He liked that she wanted to know everything about him, and even though it was uncomfortable at times and he tried to change the subject, he was glad she wasn't afraid to bring up Tory. He doubted many women would be as understanding as she was.

As he put the saw away and brushed the dust from his jeans, he realized he didn't crave time alone the way he used to. On the days she needed privacy to write, like today, he'd work on the medallion or other projects. Then he'd stop by her office with lunch when he needed his Charlotte fix. She rarely ate what he made, favoring protein bars, but yesterday she'd devoured a sandwich. He was pretty sure that was because he'd put a Twix bar between the lunch meat and the bread, thinking she'd pluck it out and get a kick out of the joke. He liked eating in the office with her while she worked. She talked about Roman and Shayna as if they were in the room with them, telling him what they wanted, what they did, how they argued. She made them feel so real, he was starting to believe they were. He'd gotten so swept up in her story lately, twice he'd woken up in the middle of the night with ideas, and they'd ended up in her office as she typed and they fleshed them out. It was exhilarating for both of them.

But *exhilarating* didn't come close to describing the all-consuming emotions of coming together each night and waking up with Charlotte in his arms every morning.

He grabbed the wood he needed to replace the rotted pieces on the deck on the south side and headed up toward the inn.

"Beau?" Charlotte's voice sounded in the distance, and his

body roared to life.

Would he ever get used to the way she affected him? He quickened his pace, and the wood he was carrying slipped. He stopped to get a better hold and heard her call his name again. He jogged up the path holding the wood with both hands, and when she called for him again, he sprinted.

He followed her voice around the side of the inn and stopped cold at the sight of Charlotte standing with her back to him, wearing thigh-high black stockings with bright blue lace at the top, a matching garter that barely covered her ass, and a pair of black heels. He recognized the thin strip of a black thong. Two black straps crossed over the center of her back and snaked over her shoulders. The legs of two blow-up dolls stuck out from beneath one arm, and she carried a whip and a feather tickler in her other hand.

The wood crashed to the ground, and his cock turned to steel.

She spun around, eyes wide, dolls bobbing, and holy fucking hell, *what* was she wearing? Black straps, no more than an inch wide, snaked over her shoulders and crossed over her breasts, covering each nipple with a bright blue bow, then wound around her back, appearing again over her hips, intersecting above her promised land. Those straps connected to her garter with tiny silver handcuffs, and a glittery blue and white bow tie sat just below her navel.

She strutted across the lawn toward him. "There you are! I have been looking all over for you."

Even though Beau knew they were alone, his protective urges had him whipping his head around, scanning the property for unwanted eyes.

"*What* are *you* looking for? I need *you*, Beau." She cocked her head to the side, looking far too innocent for that wicked outfit. "My story is too sweet. I need to sex it up."

"Out here?"

She set her hand on her hip, waving the whip, feather tickler, and two long pieces of silk he hadn't noticed before. "Wherever you want. We need a threesome, or maybe a foursome. I haven't decided."

Holy hell. "Baby, I'm totally on board with sexing you up, but I do *not* need dolls."

"Well, unless you know of a guy you can get up here in a matter of minutes, it's you, me, and the dolls. I have to do this *now* if I'm going to get my chapters done in time for our date Saturday."

He stepped closer, his hands clenching. "If you think I'm going to allow any other man's hands on you, you're dead wrong."

"You are possessive, aren't you?" she said sassily, waving the damn whip around like a wand. "We could call Cutter and Chip if you want."

He threw her over his shoulder in one swift move and stalked inside.

"Beau! I'm going to drop the dolls!"

"Good," he ground out. "I'm open to a lot of things, but sharing my woman isn't one of them."

She giggled as he tugged open the door and carried her into her bedroom. "So now I'm your woman?"

He flopped her onto her back in the center of the mattress, sending the dolls and other paraphernalia flying to the floor, and came down over her. She was grinning as he pinned her hands beside her head.

"We have woken up tangled up in each other every morning

after a series of seriously hot and emotionally intimate nights. That qualifies you as my woman and me as your man. If you're into sharing, you'd better tell me right now, so I can figure out a way to get you out of my head before we get in any deeper."

Her long lashes fluttered flirtatiously. "I like *deeper*."

He failed at stifling a growl, because, *man*, he wanted to be buried so deep inside her he could taste it.

"Does that mean you don't want to share me with Chris Pine or Hugh Jackman?"

She giggled, and he swore there was smoke coming out of his ears.

"Absofuckinglutely *not*. And while we're on the subject, have you ever *had* a threesome?"

She bit her lower lip, and an icy shock gripped him.

"A foursome, too," she said sweetly. He pushed up, and she tugged him back down. "With my *dolls!*" Laughter burst from her lungs, while the air rushed from his.

She raised her hips, rubbing against him. "I like you all crazy hot and cavemanish."

"You're going to be the death of me."

"But it'll be a really fun death, won't it?" She leaned up and kissed him. Then she wiggled out from beneath him, went up on her knees, and set her hands on her hips. "Ready, big boy?"

She was practically wearing dental floss. He wanted to gnaw it off and feast on every blessed, beautiful inch of her, and she needed to ask if he was *ready*? "Oh, I'm ready, baby."

He reached for her, and she knee-walked away, waggling her finger. "Uh-uh. We need to work out this scene, not get lost in each other."

"Are you fucking kidding me?" She'd done this to him a few times this week, and every time they'd gotten so hot they'd nearly set the room on fire. He should be used to it, but he had a feeling there was no getting used to Charlotte Sterling. And *not* getting lost in her wasn't an option. *Aw, hell.* He remembered what she'd said about working out scenes with Cutter. "Do you wear this when you work out scenes with Cutter?"

An outfit like that could change Cutter's view of her from pain-in-the-ass sister to hot-as-hell potential fuck buddy.

"No. I mean, sometimes he walks in when I'm wrapping my head around things, but I think he's only seen me in a teddy." She tapped her chin, her eyes narrowing. "No, that's not right. It wasn't a teddy. He came in when I was writing about a heroine who lived at the beach, and I was wearing a bikini."

"*Christ.* Stop. I don't want to know the rest." She was enjoying torturing him far too much. *Two can play at this game.*

He tore off his shirt and stepped from the bed. If she wanted to be sexed up, he was damn well going to sex her up so thoroughly she'd never even think about having another man's hands on her—plastic or otherwise.

"What are you doing?" she asked warily as he took off his boots and began stripping off his jeans. Her hot gaze raked hungrily down his body. "Beau…?"

"If we're getting in the mood, let's do it right." He picked up the feather tickler and silk ties and climbed onto the bed wearing only his boxer briefs. "Okay, how erotic do you want it?"

"I…um…" Crimson spread over her cheeks, turning him on even more. He loved that hint of innocence. "I was going to pose you with the dolls so I can see the mechanics of the positions."

"Not happening. I don't *do* dolls." He brushed the feather tickler up her ribs and over her breast, and her eyes flamed.

"Tell me about this Roman character. I thought you wrote erotic *love* stories, not just sex."

"I do," she insisted.

"True love doesn't need threesomes. Your hero's not in love."

"He doesn't want it. Shayna, my heroine, does."

Beau's chest constricted, wondering if that was a secret fantasy of Charlotte's. "Then she doesn't love him," he said more forcefully than he meant to. "Or maybe you don't know your characters well enough, and Roman just needs to up his game."

He dragged the feathers up her thighs and stomach and across her breasts. Her eyes turned dark as a forest, all shimmering greens and warm milk chocolate. He leaned in, taking her in a fierce kiss.

"How erotic are we allowed to play, shortcake?" His fingers circled her wrist. "You never answered me." He sank his teeth into her neck, earning a sharp gasp. "Is eroticism a secret fetish of yours?"

"*No,*" she said too quickly. "Maybe on some level. I don't know. Not *Fifty Shades* stuff, no. Definitely not."

Holding her gaze, he said, "Good, because hurting a woman is not something I will ever do, so if you want to be whipped or fucked like you mean nothing to a man, I'm not your guy."

"I don't. That's why I haven't slept with anyone since college, and even then I slept with only two guys. In my experience guys were all about the deed, and I wanted more."

"You wanted the fairy tale, which is not exactly in most college guys' repertoire." He hated that she'd been treated that way, and he was glad she hadn't slept around seeking what she probably wouldn't have found.

"But it's in yours." Her trusting eyes bored into him.

"Only for you, shortcake." The urge to make love to her, to show her how deeply and wholly he cared, gripped him. But part of the trust he'd earned grew from his respect for her career, and he didn't want to lose that. *Fuck.* Dating an erotic romance writer was as torturous as it was fantastic.

He drew back, brushed her hair over her shoulder, and said, "This is your livelihood, so let's make sure we get it right."

"You'll use the dolls?" Her eyes bloomed wide.

"No dolls, but I promise we'll nail it." He trailed kisses over her mouth and cheeks, each touch of his lips earning a tiny, sexy gasp. "Close your eyes for me. Let's get to know your characters."

Her eyes closed, and he gently tied the silk material over them. She clutched his arm, breathing harder. "Beau…?"

"Don't worry, babe. I've got you. We're just getting into their heads so you can write the best possible scene." He guided her down to her back, trying to keep his own desires in check with her laid out before him like a spectacularly stunning gift. In that moment, he knew he'd never give another man the chance to disappoint her again, and on the off chance she wanted to experience a threesome, he'd just have to convince her that he was better than any two men ever could be. "Are you okay?"

"Uh-huh," she said breathily.

"Good." He ran his hands up her stockings, following the path with his mouth, trailing kisses over her knee, along her thigh, loving the way she twitched against his lips.

She touched his hands, stopping them from moving higher. "My scene starts with Shayna lying on her side." She shifted onto her side. "Like this, with Roman behind her."

He moved behind her and began kissing her shoulder the way he knew she loved. "Like this?"

"Yeah, just like that."

She ground her ass against his cock, and he gripped her hips, holding her tight against him, gyrating and thrusting in slow, precise movements. The breath rushed from her lungs, and he sealed his mouth over the curve of her neck and sucked until she was writhing against him, making those needy sounds he loved.

"I assume the other guy would be touching her like this." He slid one hand between her legs, pushed aside the tiny swatch of thong, and teased her wetness.

"Yes" came out as a plea.

"If Shayna is into him, wouldn't she want to feel this?" He pulled his briefs off and guided his shaft between her legs.

She moaned as he thrust against her, her ass nestled against his hips, his cock sliding along her slick heat, drenched in her arousal. He pushed his arm beneath her side and reached around, pulling down the strap that covered her breast, and took his fill. He devoured her neck, while he took her nipple between his finger and thumb and squeezed, pumping his hips and teasing her clit with his other hand.

"Ohmygod, Beau—"

"Turn your head this way," he said greedily.

He crashed his mouth over hers, thrusting his tongue to the same rhythm as his cock. But he knew she wanted the full-on threesome experience, so he played the game, giving her what she needed for her scene. He tore his mouth away and shifted her onto her hands and knees.

"Beau, what—"

"Threesome, baby. You wanted it. You've got to experience

it *all*, right?" It was heaven and hell seeing her up on all fours in that sexy blindfold with her ass his for the taking. He pressed a tender kiss beside her ear and whispered, "Don't worry, baby. If you tell me to stop, I will."

"No. This is good," she panted out. "I need to feel what she'd feel in order to write it. I need to know what two guys would do."

He moved behind her, dragging his hand along her spine, down the line of her thong, and nudged her legs open wider. Then he kissed her beautiful bottom and lay on his back between her legs, bringing her sex down to his greedy mouth as he tugged that sliver of material to the side. Her back arched as he feasted on her.

She clutched at the blankets. "Beau, Beau, *Beau*—"

He took her to the edge, holding her there as a stream of sinful pleas flew from her lungs. He gave her what she needed, and she bucked and cried out, her sex pulsing hot and needy around his tongue. When she finally eased back down to earth, he moved up the bed and took her breast in his mouth, guiding her trembling hips over his hard length. He didn't enter her. Holding her hips, he moved her along his hard length, quick and rough.

"Angle yourself so you can feel it where you need it, baby," he said, and went back to devouring her breasts as she tilted her hips, pressing her clit to his erection and rocking *hard*. He grabbed her ass, brushing his fingers between her cheeks.

"*God*, Beau."

She moved faster, pressed down rougher, until her thighs flexed and shook. He clutched her ass harder, still sucking her breast. His fingers teased over her tightest hole, and in seconds she cried out, bucking wildly as her climax engulfed her.

Her entire body trembled as he pushed up beneath her. He sat with his back to the headboard, helping her straddle his hips. Her skin was flushed, her breathing shallow. Her nipples were dark pink from his mouth. She was *exquisite*.

He framed her face between his hands and kissed her deeply. "Still want to play?"

"Yes," she said shakily.

He touched the blindfold, and she covered her hand with his. "Leave it on. I have to try to picture two men. Beau One and Beau Two."

He chuckled and kissed her again. "Beau One is pretty demanding. Are you sure you're ready?"

She licked her lips. "I trust you. Beau One can be as demanding as he wants."

He lifted her from his lap, spread his legs, and set her between them on her knees. Then he sat up higher and caressed her jaw. "I need your mouth on me, baby."

She went willingly, *eagerly*, as he angled his cock to her beautiful mouth. She kissed the tip with her rosebud lips, a sweet, sensual touch, and something inside him snapped. He wasn't *Beau One* and *Beau Two*, and it felt wrong for her to need to feel that, even if only for fiction, which he knew was ridiculous. But that didn't matter, and he couldn't hold back his emotions.

He lifted her chin and peeled the blindfold off.

Her brows knitted. "What's wrong? Am I doing it wrong?"

"Hell no, baby. You do everything right all the time. I want to help you, but I don't want to be Beau One and Beau Two. I'm *one* man, *your* man, and if you're going to put your mouth on me, I need to see your beautiful eyes and know you're doing it because you want to, not for research." He felt vulnerable, laying his true emotions out between them, but he couldn't play a game at this stage. "I'm sorry. I know that's not what you anticipated, but…"

Her jaw dropped open, and she blinked several times, as if trying to make sense of what he'd said. Or maybe she was *that* disappointed. *Fuck.* Did he screw this up for her?

"Sorry. I just—"

"Beau, that's *so* romantic," she said dreamily.

"Just being honest," he said, reaching for her.

Her eyes widened, and the lusty fog in them visibly lifted, replaced with shock and elation. "Oh my God, that's it! Thank you!" She kissed him hard and jumped off the bed. "Shayna doesn't need *two* men!" She ran for the door. "She only needs one *Beau*!"

"What the…?" He looked down at his raging erection, baffled, strangely pleased that he'd helped inspire a scene, and horny as *fuck.*

CHARLOTTE STOOD IN front of her keyboard, typing as fast as she could, the sexy scene she and Beau had played out rolling through her mind like a movie. Her pulse was racing from Beau's words as much as his touch, amped up by Fleur East's "Sax" blaring from her Echo. It was one of her favorite songs, and it was perfect for this scene, given that it talks about waiting for someone to blow her mind. *Holy mother of romance, Beau Braden. You have blown my mind.*

She hated bolting from the room, but she was afraid if she stopped for even a second she'd lose her train of thought. She hadn't even taken time to wash up, which was why she was standing instead of sitting on her comfy leather chair. A damp thong made for a messy, uncomfortable situation. She should have known better than to let Beau get close after he dropped his drawers. *Good Lord,* that man could excite her with only a glance. The feel of his nakedness had set her entire body on fire. She had pretty much been a goner from that second on, but when he'd said he needed to see her eyes? *Heart-stopping.* The way he'd said it and the look in his eyes had turned her into a melty, tingly mess. And just as she was reveling in his sentiments, the scene had bloomed before her, clear as day.

She stopped typing long enough to unhook the snaps on her garter and wiggle out of her thong. Beau appeared in the doorway, his heated stare drilling into her as she kicked the sliver of material aside.

"Hey," she said, and went back to typing before he distracted her too much and she lost focus. "Sorry I ran out like that."

"Are you?" he asked in a deep, lustful voice as he stalked closer.

Her fingers moved over the keyboard a little slower. She felt his presence behind her before he moved her hair away from her shoulder and pressed a kiss there.

"Yes," she said, willing herself to continue typing. "I just had to get this scene out before it got too fuzzy."

"I knew you had to write." His erection brushed temptingly against her ass. "So I brought the scene to you."

He tossed a condom packet beside her keyboard, and her hands stilled. His arms circled her waist, and he cupped her breasts. She closed her eyes, melting at his touch. But she had to write before she lost the scene, and she knew he could shatter her ability to think in record time. She inhaled deeply, trying to remain clearheaded, and set her hands in motion again.

Focus, Charlotte. You've got this.

The pep talk didn't help. It was impossible to ignore the way he was kissing her neck, taking little sucks that sent lust spiking through her. His hands were everywhere at once, caressing her belly, her legs, her bottom, moving up her back, and tangling in her hair as his mouth worked its magic along all her pleasure points. She was breathing too hard, clenching her jaw to keep from begging him to touch her where she wanted— *needed*—him most, while simultaneously trying to convince herself *not* to want him.

Kiss, kiss, nibble, grope, kiss.

"Beau…" *I want you, but I have to write.* That was wrong on so many levels.

"Don't mind me, shortcake. You work. I'm just keeping the scene fresh in your mind."

He stepped away, and her heart sank.

"Please don't leave. I like that you're here. I just have to get this out of my head."

"Don't worry, baby. Leaving is the last thing on my mind." He rolled her desk chair behind her. "You go back to writing. I promise to be quiet."

Quiet. Great. Talking is not an issue. It's your mouth's other talents that are wreaking havoc with my brain.

He was *right* behind her. She heard him moving around and bumping the chair. Then his hand glided along her belly, radiating heat *everywhere*. She heard the distinct *snip, snip, snip* of scissors, and the straps of her lingerie fell away, leaving her in only her garter, stockings, and heels.

"Beau!" She spun around, struck speechless by his devastatingly seductive grin.

"I'll buy you fifty new sets of lingerie, but how can you write this scene if you don't know how it ends?" He gently turned her by the shoulders, guided her hands to her keyboard, and said, "You just keep on writing, babe."

Writing. Keep writing. Ohmygod...

She swallowed hard, her insides churning. Her mind ping-ponged between what she wanted and what she needed—Beau *and* to write.

He stepped back, and cooler air brought goose bumps to her flesh. He gently clutched her hips, guiding her onto his lap, his arousal hard and insistent against her bottom. She tried to turn around, but he held her in place.

"Uh-uh, you need to write, baby. Get your work done. I'll just keep inspiring ideas."

She lowered shaky hands to the keyboard and stared at the monitor, but all she saw were Beau's eyes when he'd said he'd needed to see hers.

He slicked his tongue along her neck, then drove her wild with one openmouthed kiss after another. Her body began to tremble, and her eyes fluttered closed.

"I don't hear those keys clicking," he said in a voice full of restraint.

"Hard to concentrate."

"Oh, you want it *harder* so you can concentrate?" He rocked his hips. "*Write*, baby."

"Writing," she said absently as he continued kissing and grinding until she was panting and breathless, her eyes closed.

He clutched her thighs, spreading them open wider, his fingertips grazing her sex.

"Oh God, Beau. I can't think."

She pushed to her feet, leaning her palms on the desk, and her head dipped between her shoulders. She was shaking from head to toe. Her thighs were wet with desire. He was right there with her, both hands teasing between her legs, his mouth wreaking havoc on her hips.

"You know what?" he said in a gravelly voice that raked down her core. "This isn't fair. You go back to writing, baby. I'll just sit here *without* touching you."

Noooooooo!

She heard him moving around again and closed her eyes to catch her breath. She couldn't do this. She didn't want to resist him or let him think she was only interested in him for research. She turned around, and holy mother of hotness, he was sitting naked in the chair, his talented love machine there for the taking.

"Fuck it." She grabbed the condom. "I want you, Beau. *You*, not research, not writing. Just you." She tried to rip the package open with her teeth like the heroes did in her books, but the more she tugged, the wetter and slipperier it became. "Ugh!"

Chuckling, he slid his hand beneath her hair and rose, taking her in a toe-curling kiss.

"I want you, too, beautiful." He took the package from her hand, tore it with one quick rip of his teeth, and sheathed himself faster than she thought possible. "I want to do so many things with you right now—bend you over the desk, have you straddle me on the chair, and come down over you on your couch."

"Yes, yes, and *yes*, please, but in reverse order," flew from her lips. "Couch first. You need to see my eyes, because it's *you* I want, Beau. Only you."

Torrents of emotions stormed in his eyes. "You utterly and completely destroy everything I thought I knew about myself."

Worry rose in her chest as he swept her into his arms and

carried her to the couch. She kicked off her heels, and when he laid her down, she reached for him, full of want and worry.

"I don't want to be bad for you," she said. "I don't want to destroy anything about you."

He cradled her against him, and the storm in his eyes burned away, leaving emotions so intense, so consuming, her world spun on its axis.

"Don't worry, baby," he said as their bodies came together. "Everything I thought I knew wasn't *anything* compared to what I'm discovering with you."

He lowered his lips to hers, kissing her deeply as he began a slow grind. She became aware of everything—the mintiness of his breath and the eager exploration of his tongue, the strength of his arms and press of his thighs. Together they found their groove, their bodies bound by their greediness, thrusting and gyrating, until the rest of the world faded away, and there was only the two of them and the pure, explosive pleasures between them.

Her man of his word fulfilled each and every naughty promise, making love to her on her chair, her desk, and even against the wall. Each time she came was more explosive than the last, until she felt boneless.

When they finally fell into bed, Beau gathered her in his arms and pressed his lips to hers. Lulled by the even cadence of his breathing, she was too sated to move, hovering peacefully in that gray space between wakefulness and sleep.

"Charlotte," he whispered.

She was too worn out to even make a sound. He was quiet for so long, she felt herself dozing off. Just as the world went dark, he whispered, "I'm falling hard for you, baby."

Happiness flowed through her as she fell asleep with her head tucked against his chest and her heart in his hands.

Chapter Fourteen

CHARLOTTE WORKED TIRELESSLY from nearly sunup until late at night to finish her chapters over the next week, while Beau prepared for Charlotte's surprise and went through emotions like they grew on trees. He stood in the doorway to her office Saturday afternoon thinking about how much he'd miss her when he left. It was hard to believe he'd been there only three weeks. In that time Charlotte had seamlessly and effortlessly become his other half. They'd moved his things into her room and adjusted their schedules to accommodate her long hours of writing, waking up earlier so they didn't have to give up their steamy mornings or their walks. When they fell into bed at night, they laughed as much as they loved, which was new for both of them. Beau felt so much for her, he had trouble keeping it inside. He'd been in love only once before, and it had been nothing like this. Was there a difference between loving a person you'd known your whole life and *falling* in love with someone? He didn't know the answer, but what he felt for Charlotte was more powerful than anything he'd ever experienced. Even the guilt that usually hovered over him like a winter storm didn't feel so heavy when he was with her, giving him hope that maybe he could have, or even deserved, a second chance at happiness.

Charlotte glanced over with the phone to her ear and held a finger up, indicating she'd be only a minute.

She'd been writing all morning, and she looked sexy and sweet wearing one of her father's button-downs and a pair of cutoffs, barefoot as always. He didn't know when he'd begun tucking away information about her like cherished charms, but he already had a stockpile, and he never wanted to stop adding to it. He loved knowing that she sometimes woke up at night and scribbled notes on her hand when she couldn't find a pad of paper, and that her middle name was Marie-Nöelle, after her maternal grandmother whom she'd never met. Charlotte loved harder than anyone he'd ever known, and she never let the people she loved go, keeping pieces of who they were alive in her heart. He'd learned that Twix bars had been her grandfather's favorite junk food, and she used to sneak them to him when his doctors tried to cut them out of his diet. Last night she'd told him that she always wished she'd had a baby sister to look after and an older brother to watch over her, which explained her and Cutter's close platonic relationship.

"Okay, yes!" Charlotte said into the phone. "I can't wait to meet you both. We'll see you then." She ended the call, her smile a mile wide. "I'm ready for our big date!"

She was so damn addicting he was beginning to wonder how he'd make it through a day without her, much less *every* day.

"That was your brother Nick on the phone," she said as she moved papers around on her desk. "He's so nice! He and Jilly are coming to the Mad Prix awards ceremony to support Graham and Ty. They're on the same flight as Aiyla. I can't wait to meet them. And shame on you for not calling him back all this time."

Beau tried to process what she said. "They're coming *here?*" He'd spoken to Jillian recently, and to Aiyla last night, and neither of them had mentioned Jillian and Nick coming to the inn. He thought about the call from Ty and realized he'd been set up. Ty had used Aiyla as an excuse to make sure Beau would be there when Nick and Jillian arrived.

"Yes! Isn't it great?" she said as she shut down her computer. "They'll be here Saturday afternoon, hopefully in time to see Graham and Ty cross the finish line. I tried to get them to come sooner, but Nick said he had to work. I can't believe they're coming all that way for a weekend. You have the greatest family." She turned around, and her vibrant smile faded. "What's wrong?"

"I have *nosy* siblings," he said distractedly. "Why don't you throw on some jeans; we're going into the woods."

"I go into the woods in shorts all the time. I'm fine."

"Not this time," he said too gruffly.

"I see *bossy Beau* is back," she said as she walked past him and reached for the light switch. "Lights," she whispered with a waggle of her brows. "My boyfriend fixed them for me."

She flicked the lights on and off, and he swatted her ass. "*Jeans*, shortcake."

"Do I get to dress you, too?" She pointed to his body. "Pants and shirt *off*, please," she said as she headed out of her office. Then she called from the hall, "Construction boots *optional.*"

He liked the sound of that despite roiling over Nick and Jillian's arrival. *Cheer on Graham and Ty, my ass.* They were checking on him. He sent a quick text to Nick. *You and Jilly don't need to come out here.*

His phone rang a second later, and Nick's name flashed on the screen. He answered it as he left Charlotte's office and headed in the opposite direction of her suite. "What the hell, Nick?"

"You tell me," Nick demanded. "You ghosted me this week, and Jilly's worried about you."

"I'm fine. Better than fine, and I talked to Jilly last night." He eyed the door to Charlotte's suite. "You don't need to come out here. And why would you call *Charlotte?*"

"If you'd answered your damn phone I wouldn't have. But I've gone ten years watching you beat yourself up for something that's not your fault. You can run, but until you deal with this shit, you're never going to move on."

Beau paced, envisioning his brother's cold, dark stare. "Back off, Nick. I'm fine."

"Then come home before you go to L.A., man. Or sign the damn contract and then come back. Show us you can be here this time of year, and we won't worry about you."

"No, and you coming here will not change my mind." They used to go at each other's throats over this subject until it came to blows. Nick had tried on more than one occasion to beat some sense into Beau, but despite Nick's twenty-pound advantage, Beau had held his own. Eventually Nick had gone from talking with his fists to doing shit like this, getting in his face. Beau preferred the fists.

"We'll see." Nick paused long enough for his challenge to grate on Beau's nerves. "On a lighter note, Charlotte sounds *hot.* Maybe she'll make it worth my trip."

Beau ground his back teeth. "Jesus, Nick. She's *off*-limits."

Nick scoffed. "Unless she's yours, she's not off-limits, and considering you're leaving in a week and you haven't claimed a woman in a decade, how about we let her make that decision? See if she wants to play with a real man."

Charlotte's door flew open, and seeing her gorgeous face amped up his protective urges. If his brother thought he was getting anywhere near her, he had another thing coming.

"I mean it, Nick. *Back off.*"

"Why should I?"

"Just do it and maybe I won't kill you for coming out here." He ended the call and stuffed the phone in his pocket, trying to bury his irritation. "All set?"

"Yes." She tugged on his shirt as they headed outside. "But I see you didn't follow *my* instructions."

"I don't take orders well."

"Clearly. Where are we going?" she asked as they crossed the lawn toward the woods.

"Woods," he said, his tone too clipped. *Damn it.* She didn't deserve to take the brunt of his frustration. He took a few deep breaths to clear his head, and then he lightened his tone and said, "We need to stop by the barn for a sec before you see your surprise. I think I left something there when I went down the other day."

"I love that I'm the one who lives here and you're surprising me. You just might be the best boyfriend ever."

His mind reeled back to the missed texts from Tory, and he stifled the familiar reaction to fend off her compliment. "I don't know about best boyfriend ever, but I do like to see your smile." He leaned in for a kiss, and just like that, his entire body exhaled. "I'm sorry for being short with you."

"It's okay. I get it. You've been avoiding your family because they smother you this time of year. But Nick was really nice, and I think it's sweet that he and Jilly are coming out to cheer the guys on. I'd give anything to have siblings that would show up out of the blue."

"You can borrow my brothers and sister anytime you'd like."

As they followed the trail through the woods, he picked apart the way Nick's visit had upended his good mood. He was sick of ping-ponging back and forth between guilt and the pressure to get over it. He was finally making headway, seeing beyond the smoke of the past and wanting something more. How could one conversation with Nick bring it all careening forward again?

"Are you looking forward to the Mad Prix weekend?" he asked, hoping to veer away from talk of his family. "Or will the chaos of having all those people around bother you? It's so peaceful here."

"Yes and no. I'm looking forward to it mainly because it reminds me of when my parents were alive, and I'll see lots of people who knew them," she said as they followed the trail through the woods.

It wasn't lost on him that she longed for connections to the people who knew her family, while he did everything he could to get away from the people who knew Tory. It dawned on him that just as the guilt had become a part of him, so had his reactions to those people. Of course his family was smothering him. By avoiding them, he'd made his guilt not only his problem, but theirs, too. *Holy fuck. Why didn't I see that before?* It was time for him to start to figure some of his shit out.

"I love the excitement of the crowds," Charlotte said, bringing his mind back to their conversation. "This year we're changing things up a little. Instead of having the awards ceremony the next morning, we're doing it the evening of the race, and after dinner there's live music and dancing."

He was glad he'd brought a sport coat for his meeting in L.A. He could only imagine how stunning Charlotte would look all dolled up.

She looked up at him and said, "I can't wait to dance with you. But it's our last weekend together, and to be honest, I'm not thrilled about losing that time alone with you. Especially since chefs, housekeepers, and groundskeepers will begin arriving midweek to prepare for the event. I've gotten used to our time alone."

He pulled her closer and said, "We'll find time alone. Don't worry."

"I'm not ready for you to leave," she said forlornly. "I wish I could change my trip to New York. I'll be gone Sunday afternoon until Tuesday for the meeting with my editor. I hate that I'll miss that time with you."

"I hate it, too, but this isn't it for us, babe. I'm coming back to see you."

"Promise?" She bounced on her toes, turning those doe eyes up to him.

"Do you really think I could stay away from you?" He draped an arm around her as they descended the last hill toward the barn and said, "But you can't blame me if you come back from New York and find your dolls hanging from nooses in the trees."

"I can totally see you doing that and using them for target practice with a nail gun or something. But then I'll be up the creek without a paddle after you leave."

"That's another great reason for me to come back and visit," he said as they headed across the grass by the brook.

"Often?" she asked with hope in her eyes. "I might need to

work out scenes on a weekly basis."

He chuckled. "As often as you'll have me, shortcake."

He crushed her to him and pressed his lips to hers, chasing away the reminder that their days together were numbered.

THE SUN WARMED their faces as Beau kissed Charlotte. She didn't want to think about what might come next, or if they could make a long-distance relationship work, and as he took the kiss deeper, thinking was no longer an option. When their lips finally parted, he drew back for only a second before recapturing her lips, leaving her breathless.

"I need to stock up on your kisses," he said in a heated whisper. "And we need to act out as many scenes as you can think up so you never want to go back to using those dolls."

"You blow my dolls out of the water. Out of this *world*."

"Damn right I do." He led her up to the barn. "I can picture you sitting there by the brook, your toes dangling in the water, having a Twix and protein bar picnic."

She gazed up at him and asked, "Are you in this picture?"

"I never thought I'd want to be in anyone's picture ever again, but you make me want to be in yours. I like who we are together and who I am when I'm with you."

He was saying so many hopeful things, she wanted to cling to each and every one. But she was afraid to get her hopes up too high. He was about to embark on a life-changing, jet-setting adventure, and she had a feeling his life would become a hundred times more complicated than he anticipated. She tucked that unhappy thought away as he pushed the barn door open, and the pungent smell of horses, leather, and hay wafted out.

He bowed like a prince welcoming her to a ball. "After you, shortcake."

She walked into the barn and said, "Well, aren't you fancy—"

Her knees nearly gave out at the sight of two beautiful horses. One of them nickered, its big head bobbing to greet her. "Oh my gosh. Beau! How did you do this without me knowing?"

"Once you're in your office, you don't exactly notice much else." He took her hand and led her to a beautiful chestnut mare.

She reached up to pet the horse, and it nudged her with its muzzle, just like Winter used to do. Tears burned her eyes. "Hi, pretty girl." She stroked her cheek and pressed a kiss there, inhaling the familiar scents of her childhood. "What's her name?"

"Ginger, and that gorgeous girl"—he pointed to the dark brown horse in the next stall—"is Spice. I borrowed them from Hal and told him I'd bring them back tomorrow evening. I've got everything we need in the tack room. But first..." He went into an empty stall and came out with his hands behind his back. "These are for my fairy-tale-loving girl."

He handed her a pair of pink leather riding boots embellished with brown-and-white butterflies and flowers. Completely overwhelmed, she launched herself into his arms, happy tears tumbling down her cheeks.

"There are no words for the sweetness that is you, Beau Braden. Thank you!"

Their happiness radiated into their kisses, and when he set

her down, she hugged him again.

"How did you know my shoe size?" she asked as she tugged off her sandals and slipped her feet into the boots. They fit perfectly.

"You know those adorable rubber boots you kick off by the door every morning?" He shrugged.

"*Sneaky.* I like that about you." She stood up and twirled on her heels. "Well? How do they look?"

"They look cute, but you look like you belong on a horse way more often than once in a blue moon. When I visit, we're going riding again."

She tried to hold back her fears, but her emotions were on overdrive, and the truth poured out. "I'm afraid to believe in this," she whispered. "In *us.*"

His brows knitted. "Why?"

"Because I'm so happy, but you're going to be busy when you go back to your real life, and I'll dive into one book after the next. And I know I'm rambling about long-term when we've only been together a short time, but we have less than a week left. And I want that week, but it's also scary because then I'll like you that much more. All this time with you has filled me up with so much happiness, it feels like some kind of spectacular fantasy."

"Breathe, baby. Slow down and breathe." He embraced her. "It is spectacular, but it's not a fantasy. I'm not a put-down-roots kind of guy, and I can't make promises for something I'm not sure I can do, but I promise you this. Whatever this is between us is real, and it's the one thing I don't want to run from."

"Then you think you really will come visit? Between shows, or something?"

"Nothing could keep me away. And I want to do a few things around here to keep you safe before I go. The thought of anything happening to you..."

"Bodyguard?" she teased.

He raised his brows. "That's a great idea."

"Beau!" She swatted his arm.

"Okay, I'll cancel the bodyguard. I ordered a driveway alarm that I'm going to install before I leave so you'll be alerted if anyone drives up to the inn."

"Seriously? They make those?"

"Hell yes. And I'm getting you a dog, too. A big one."

"It'll have to learn to feed itself," she teased. "You know I'm not very good in that department."

"You're right. Maybe I'll let you keep Bandit. At least he knows how to steal food."

She had a feeling she'd fall just as hard for his thieving dog as she had for him. "I love that you worry about me." She looked at the horses, then back at the man who made her head spin, and said, "And I still can't believe you did all of this for me. You brought in horses, cleaned the barn, and got me gorgeous boots. Beau...?"

"When you told me about Winter and how much you loved riding, you lit up the same way you do when you talk about your walks with your grandfather and your life here, your writing. You've done so much for me. I wanted to bring those feelings back for you."

Her eyes dampened again. "I haven't done anything for you except build a funky dreamscape that *you* had to help me take down." After they'd cleaned up, he'd set the jars she'd given him on her dresser, and then he'd written, *More Charlotte* on a piece of paper and put it in his Hopes and Dreams jar. It was another night she'd never forget.

"You've made me *feel* so many things that I thought were lost to me, and you always make me smile, which doesn't come easily for me this time of year. Or maybe *ever*, I don't know." He cupped her face and brushed his thumb over her cheek. "You've made me happier in these last three weeks than I've been in a decade." He gave her a quick kiss and said, "Now, let's put those pretty boots to the test. I want to see all your favorite riding spots."

Emotions bubbled up inside her as she went up on her toes and kissed the center of his chin. His scruff prickled her lips. She liked it so much, she did it again, and he pulled her closer. "I will show you my old favorites, but I think it's time for new ones. I want to find our own favorite places."

"That sounds even better."

It had been so many years since she'd ridden, as they saddled the horses she wondered if she'd forgotten how. But when she mounted Ginger, a familiar sense of peace came over her. The saddle cradled her hips as she shifted her bottom and positioned her legs to accommodate the breadth of the horse.

"Ready to ride, beautiful?" Beau looked regal on the dark horse.

"The horse, or you?" she teased as the horses walked at an easy pace away from the barn.

A wolfish grin slid into place. "The horse now, me later."

Charlotte's mind wandered as they explored the trails and hills of the property she'd once known by heart. They galloped in the meadows, the breeze sweeping across her cheeks. The rhythmic sounds of the horses' hooves brought a euphoric sensation of freedom and a sense of adventure she'd forgotten she had. The horses walked side by side, giving Beau and

Charlotte a chance to talk. They cracked up like fools as they tried to kiss without falling off. Beau's strong hands kept her steady as his lips landed on hers, and as the sun drifted toward the horizon, they came upon an overlook. They tied the horses to trees and sat on a rocky ledge.

"Come here, babe." He wrapped his arms around her, bringing her back against his chest, his legs cradling her hips.

He kissed the top of her head, but he didn't say a word as ribbons of blues and purples painted the sky. That was the thing about Beau. He didn't need to talk to get his point across. She could feel how happy he was, the same way she'd felt his tension when he'd first arrived.

She reached behind her and rested her hand on his neck, thinking about how much had changed between them. How much she'd changed, proven by the fact that she was there, enjoying an entire afternoon and evening without panicking over missed word counts. She owed that to Beau.

"I didn't realize how much I missed riding," she said, snuggling closer and admiring her pretty new boots. "I forgot how rejuvenating it was. It gives me such a *high*."

"Being with you does that to me." He leaned to the side, tipped her chin up, and kissed her.

"I really like when you tip my face to yours."

He did it again, kissing her sweetly, contradicting the seriousness in his eyes. "Then I'll do it more often. I've been trying to figure out how to say something to you, and I'm not great with words or expressing my feelings, but I need to say this."

She turned sideways, putting her legs over one of his so she could see him more clearly. "Okay."

"I like that you're not afraid to talk about Tory, and I'm sorry that sometimes I dodge your questions, but it's not because…" His brows knitted, as if he were grasping for the right words. "I was so young when she and I started going out. We were always 'Beau and Tory,' as if we were one entity. That's how people around town referred to us, like we were one human being. Even though I went away to college, she was part of my life there because she was always in my head, and my heart," he said with a hint of apology in his voice and his eyes.

"I understand," she said, feeling a little pang of sadness that she hadn't been that girl.

"Until I met you, I didn't think about who I was *without* her, which seems ridiculous since it's been so long. But I've lived with this guilt that has overshadowed everything in my life."

"I know—"

"Hear me out, please, because that's not what I wanted to tell you, but it's just as important. What I wanted you to know is that things between me and her were very different from what is between you and me. I don't want you to think that we, *you and I*, are a rerun of what she and I were. Everything about who I am with you is different from who I was back then or who I have ever been. I'm not a reckless kid, and I was never the type of boyfriend who would do things like borrow horses or buy boots. That wasn't me back then. That's who I am with you, Charlotte, and I want you to know how big, or important, or…"

He was trying so hard to show her who he was, and she already knew. "Different?" she suggested.

"Yes, *different*, that's it."

"Beau, I haven't even once worried that I was a substitute, and I'm not jealous of what you had with her. Not in a bad sense anyway. I really like you, so of course I wish I had history with you. And I probably would be jealous if she were still alive because you clearly still love her."

"I do, but I'm not in love with her in an active way. I'm not pining for a woman I can't have."

"I know," she reassured him. "You explained that to me. I meant you love her in a good way, though. I'm glad she was loved before she died. It would be even sadder if she hadn't ever experienced it. That said, I do hope that one day you will find a way to forgive yourself for not seeing her texts, because if she truly loved you, she wouldn't want you to carry that burden forever."

Relief eased the tension around his eyes for only a moment before seriousness overtook him again. She could see he wanted to say more, but he remained quiet as his arms came around her.

She didn't want to push him, but she truly believed he needed some type of closure in order to really move on, no matter how much she wished otherwise. As they gazed over the picturesque mountains, her thoughts turned inward. In all the years she'd lived at the inn, she'd never longed for human touch, or the type of intimacy she and Beau shared. She'd never experienced it firsthand to know what she was missing. Nestled within the safety of his arms, she knew she'd long for him when he left, and she could only imagine the sense of emptiness Tory had left behind. It was different, but in some respects, it was the same.

She rested her cheek on his chest, thinking about the complexities of love, and she wondered what was worse—having only dreamed of finding love, finding it and letting it slip away, or loving someone so completely that a decade later you were still punishing yourself for having made a mistake?

Chapter Fifteen

THE DAYS LEADING up to the Mad Prix awards ceremony passed in a flurry of preparations, but it never overshadowed the closeness or the deepening of Beau and Charlotte's relationship. Charlotte had surprised him and put aside her work last Sunday to spend the day horseback riding with him again before they'd had to return the horses that evening. They'd packed a picnic, and spent the entire day enjoying each other. It was the calm before the awards-ceremony storm. While chefs, waitstaff, housekeepers, groundskeepers, and valets took over the inn, Beau raced through a number of smaller repairs he'd noticed needed tending to, which had turned into bigger jobs, like reframing a window instead of simply replacing a sill. Charlotte was knee-deep in writing again. She'd failed to mention that in addition to innkeepers came a group of massage therapists and an entire office and concierge staff who took over the study, managing phone calls, registrations, and it seemed to Beau, everything else under the sun. Most everyone greeted Charlotte with warm hugs and intimate conversations, catching up on one another's lives like old friends. She might not have a biological family, but she was clearly loved by many, and he was glad for that.

Beau paced the terrace Saturday afternoon, waiting for Nick, Jillian, and Aiyla to arrive. Nick had called from the airport, and Beau had been tense ever since. Hopefully Nick wasn't dead set on harassing him the whole time he was there, because if he was, he had another thing coming.

The grounds were crawling with charitable contributors, race staff, and spectators sipping champagne and nibbling on finger foods while they waited for the racers to ascend the last hill before heading down to the finish line. Charlotte was mingling among them.

Cheers told Beau the racers weren't far off. He descended the steps, excited to see where Ty and Graham would place, and scanned the crowd for Charlotte. Colorful banners emblazoned with sponsors and charity names flapped in the breeze, and just beyond, his beautiful girl stood by the podium, looking carefree and gorgeous in a sexy blue halter dress as she spoke with Parker and Grayson Lacroux and Eric and Kat James. Parker was the founder of the Collins Children's Foundation, and Grayson was her husband. Eric had started the Foundation for Whole Families. The money earned from the race benefited their charities. Beau knew Eric and Kat well, and he'd been thrilled to meet their six-month-old son, Denny, whom Charlotte was now fawning over with that dreamy expression women got around babies.

Beau stopped to admire her, remembering how she'd said she'd once dreamed of finding Mr. Right and having a family of her own. He wondered what she was thinking as she shifted her attention to Parker and Grayson's baby girl, Miriam, who hadn't left her daddy's protective arms since they arrived.

It had been ages since Beau had given any thought to having a girlfriend, much less a family. But when he'd held Eric's adorable son and felt the weight of the precious baby in his arms, he'd been hit by a pang of unexpected longing, just like a fucking chick, and had become aware of a void he hadn't realized existed. Maybe he was misreading it or was just messed up by the tension of Nick showing up today, but for whatever reason, the awareness had burrowed itself under his skin like a tick and he had yet to shake it loose.

Charlotte headed his way, her long dark hair drifting over her shoulders. Her easy manner made his chest feel full. She was leaving for New York tomorrow afternoon, and he knew there weren't enough renovations on earth to keep him distracted from missing her.

"Hey, beautiful." He kissed her softly. "Nick called. They should be here any minute."

"I can't wait to meet him and Jillian, and to see Aiyla again."

More cheers rang out. "Sounds like the contestants are nearing the last climb."

"You can bet Ty is at the front of the pack," she said. "But it'll take him some time to breach the hill, and competitors will be coming in for the next few hours. I hope your family makes it in time to see them cross the finish line."

"My money's on Graham taking first. My brother has got a competitive streak a mile wide." He gathered her in his arms. Her skin was warm from the sun and smelled of the lilac body wash he'd lathered on her in the shower earlier that morning. "You did an amazing job. The event came together perfectly."

"Thanks, but you know I have nothing to do with it. It's all these wonderful people. Most of them knew my family and they do it for them. I'm glad, though. It's the one time of year I get to hear stories from my parents' friends."

"What about when you go back to Port Hudson tomorrow? Will you see old neighbors? People who knew your family?"

"Not this trip. My editor, Chelsea, emailed earlier. They're setting up a meeting with the marketing department before I meet with her. My publicist, Luce Palmer, will be there for that, and then I'll meet with Chelsea in the afternoon. And *then* it's me and the LWW girls *all night long*. We have a *lot* to catch up on." She ran her finger down his chest and said, "I have a boyfriend to rave about, you know."

"Are you nervous?"

"No. *Yes.* A little, because I'm not sure my book is perfect, but we'll see. This is my fifth book, and I still worry with every one, so that's normal."

"I'm sure it's great, and if it needs tweaking, you'll tweak it. I wish I could be there to watch you in action."

Heat brimmed in her eyes, and she whispered, "You got to watch me in action last night."

"Man, did I ever." His cock twitched with the memory of her riding him rough and wild.

"Hey." She touched his cheek, bringing his eyes to hers. "Stop thinking about me naked."

He brushed his lips over hers and said, "But it's such an awesome visual. I love seeing you in the throes of passion."

"Okay," she said in a singsong voice. "If you want your brother, sister, and Aiyla to see you with tented pants, because either that's Jilly and Nick, or you have a fan club led by another burgundy-haired woman."

He turned around just in time to catch Jillian throwing her arms around him.

"Beau!" She acted like she hadn't seen him in years. The air around her buzzed with excitement. "Jax wanted to come with us to see Graham run, but he's got a huge wedding this weekend, and you know how anal he is about being available for the brides on their big day. Can't have any bridal gown mishaps."

Aiyla waved, the calm to Jillian's whirlwind, while Nick stood protectively beside her, giving off a don't-fuck-with-me vibe. His thick dark hair sprouted out from beneath his ever-present black cowboy hat, brushing the collar of his tight T-shirt. Tight was the only type of shirt he owned. Where Beau was fit, Nick had insanely large, bulbous muscles.

"I'm sure Aiyla will take enough pictures that he'll feel like he was here," Beau said as Aiyla hugged Charlotte.

"You look amazing," Charlotte said. "I'm sorry you're not racing this year."

"Next year it's *mine*," Aiyla said confidently. "I've been training, and next year it's me and Ty again all the way." Her shirt had TY BRADEN'S #1 FAN emblazoned across the chest, and her shorts revealed her flesh-colored prosthetic leg, on which she'd written #TEAMTY and #TEAMBRADEN in red marker. She carried a camera over one shoulder and moved it out of the way as she hugged Charlotte. Her honey-blond hair was as light as Charlotte's hair was dark.

Beau placed a hand on Charlotte's back and said, "Jilly, Nick, this is—"

"Only the most amazing romance writer on the planet!" Jillian said excitedly as she hugged Charlotte. "I love your books so much. I want a man just like your hero Daryl Magnum from *Crazy, Sexy, Sinful*. Think you can whip one up for me?"

Nick and Beau shook their heads.

"Daryl is a fan favorite. Everyone loves the mysterious, stoic bad boy," Charlotte said. "My social media pages are always filled with fans wanting more of him." She glanced at Beau and then leaned closer to Jillian, lowered her voice, and said, "I think we'd better talk about that when Paul Bunyan and Burly Beau aren't around," Charlotte said.

"Burly Beau!" Jillian laughed. "They're growly, but they're softies at heart."

"Bullshit," Nick said at the same time Beau said, "Softy, my ass."

The girls giggled.

"Remind me to corner you later," Jillian said to Charlotte. "I brought a copy of *Crazy, Sexy, Sinful* that I was hoping you'd autograph. Beau said he'd get me your autograph, but last night he said he forgot, which is guy code for he hadn't done it because he was too embarrassed to ask."

Beau locked eyes with Charlotte. "We've been a little *busy*."

Nick slid him a curious look.

"Yeah, yeah. Whatever. I hope we didn't miss the guys crossing the finish line," Jillian said as she smoothed her hand down her black sleeveless blouse. "Nicky got into it with a hot cowboy at the gas station."

Nick shook his head with a tight expression. "The jackoff was staring at her ass."

"I have a nice ass." Jillian wiggled her butt. "It should be admired."

Beau and Nick both mumbled, "Jesus, Jilly."

"We are going to get along *so* well," Charlotte said with a big grin.

Beau embraced Nick. "Good to see you, little brother. Don't make me regret saying that."

Nick mumbled something indiscernible. Then he tipped his cowboy hat to Charlotte and said, "Nice to meet you, sweetheart." He gave her a quick hug, smirking at Beau over her shoulder.

Bastard.

"I'm excited to finally meet both of you." Charlotte flashed her killer smile, and Beau put his arm proprietarily around her, pulling her closer.

Jillian's eyes widened, and before Beau could say a word, she blurted out, "You two are *together*? I didn't know you were *that* kind of *busy*!"

Shock registered on Nick's face.

"We are," Beau said proudly, meeting Nick's scrutinizing eyes. "Like I said, back off, bro."

"Hey, Nick, maybe if you ask nicely Char will let you play with her blow-up dolls," Aiyla said, earning a sideways glance from Nick. "When Ty and I were here last summer, Charlotte pulled us into her office and made us get down and dirty with them."

"Really?" Nick's interest was obviously piqued.

"For research, asshole." Beau glared at him. "And she doesn't need to use them now that I'm here."

Cheers drew their attention to the far end of the property, where hordes of people were waving flags and shouting happily. Spectators lined up between the final hill and the finish line hooting and hollering, unwilling to relinquish their front-row view.

"We'd better hurry," Aiyla said. "I want to get pictures of Ty."

"Come on!" Jillian grabbed Aiyla's and Charlotte's hands, and they ran toward the crowd.

Nick sidled up to Beau and said, "You *are* leaving at the end of next week, right? Meaning Charlotte will be available once you're gone? Because I'm feeling a need for a mountainside-inn vacation." He chuckled.

Beau glowered.

"HURRY UP, YOU guys!" Aiyla urged as she ran toward the hill, camera in hand. She was faster with her prosthesis than either Jillian or Charlotte were in their sandals.

"Go! We'll catch up!" Jillian said, still clinging to Charlotte's hands like they were best friends. "Get pics of Graham, too!"

Aiyla blew them a kiss and took off running at full speed.

"God, I love her," Jillian said as Aiyla disappeared into the crowd at the top of the hill. "She and Ty are so in love."

"You should have been here after last year's race. Ty took such amazing care of her." Charlotte smiled to herself, thinking about Beau and the way he was always looking out for her.

Jillian looked over her shoulder at Nick and Beau, then dragged Charlotte away from the crowds. "Okay, you have to tell me what you've done to my brother. The man has stars in his eyes when he looks at you and *fire* in them when Nick looks at you."

"Fire, huh?" She stole a glance at Beau, who was watching her, his jaw tense as he listened to something Nick was saying. Beau lifted his chin, the edges of his mouth quirking up, and she felt herself blushing. *From a glance!* She looked at Jillian, who was grinning like a Cheshire cat.

"See what I mean?" Jillian hugged her. "Thank you! Beau hasn't made time for anything in his life but work for as long as

I can remember. He doesn't usually give women a second glance, and look at him! The man cannot take his eyes off you, and clearly it's mutual."

Charlotte realized she was staring at Beau. But how could she not? He was everything she'd ever dreamed of and more. "It's definitely mutual." *And I can't imagine how sad I'm going to be when he leaves.*

"I don't know how serious you guys are, but please don't hurt him. He's been through a lot."

Charlotte was touched by how deeply Jillian cared for her brother. "Hurting him is the last thing I'd ever want to do. He told me about Tory."

"He *told* you? Okay, then, you two must be serious. He won't talk about her with anyone."

"I know," she said as Aiyla raced past them in the other direction.

"Where are you going?" Jillian called after her.

Aiyla lifted her camera and yelled, "Finish line pictures!"

"Come on!" Jillian grabbed Charlotte's arm and ran toward the finish line. "She's right! We need to see them cross!"

"What's wrong?" Beau asked as they approached.

Charlotte grabbed his hand as they ran past, dragging him with them. "We're waiting at the finish line! Run!"

Nick fell into step beside them, glaring challengingly at Beau, like a bull preparing to charge. Beau's nostrils flared.

"You two are ridiculous!" Jillian said.

Charlotte was totally confused. "What—"

Beau dropped her hand and took off toward the finish line. Nick was right there with him, neck and neck. Their hulking bodies and powerful legs ate up the distance so fast, Charlotte couldn't believe her eyes as she and Jillian ran after them.

"I thought Beau was a walker!" she said as Beau kicked up his speed even faster, leaving Nick in his dust.

"Beau was a runner in high school. He won all sorts of awards. Nick never runs. He's all about muscle." Jillian grabbed her side and doubled over, panting.

"Are you okay?" Charlotte asked.

"Fine. Not used to running."

Beau sprinted over the finish line, and Charlotte screamed, jumping up and down. She and Jillian hugged and cheered. Beau and Nick high-fived, and Beau headed straight for Charlotte with a look of satisfaction on his ruggedly handsome face. She wanted to run to him, but she hated to leave Jillian hanging.

"Oh my God. Go before you burst!" Jillian shoved her toward Beau.

Charlotte ran as fast as her legs would allow. Beau reached her in seconds, sweeping her into his arms as Ty and another guy raced past with a pack of other runners on their heels.

"You were a runner!" she said between happy kisses.

"Long time ago. That win was for you, baby." He kissed her hard, then set her on her feet out of the way of the competitors. "That's Ty and Graham in the lead. Come on." He looked over his shoulder at Jillian and said, "Need a carry, sis?"

She waved him on. "Not unless you know a hot single guy!"

Beau made a growling noise. Charlotte loved the way Jillian purposely poked his protective side. They weaved through the crowd. Ty and Graham sprinted shoulder to shoulder.

Aiyla cheered Ty on as she took pictures.

"Push it, Graham!" Nick hollered.

Beau cheered for both Ty and Graham, holding tightly to Charlotte's hand.

Suddenly Ty bolted off to the side and scooped up Aiyla, carrying her toward the finish line. The crowd roared, waving flags and hollering as Ty passed three runners, still behind Graham and a handful of others. Nick whistled, Beau and Jillian cracked up, and Charlotte was in love with them all.

"That is going in a book!" Charlotte exclaimed.

Graham crossed the finish line, and the crowd went wild. Charlotte and the others screamed, cheering and hugging each other as more runners crossed the line. Ty and Aiyla took sixth place, but Ty didn't seem to mind giving up the gold. He was too busy lip-locking with his wife.

"Come on, baby. I want you to meet Graham." Beau led her through the crowd.

They caught up with the others, and Beau hung back, letting everyone else congratulate Graham first. Graham looked so much like Beau, he could have been his leaner, younger doppelgänger, with the same short brown hair and dark eyes, which seemed to be a Braden trait. He had a nice smile, and as Beau embraced him and they hugged for a beat longer than the others, Beau said something that made Graham pull back and search Beau's eyes.

"Really?" Graham asked.

Beau gave a curt nod. He reached for Charlotte's hand and said, "Charlotte, this is my little brother Graham."

"Little, my ass, old man." Graham opened his arms and said, "I'm sweaty, but pleased to meet you."

"I don't mind sweat." Charlotte embraced him. "Congratulations. That was awesome!"

"You and Ty were both awesome." Beau put his arm around Charlotte.

"I'm not sure I would have taken first if not for my lovesick cousin missing his girl," Graham teased.

"You won fair and square." Ty grabbed two Gatorades from a volunteer and handed one to Graham. "You got the gold, but I got the girl." He pulled Aiyla into a kiss.

"Get a room," Nick teased. "And a shower."

"The awards ceremony isn't until four o'clock," Charlotte reminded them. "The dinner and dance start at seven, so you guys have plenty of time to shower and get a massage if you want to."

Jillian wrinkled her nose at Ty and Graham and said, "You guys *are* pretty dirty."

"Hey, I like my man dirty," Aiyla said, leaning in for another kiss, which Ty was more than happy to give her.

"Speaking of *dirty*, where's Butterscotch?" Nick asked. "He's usually right up there with you guys."

"Jon?" Charlotte asked. Jon Butterscotch was a physician and Ty's brother's business partner.

"You know Jon?" Beau asked.

"Oh, please," Charlotte said. "There's not a single female on earth who can get within a hundred feet of 'Mr. Fifty Shades of Sweetness at Your Service' without knowing him."

Beau grimaced.

"He's harmless," Ty assured him. "He's the one who helped Aiyla after the race and worked through her diagnosis. He was there every step of the way. He's a good guy, and last year he stayed back during this stretch of the race to help one of my friends with a sore ankle."

Nick's eyes narrowed. "Yeah, Trixie Jericho. She's a friend of mine, and Jon better keep his paws off her."

"You know Trixie?" Charlotte asked, wide-eyed. "I *love* her!"

Beau chuckled. "Nick, I thought you had no interest in her. I knew there was more to you two than met the eye."

"She's a *friend*," Nick sneered. "And Butterscotch thinks he's God's gift to women. He's not right for her."

Jillian crossed her arms and flipped her hair over her shoulder. "Are you right for her? Because she's all cowgirl and you're full-on cowboy."

"Come to think of it," Ty said with a glimmer of mischief in his eyes, "I think Jon was with Trixie earlier today."

As Jillian and Ty harassed Nick, Beau whispered in Charlotte's ear, "How's my girl holding up?"

"Good. I *love* your family. You're so lucky to have so many of them around."

His eyes shifted to the others, who were talking and clapping as runners crossed the finish line. "I am pretty lucky. But I'm luckiest because I found you." His lips came tenderly down over hers.

"Speaking of getting the girl and getting a room," Graham said, earning cheers from everyone and a sneer from Beau. "I thought you were just here to do repairs."

"I am," Beau answered. "Charlotte's really good at repairing broken thirty-year-olds."

He pressed his lips to hers, and she felt the approving eyes of his family on them.

"Who the hell are you, and what have you done with my brother?" Nick asked.

Beau glared at him.

"Actually, what Beau said isn't really true." Charlotte gazed up at him and said, "You weren't broken. You were just lying in wait, like Sleeping Beauty, waiting for the right kiss."

"Sleeping Beauty." Nick's deep laugh rose above everyone

else's. "That's about right."

"Christ, shortcake. Couldn't you have said *Thor?*"

"Mm, Thor," Jillian said, earning another slant-browed stare from Beau.

"I never saw that movie, but I don't think the analogy would work," Charlotte said. "Besides, I can't compare you to Chris Hemsworth. I mean, just look at you." She waved at his body.

"Damn," Graham said. "That's harsh."

"I know, right?" Charlotte put her arms around Beau and said, "Beau is about a *million* times hotter than Chris." She looked pointedly at Nick and added, "And my man wields a much bigger *hammer.*"

Chapter Sixteen

CHARLOTTE AND BEAU had watched most of the race and had seen Trixie and Jon cross the finish line, *separately*, which Nick seemed overly pleased about. They hung out with everyone during the awards ceremony and were meeting them in ten minutes for dinner. Beau put on his sport coat and headed to Charlotte's suite. He pushed open the door just as she was coming out of the bedroom. Their eyes connected, and his thoughts stuttered. They both stood stock-still, each taking in the other. Charlotte looked elegant in a short black dress that cinched at her waist and flared to just above her knees. Lace covered her beautiful shoulders, and her hair was pinned up in some kind of twist with a few pretty tendrils framing her face. She never wore makeup, and she didn't need it, but tonight her eyes were smoky, her lips a soft shade of red.

"Wow," fell from Beau's lips as he closed the distance between them.

Charlotte twirled slowly in her high heels, revealing racy, bold cutouts along the back of the dress. "You like?"

"No, baby. I *love*." He took her in his arms, his hand drifting down her back. Her skin was like warm velvet, and her lips curved up in a sweet, effortless smile. He remembered the first time he'd held her, really held her, not when they were challenging each other. The first time she'd touched his face, his *body*. He wasn't sure how it had happened, but sometime over the last few weeks he'd free-fallen into love with her. A love so true and real, and so vastly different from anything he'd ever known, but he had seen this kind of love between his parents his whole life. He may never have noticed it the way he did if not for the amazing woman in his arms.

"Why are you looking at me like that?" she asked shyly.

He pulled her closer and said, "Because you are exquisite. You're always beautiful, but *wow*, baby. You take my breath away."

"As you do, me." She ran her hand down his arm and said, "I feel like we're going to prom or something."

He kissed her neck, not wanting to mess up her lipstick, and said, "I'm not sure I want to leave this room." He held her tight against him as he lowered his mouth to her shoulder.

"Mm. I love when you kiss me."

"I love when you wear your hair up like this." He continued kissing and tasting. "You're going to New York tomorrow, and I want to memorize everything about you." Her skin warmed even more. He put his mouth beside her ear, inhaling her intoxicating scent, and whispered, "Two days apart will seem like forever."

"For me, too," she said breathlessly as he kissed her jaw.

He'd been holding in his emotions for so long, but he no longer wanted to try, and the truth poured out. "I'm falling so in love with you, shortcake. I don't know what you've done to me, but please don't stop doing it."

"You're…"

He drew back and gazed into her glassy eyes. "Falling in

love with you."

A single tear slipped down her cheek, and he kissed it away.

"But you said you can't put down roots."

He heard the worry in her voice, and as much as he wanted to promise her the world, he went with the truth, because when it came to Charlotte, he would always do the right thing. "I don't know if I ever can, but I love you. I love who we are together, and I want you to know that before you leave."

He slid his hand to the back of her neck, drawing her in to a kiss.

The door flew open, and they startled apart as Jillian burst in. She hurried toward them wearing a tight sparkly gray minidress with fringe at the bottom and holding her phone straight out toward them.

"See, Mom?" Jillian said excitedly to her parents, who were on FaceTime on her phone. "I told you he had a girlfriend!"

"Jesus, Jilly. Ever heard of knocking?" Beau put his arm around Charlotte, but she was busy smiling and waving at his parents.

"You wouldn't have heard me," Jillian said. "You were too busy making out." She moved next to Charlotte, turning the phone toward them. "Amazing dress!"

"Thanks! Yours, too," Charlotte said. Her eyes flicked to Beau, her cheeks pink, which he knew was from his confession, and it made him love her even more.

"It's one of my original designs. Isn't it fun?" Jillian wiggled her hips, and the fringe shifted around her thighs.

"Hi, Beau honey," his mother said. "Sorry to interrupt you two. Jillian said you wouldn't mind."

Beau glared at Jillian, then shifted a softer expression to his parents. As the shock of the interruption wore off, excitement and nervousness swelled inside him over introducing his family to his *girlfriend.* "It's okay. Mom, Dad, this is Charlotte Sterling. Charlotte, this is my mom, Lily, and my father, Clint."

Bandit barked, and his big, beautiful dog went paws-up on his father's lap, sniffing at the screen.

"Aw, he's so cute!" Charlotte squeezed Beau's hand. "Hi, Bandit. Hi, sweetie." She leaned closer to Beau and whispered, "I want to pet him."

"He's a kleptomaniac," Jillian said. "He steals everything."

"Hey, buddy boy. I miss you," Beau said, wishing he could pet him, too. Bandit whimpered and sniffed the monitor. "Make sure you steal Jillian's stuff when she gets home."

Jillian swatted Beau's arm. "Brat."

Bandit barked. He was a great dog. If he'd been there, he'd get right between Jillian and Beau, protecting Beau.

"Okay, Bandit, down boy." His father bent to love him up, and his mother's face filled the screen.

"He misses you, Beau. But I'm glad you let him stay with us," she said. "I'll miss the thieving guy when you move. Charlotte, it's so nice to meet you, sweetheart. I read all of your books, and we've heard so much about you from Ty and Aiyla. It's wonderful that you open the inn for this event. And you all look so gorgeous. Beau, I haven't seen you dressed up in years."

"Doesn't he look amazing?" Charlotte said. "I'm so happy to meet you guys. I heard all about how you two met at the vineyard. It's such a romantic story."

"More like a romantic *chase,*" his father said. "Hal introduced us, just like you two. He's quite the matchmaker. But my wife played hard to get."

"Only because I wanted to make sure you were not one of those fickle men who went after every skirt they saw," his mother said. "But I quickly learned that Bradens are fiercely loyal."

Charlotte glanced at Beau with so much love in her eyes, he was sure his parents could see it as she said, "The apple didn't fall far from the tree."

They talked for a few minutes longer, and as Jillian filled in his parents about the race, Charlotte whispered in Beau's ear, "I love you, too."

Beau lowered his lips to hers, sealing their confessions with a kiss.

Jillian and his mother said, "Aw," in unison.

"Okay, enough," Beau said. "Mom, Dad, we have to get to dinner. Jillian, let's go."

THE MAIN FLOOR of the inn had been transformed into a luxurious banquet area, with round tables draped in white linen, fine china, and sparkling silver. Floral centerpieces adorned the tables, and white lights ran along the exposed beams in the ceiling. Beau sat between Graham and Charlotte, surrounded by his family and friends after dinner, enjoying the get-together but wishing he could sneak away with Charlotte. Music from the band drifted in through the open terrace doors, where people were dancing, drinking, and celebrating, reminding Beau of the evening he and Charlotte had danced at the restaurant, the first night they'd been intimate. It was a night he'd never forget.

Who was he kidding? He'd never forget a minute of their time together.

Charlotte was busy talking with Aiyla and Jillian about

dresses. The three of them, along with Trixie, had clicked like sisters. He loved seeing this playful, girlie side of her. Seeing her with his family and friends brought an element of unexpected relief. In the back of his mind, he must have worried about how he'd feel bringing a woman around the people who had known how much he'd loved Tory. It was obvious that he needn't have worried. He'd never been happier to see his family embrace anyone.

Graham nudged his arm and nodded toward Nick, who looked like he was chewing on nails. Beau followed his gaze and saw Trixie dancing with Jon.

"Go cut in," he said to Nick, who was sitting on the other side of Graham.

Nick scoffed. "I don't chase."

"Good luck with that," Beau said.

The song ended, and Trixie and Jon returned to the table. They were all used to seeing Trixie in cutoffs or jeans and cowgirl boots, not tight minidresses and sky-high heels. And Jon looked more like a surfer than a doctor, wearing a black dress shirt, open one button too far, with his blond hair, bright blue eyes, deep bronze tan, and ever-present cocky demeanor. No wonder Nick was ready to cause some trouble.

"Come on, y'all." Trixie pushed her long dark hair over her shoulder and said, "Time for tequila shots." She pulled Nick up to his feet. "I need you to keep me from doing something stupid, like body shots."

"I'm in!" Jillian popped up to her feet.

"Oh yeah." Jon grabbed Ty by the arm and hauled him to his feet. "Body shots with two hot babes. You'd better keep me under control."

Ty glanced at Nick, who was watching Jon like a hawk, and

said, "I think that job's already taken."

Graham stood, pulling Beau up with him. "Come on. We haven't done shots together in forever. Let's get you nice and drunk so Char can take advantage of you."

"If you think I need to be drunk for that, you're crazy." Beau touched Charlotte's shoulder and said, "Babe? Feel like drinking?"

"Only if they can make tequila taste like candy," she said as she rose to her feet.

"Cherry cheesecake shooters," Aiyla said as they made their way to the bar. "It's the only thing my friends will drink."

"Think you can outdrink me, Nicky boy?" Jon asked.

Nick scoffed. "I can out-anything you."

"Game. On." Jon put his arm around Jillian and said, "Let's get this party started."

CHARLOTTE'S PULSE HADN'T stopped racing since Beau had told her he loved her. Her emotions were heightened by how enamored she was by his family. These were the moments she'd always dreamed of. The things she'd thought she'd never have—a man who adored her so much that she could feel it in his every breath and friends who treated her like family instead of like the girl who once had a family. But as everyone gathered around the bar and Graham and Ty each slung an arm over Beau's shoulder, worries trickled in about what loving each other really meant. His family loved him so much, and she didn't know if he avoided them all summer or just for a few weeks. Or was it only in his hometown? Or everywhere? Were there other things he avoided to escape the guilt over Tory? Places they would have to avoid besides his hometown?

Charlotte felt a hand on her arm as Aiyla guided her a few feet away from the others and asked, "Are you okay?"

"Yeah. Fine," she lied.

"You look green all of a sudden. Do you need to sit down?"

"No, thanks. I just need a road map for relationships." She tried to school her expression and said, "I'm okay, really."

Aiyla stole a glance at Beau. "Ty told me what happened with Beau."

Relief swept through Charlotte. She didn't want to lie to her friend again, but still she didn't know what to say.

"You should know what else Ty said. He and Graham and I went for a walk around the lake, and Beau was all they talked about. How different he is with you, how happy. They said they'd never seen him like this. *Ever*, Char. That's a long time."

She knew what Aiyla was implying, that he was happier than he'd been with Tory. Char didn't know if she believed that, but she didn't need to. She wasn't worried about replacing Tory or living up to what they had. Beau was an honest man, and he'd already told her that what they had was different from what he'd had with Tory, and she'd never want to take away from what they'd had. That was then, and this was now. She believed in Beau, and she believed in what they had now. She just wanted to be sure that at some point they'd have a life without bounds.

"We're both happy," she said. "But he has a lot to get past."

Aiyla lifted the hem of her maxi dress, showing Charlotte her prosthetic. "So did we."

Charlotte knew how much Aiyla and Ty had gone through, and though different, it was also similar. Aiyla's prosthesis had changed their lives dramatically. She and Ty were both extreme sports fanatics, and she'd gone through extended therapy to learn to walk again and manage life with a prosthesis. He'd been with her every step of the way, and Char wanted to be there for Beau.

She glanced at him, with his clean-shaven cheeks and a glimmer of happiness in his eyes that hadn't dimmed since he'd told her he loved her, and her love for him swelled. "I want to help him but not push. Look at how much everyone loves him. How can he stay away from them? I want to wrap myself up in all of them."

"Sometimes it just takes the right person to lead the way." Aiyla reached for her hand and said, "Come on, let's see if we can nudge him in the right direction."

He'd already been nudged. The man needed a good hard shove. But that had to come from within, not from Charlotte or anyone else.

"There's my girl." Beau reached for her.

As he nuzzled against her neck, she realized she was getting way ahead of herself. They were in love, hoping to make a long-distance relationship work, not getting married.

"Everything okay?" he asked.

She looked into his honest eyes. He'd never let her down, and she had a feeling he never would. "Better than okay. I just needed a moment to wrap my head around tonight."

"I'd like to wrap my body around yours right this very second." He pulled her against him and kissed her hard.

"There goes bachelor number one," Jon said.

"Give it up, Butterscotch. We don't do that shit." Nick handed Charlotte a shot glass. "Cherry cheesecake shooter, sweetheart. Your boyfriend told us to keep them coming."

"Thanks. What does he mean by bachelor number one?"

"Our uncle does a bachelor auction for charity every year," Nick explained. "Jon's always trying to get us to participate."

"You should do it, Nicky!" Jillian chimed in. "Now that Ty and all his siblings are spoken for, it makes sense. Carry on the family tradition."

"Wait!" Trixie pushed between Jillian and Nick, her eyes bright with mischief. "Let's get them to do a bachelorette auction! I'd totally do that. Wouldn't you, Jilly?"

Jillian said, "Yes," at the same time Beau and Nick said, "No," causing everyone to laugh.

"I'd do it as long as Beau has enough money to win me," Charlotte said. "That sounds like fun."

"I'll give him a run for his money," Jon said with a smirk.

Beau gave him an *over my dead body* glare. "I'd sell my house if I had to."

"To Beau finally getting a life." Graham held up his drink, and everyone toasted.

That sparked a flurry of conversations about bachelor and bachelorette auctions, during which they toasted two more times. Jillian and Trixie took charge of ordering and handing out shots as the men tossed out barbs. Beau laughed harder than Charlotte had ever heard. It was untethered and carefree, and she knew these people were key to him rediscovering this side of himself.

"Speaking of going home," Beau said, and everyone fell silent.

Including Charlotte. Hope bloomed inside her, but she quickly tempered it. She, of all people, knew he'd only begun healing, and look how far he'd come. He'd shared things with her that he'd had bottled up for years, and he loved her. Truly, deeply loved her in a way she doubted many people who hadn't suffered loss would be capable of loving a person. She knew he wasn't going to say what they all wanted to hear—that he'd head back to Pleasant Hill soon—and that was okay. Love didn't have a deadline.

"Char's going to New York, and I could use an extra set of hands on a few projects while she's gone. Anyone able to stay?"

Everyone answered at once. Most had to get back to work, but Nick and Graham both offered to stay and help. She didn't understand the grateful look on his brothers' faces, but she was happy they'd get time together.

"How many Bradens does it take to renovate an inn?" Jon held up his drink, and everyone lifted their glasses. "Who the fuck knows!"

They all cheered and drank.

And so went the next hour. The guys hanging on one another, laughing, joking, and challenging one another about everything under the sun, while Charlotte and the girls discussed potential story lines for Charlotte's upcoming novels.

"I want to be a heroine named Daphne." Trixie swayed on her heels. "And I want my hero to have a really manly name, like Rock or Stone."

"No!" Jillian said with wide eyes. "You need a better name. Daphne is so...*blah*. You're wild and free, and you're thinking about starting that mini-pony business, which is going to take you all over creation. You need to be Esmerelda or—"

"Just name me *Trixie*," Trixie said. "Give me a hard-bodied hero who isn't a dick—"

"But has a *big* one," Aiyla chimed in.

"Whoa, baby cakes," Ty said as he took Aiyla's hand. "Time for me to put my girl to bed before she starts trash talking."

"Oh, come on," Jillian begged. "She's just having fun."

Charlotte's head was spinning as Beau swept her into his arms and away from the others. He smelled delicious as he guided her arms around his neck and began slow dancing.

"I love you," she said, or at least she thought she did. She wasn't sure. Her mouth felt a little numb, and Beau was smiling at her like she'd said something funny. *I love you* wasn't funny, but what if she'd said something else and just thought she'd said that?

"I love you too, beautiful," he said, putting her worries to rest. "Are you having fun?"

"Yes! I love your family, and I love tonight. I love you all dressed up, and I love you in your birthday suit."

He chuckled. "Funny, I love you in your birthday suit, too. But I can't take advantage of you if you're drunk. Are you drunk?"

"A little," she whispered. "Are you drunk?"

He chuckled. "No."

"Good. Then I *can* take advantage of you." She tugged his mouth down to hers.

His lips were firm and insistent, his mouth sweet and delicious. As they made out, swaying to the music, somewhere in the recesses of her mind, she worried about what his family and the patrons who had known her family might think of her. But she was happy, and they were in love, and tonight was all they had before she was gone for two days, so she pushed those worries away and enjoyed dancing, and kissing, her man.

Chapter Seventeen

CHARLOTTE AWOKE WITH a groan and begrudgingly opened her eyes, meeting Beau's all-too-alert gaze. His naked body warmed her side as he leaned down for a kiss.

"Now I remember why I hardly ever drink," she said.

"Don't worry, baby. I've got you covered." He helped her sit up and handed her ibuprofen and a glass of water. "Start with this."

"You're a savior." She took the medicine and set the water beside her lamp. "That was so much fun last night. I hope I didn't do anything embarrassing."

"No more embarrassing than anyone else."

"Oh *God*."

She flopped onto her back with her arm over her eyes, and the sheet fell away, exposing her to cooler air *and* to Beau's hungry mouth. He kissed the swell of her breast, and despite the dull ache in her head, her whole body responded.

"You were sexy, baby." He dragged his tongue over her nipple, and she moaned with the titillating pleasures it sent sizzling through her. "And adorable."

He sealed his wicked mouth over the taut peak and sucked. His arousal pressed against her leg as he brought his hands into play, teasing her and driving her to the edge of insanity.

"And delicious," he said as he moved down her body, reminding her that they'd made out on the dance floor.

He kissed her belly, nipping at her tender skin as he lifted her legs at the knees and settled them over his shoulders. His gaze raked boldly over her sex, and her whole body flamed in anticipation. He kissed each of her inner thighs. Then he placed the softest of kisses to her sex, teasing her with fluttery flicks of his tongue until her insides reached for him and her back bowed off the bed. He pushed his hands under her bottom, holding her up as his mouth covered her. He feasted on her, fucking her with his tongue, sucking and kissing and biting. Heat and tingles spiked up her limbs, lust pooled in her lower belly, and she clung to the sheets, gasping for breath.

"I need to drink more often."

He lifted his smiling face.

"Don't stop! Geez! I didn't mean to say it out loud, but I do think this isn't just the cure for a hangover. I think it's the cure for *everything*."

"God, I love you, Charlotte Sterling."

She pointed between her legs and said, "Then get busy, and if you take away my hangover, I'll even reciprocate."

He got more than busy. He took her to paradise and back twice, leaving her ragged and trembling. And when he reached for a condom, she shook her head and said, "My turn."

"No, baby. I want to be inside you, and if you put that sexy mouth of yours on me, I'll come."

"Then I won't let you." Rejuvenated by his desires, she rolled him onto his back visually feasting on his broad chest and hard cock. "Where to start," she said innocently, teasingly, as she lowered her mouth to his pecs.

She wanted to go slow, to drag out his pleasure, but the second her lips touched his hot skin, she wanted *more*. She sucked his nipple as he'd done to her and wrapped her fingers around his hard length, stroking him as she sucked. His hips pistoned with every stroke, fucking her fist as she devoured his body. She kissed and nipped as she moved lower. When she reached his cock, she teased him as he'd so often teased her, licking and sucking his inner thighs, the tender skin around the nest of hair at the base of his shaft. She lifted his balls and sucked them into her mouth.

"Jesus, fuck—" He grabbed his shaft and stroked as she sucked and licked his balls.

The sight of his strong hand wrapped around himself made her even hotter.

"Don't stop," she said, and then she lowered her mouth over his thick length, following his hand up and down.

He groaned and thrust.

"Don't come," she pleaded, earning a frustrated moan. "Not yet."

She moved between his legs, loving his sac again, and put her hand around his, wanting to feel his strength wrapped around himself. She'd never wanted to explore like this, but when he said, "Touch yourself," she obeyed without hesitation.

And he watched, stroking himself as she teased her wetness with one hand and placed her other hand over his, stroking his cock with him.

"Suck me, baby. Suck me and ride my face."

She could come just from hearing him talk like that. It was so naughty, so *hot*. The sight of his dark eyes boring into her emboldened her even more.

"Okay, but you can't come. I want to feel you inside me

when you come."

"How about if I come in your mouth, you come on mine, and then you get me hard again?"

Oh, how she loved *that* option! "Can you…?"

"Have I ever failed you before?"

She scrambled over him. He wrapped one arm around her hips as he ate at her sex and fucked her mouth, hard and fast. Her entire body vibrated, heat and ice coursing through her as they drove each other out of their minds. Her senses reeled, short-circuiting, and she couldn't hold on to a single thought beyond the mounting pleasures inside her and the feel of his thickness pushing in and out of her mouth. She felt him flex beneath her at the same moment he did something incredible with his tongue, and they both surrendered to their passion and spiraled over the edge. Pleasure exploded inside her as she swallowed the proof of his arousal, and she collapsed beside him.

He came down over her and captured her mouth with savage intensity, his half-hard cock grinding against her center, making her want and need him again. It took only a minute, and then his hard length was riding her slickness and they were both clamoring for more. He sheathed himself and drove into her in one hard thrust.

She cried out with the ferocity of erotic pain and pleasure engulfing her. "Again!"

He held her tight, taking her harder, deeper, and kissing her like she'd never been kissed before. Waves of pleasure crashed over her with every stroke of his tongue, every thrust of his hips. Their bodies smoldered as they gave in to their carnal desires, soaring higher until they shattered into a million sated pieces, bound together in a tempo all their own.

A LONG WHILE later Beau and Charlotte showered, loving on each other even more, and finally dressed to join the others. Everyone was waiting for them, and they'd probably missed breakfast, but Charlotte didn't care. Even though she wanted to see everyone, she was in no hurry to leave their suite. She packed her bag, knowing she had to leave soon but wanting every minute alone with Beau that she could get.

Beau gathered her in his arms, gazing lovingly into her eyes. He did that so often, looked at her like he had a million things to say, but said nothing, or little. She liked that thoughtful side of him.

"Two days?" He pressed his lips to hers.

"Two days. Then we'll have until you leave for L.A. Thursday."

His eyes turned from sated to serious. "I want to drive you to the airport."

She'd known he would. She didn't want to feed in to his worries any more than she wanted to negate them. But their lives were soon going to be far apart, and she didn't want him to worry every time she went somewhere that he'd lose her like he'd lost Tory.

Treading carefully, she said, "Jilly and Aiyla and everyone are going together, and your brothers are staying to spend time with *you*. You should be with them."

His grip on her tightened, and his jaw followed. "Char—"

She silenced him with a kiss. "I know you worry, but Ty would never let anything happen to Aiyla, and he'd never let anything happen to me. Your mistake wasn't that you caused an accident. You were busy with your brother and you missed texts. You never miss a thing with me, Beau. *Ever.* And you're picking me up Tuesday, right?"

He nodded, his jaw working overtime. "But my brothers can wait."

"I know, but they don't have to."

He exhaled and touched his forehead to hers. "This shouldn't be so hard."

"Yes, it should. After my parents' plane went down, I was petrified of flying. My grandfather basically forced me to fly here. You know he could have afforded to hire a driver, or he could have allowed me to drive, but he knew that would only further instill a fear of flying."

"How did I miss that? My brave girl is even more courageous than I thought. Guess that makes me a wimp." His lips curved up confidently despite his words. "You're right. You'll text me when you get to the airport?"

"Yes, and when I land in New York, and when I get to my hotel, and by then your brothers will be so sick of me texting you, you'll want me to stop."

"Never." He kissed her then, slow and tender. "You are great at fixing thirty-year-olds."

"I only need to be good at loving you."

His expression warmed, and he said, "I have to ask you something. Where do you keep your car?"

"What car?"

His brows shot up. "You don't have one? What if there's an emergency?"

She shrugged. "I had one, but it died a few months ago. I just haven't gotten around to picking out a new one."

He uttered a curse. "That's what we're doing Wednesday.

You can't be here without a car."

"Shh. No more worry talk."

"We're getting you a car. A good one. A four-wheel drive."

"Maybe if you kiss me again, I'll think about it." She pursed her lips like a fish, and he kissed her *hard*.

There was a knock at the door, and before they could answer it, Jillian peeked her head in, eyes closed. "Are you dressed? It's time for us to get going so you and the guys can have your penis party."

Charlotte burst out in hysterics.

Beau shook his head. "Since when do I have a sister with a trucker mouth?"

Nick stuck his head in over Jillian's. "She's always had a trucker mouth. You're just never around enough to hear it."

Beau carried Charlotte's bags, and Jillian slipped her arm through hers, heading down the hall in front of Beau and Nick.

"You look very blissed out, and I do *not* want the details. But on the way to the airport we're going to discuss how you come up with so many amazing sex scenes. I swear you should sell your stories to men as how-to guides."

Chapter Eighteen

WAKING UP WITHOUT Charlotte sucked. Showering without her was even worse. Not because Beau needed sex, although that was a nice bonus, but because waking with her in his arms, showering with her, and spending the morning with her had become as much a part of him as the oxygen he breathed. He wanted to call her, but she was having breakfast with her publicist, so he sent her a text. *How's my shortcake? Good luck today, and have fun with your friends tonight. Miss you.* He stared at the screen for a long moment, and then he did something he'd never thought he'd do. He added a heart emoji and then he added a kissing emoji. He sent it off, picturing her rosebud lips curved up as he headed upstairs to find his brothers.

They'd spent the afternoon in town yesterday buying supplies. Then they'd swung by Hal's ranch for a quick visit, since they didn't see him very often. They'd ended up staying for dinner and hanging out with their cousins Treat, Rex, and Josh, and their wives and children. When they'd returned to the inn, they'd unloaded the truck and brought tools up from the workshop. Today they'd work their fingers to the bone, but it'd be worth it.

The event staff had left them with a full refrigerator. Like bread crumbs marking his brothers' way, he found two coffee mugs and plates drying on a towel next to the sink.

"Hey," Graham said as he came in from the terrace wearing his favorite gray MIT baseball cap. "Nick's outside on the phone. He said he wanted to see the grounds."

Beau poured himself a cup of coffee. "I have to go down and collect the eggs. Come with me. We'll grab him on the way."

"Eggs? You have a refrigerator full of food."

"We also have a coop full of chickens."

"We?" Graham said as they headed out to the yard.

Beau didn't know how to respond. He'd taken himself by surprise, too. When they came around the side of the inn, he spotted Nick pacing by the woods. "Everything all right with him?"

"Knowing Nick, he's got one of his ranch hands holding the phone up to one of the horse's ears so he can talk to them."

Beau laughed. "He does love his horses. I really appreciate you guys sticking around to help. I can't hang Charlotte's chandelier by myself, and with the three of us, I think we can get both the study and her bedroom done."

"When's the last time you asked anyone for help? That told us how important this was to you."

Nick ended his call and said, "Sleeping Beauty awoke without a kiss?" He shoved his phone in his pocket and said, "Or did Graham cuddle you awake?"

"Bite me." Beau motioned toward a trailhead. "Come on. We're going to visit the Chickendales."

Graham and Nick exchanged a glance.

"Dude...?" Nick scoffed. "What the hell is a *Chickendale*?"

That was just the first in a long line of questions about *Charlotteisms*. They collected the eggs, and as Beau showed them the rest of the property, he detailed each of the things he'd like to fix, starting with the barn roof and ending with repairing the floors, steps, walls, ceilings, and repointing the fireplaces in Snow White's cabin. The workshop was also on his list. He'd replaced most of the rotted wood, but it needed a new roof.

"You realize you just listed weeks' worth of work, not two days," Nick pointed out on the way back to the inn.

"No shit. I'm not talking about now. I just need your help with the study and her bedroom."

When they reached the inn, Graham said, "I still can't get over that cabin. I would have liked to have met her great-grandfather. What a skilled visionary. No wonder she doesn't want to leave this place."

"It's all she's got left of her family. That's why I want to get these rooms done before I take off for L.A. I'll come back and finish up the rest over time."

"You sure you want to do that?" Graham asked. "Move to L.A.? Work on a reality show? It's a great opportunity if you want a public life, but…"

Beau had been wrestling with accepting the public aspect of the offer from the get-go. Now that he was with Charlotte, the traveling wasn't as appealing as it once was. Before Charlotte had come into his life, he'd worked himself to exhaustion just to be able to sleep at night. She'd calmed those demons. But what if everything was easy and right with Charlotte only because they were far away from the ghosts and memories in his hometown? If he wasn't moving from one project to the next, would all those memories come crashing down on him again? Was it fair to put Charlotte in that position? And even if it was, he'd been dead set on taking the job and had cleared his professional slate for the next two years.

Nick was watching him. His brother had been quiet throughout their walk, eyeing Beau like he had something to say. Beau was uptight enough from missing Charlotte. Knowing he was leaving at the end of the week for God only knew how long didn't help. He was in no rush to butt heads with Nick.

"The wheels are already in motion," Beau said, and changed the subject to give himself something else to focus on. "We've got to get this done before Char gets back." He led them into the study. "I figured we'd start with moving the shelving units and furniture to the suite she uses for storage upstairs. Then we can paint the room. The new furniture is being delivered this afternoon, and once that's in, we can move down to the bedroom."

"You ordered her *furniture*?" Nick slid a worried look to Graham.

Beau crossed his arms and set a steely gaze on Nick. "Yes. I ordered her furniture. You have a problem with that?"

"Nope," Nick said tightly. "Let's do this."

He and Nick began packing the contents of the shelves into boxes while Graham emptied the desk drawers.

"How many Bradens does it take to renovate a study and a bedroom?" Nick said with his first smile of the day.

Beau was glad for his levity. "I appreciate the help, man. Three sets of hands will make this process go much quicker."

"Hey, Beau? How long has she lived here? There are old check registers from several years ago, and all sorts of shit in here." Graham handed Beau a birthday card. "Look inside."

"When I said she never leaves her office, I meant it. I doubt she's ever gone through these drawers." He opened and read the childlike handwriting. *Dear Grandpa, happy birthday. I love you, Charlotte.* "Why don't you let me go through the drawers? You can help Nick."

"You think it's okay?" Graham asked. "Packing up her stuff like this? What if it was just an offhand comment about using the study as an office?"

"Every comment she makes is offhand. It's one of the things that makes her Charlotte." *And one of the things I love about her.* "We're not going through her stuff, just packing it up temporarily. We're going to put it all back. Besides, asking would have ruined the surprise."

As he emptied the drawers, he found Charlotte's grade school pictures. She was adorable, with a gap-toothed smile and pigtails. He found anniversary cards from her grandmother to her grandfather and a few more birthday cards. He didn't read the cards from her grandparents, but he peeked at the ones from Charlotte, filling his heart up with pieces of her past.

The bottom drawer of the desk was locked. "You guys haven't found a desk key, have you?"

"Nope," Nick said. "But I found a bunch of old Twix bars in a jar on the bottom shelf. Guess her grandfather was a chocolate lover."

"Did you check underneath?" Graham asked.

Beau ran his hand under the desk, shocked when his fingers ran over a key taped to the bottom of the drawer. "I'll be damned." He held the fancy old-fashioned key up to show them.

"When in doubt, go with whatever's simplest." Graham went back to packing.

Beau couldn't remember a time when anything had been simple.

He unlocked the drawer and found a thick, leather-bound book with *Once Upon a Time* embossed in gold script across the front. He imagined Charlotte as a young girl sitting on her grandfather's lap, listening to him read her fairy tales. He withdrew it from the drawer, and a handful of loose pages slipped out. As he collected them, he realized what he'd found. Within the tattered pages of the book were Charlotte's drawings of fairy-tale-themed rooms. He sat in the leather chair carefully looking through them, marveling at the thick, uneven crayon images she'd described, the detailed faded pencil marks of a teenager, and the careful, intricate drawings of a young woman breathing life into her dream and feeding her grandfather's happiness. She'd drawn frilly canopies, garden murals, castle beds, and dozens of other pictures. Each page was labeled: Thumbelina Room, Henny Penny Room, Cinderella Room, and many more, including some he'd never heard of, like the Town Musicians of Bremen Room and the Elf Mound Room.

"I'm ready to haul this stuff upstairs." Nick peered over Beau's shoulder. "What's that?"

"This?" *Is everything that matters.* He carefully tucked the pages back into the book and said, "This is the very heart of my girl."

CHARLOTTE MARCHED OUT of her editor's office and straight to the seventh floor of LWW Enterprises. It was six thirty, and the offices were still buzzing with employees. *See? It's normal to work long hours*, she fumed as she stormed off the elevator toward Aubrey's department. Her editor thought her writing had changed. *It's not erotic or edgy enough, and it might disappoint your fans.* She'd blamed it on Charlotte working too hard. *Ha!* If she only knew how much fun she'd been having lately!

Becca shot to her feet as Charlotte approached, her blond, side-swept barrel curls bouncing around her shoulders. Her skirt was tight, her leopard-print blouse was low-cut, and her cherry-red lips curled up into a smile as warm and welcoming as any Charlotte had ever seen. She *loved* Becca, and every time she saw her, she mentally added to the story line she wanted to write featuring Becca as the heroine.

"Charlotte, so good to see you."

Charlotte embraced her. "You, too. How are things?"

"First of all, your fans are chomping at the bit for Roman! Have you looked at your Instagram page lately? They're making bets about who is a better lover, Roman or Daryl." She waggled her brows and said, "I'd love to be in the middle of that *manwich.* How's it going with Roman? Is he everything you hoped and more?"

When she thought of Roman, she immediately envisioned Beau. "Yes, but unfortunately, Chelsea thinks otherwise."

Becca winced. "Sorry. She's a tough cookie, but she knows her stuff, so…"

"I know I have to give her criticism the weight it deserves, but that doesn't mean it doesn't sting."

"Aubrey and Presley are waiting for you in Aubrey's office." She leaned closer and whispered, "But you had a rough time down in the lion's den. Wait here one second. I have something to ease the pain." She sashayed across the room, rockin' the 1940s pinup style better than Gwen Stefani. She returned with a wine cooler and a Twix bar.

"You are a goddess!"

"I know, right?" Becca shrugged one shoulder and handed her the goodies. "Do you need me to take care of anything for you before I head out? Do you need a car for later, or...?"

Charlotte held up her wine cooler. "You've already made my day. I'm fine, thanks. I'm going to drag the bigwigs out for a drink. Want to join us?"

"Can't, but thanks. I have to meet my trainer in twenty minutes. I *love* kicking his ass." She grabbed her purse and said, "Buy Aubrey extra drinks tonight, please. She's been hell on wheels since finding out that boy toy of yours is going to be the new face of *Shack to Chic*."

"What? She *knows*?" She hadn't had a chance to tell Aubrey yet.

"Honey, *nothing* is a secret in the entertainment world. *Ciao*."

Charlotte peeked into Aubrey's office. Aubrey and Presley were sitting with their backs to the door, whispering, with their foreheads nearly touching. Aubrey's hair looked even blonder next to Presley's dark burgundy tresses. Charlotte realized that Presley and Jillian both had the same hair color, which fit, since they were equally bold.

"It's not nice to tell secrets," she said as she entered the room.

They both squealed and jumped up for a group hug.

"Careful not to spill my drink!" Charlotte laughed. "God, I've missed you guys *so* much. Where's Libby?"

"She couldn't make it, but don't worry. I gave her hell about needing some fun in her life. She's so serious sometimes. I worry about her," Aubrey said. "The same way I worry about you all alone on that mountain."

"She just needs to meet someone who inspires her to break out of her shell. Beau's serious like that, but he's less serious when he's with me, and believe it or not, I actually leave the house every day for more than just collecting eggs."

Her friends crossed their arms and feigned seriousness with narrowed eyes and pinched expressions.

"Uh-oh." She looked down at her green pencil skirt and off-white blouse. The skirt was a little tight, but not slutty.

"It's not your clothes," Presley said. "You look like a million bucks, and that blouse makes your boobs look amazing." That was a huge compliment coming from her fashionista friend.

"Thank you. Then what did I do? Wait. Don't tell me yet." Charlotte guzzled her wine cooler and tossed the empty bottle in the trash can. "Okay, give it to me."

"You didn't tell us that your *big distraction* was the new face of *Shack to Chic*," Aubrey said.

"He hasn't officially taken the job yet, but how did you know? I haven't told anyone. I've been too busy to think."

"We're putting together a competing reality show, and the *Shack to Chic* producers have kept their intended hire a secret," Aubrey explained as she grabbed her purse and handed Presley her bag. "But my source at the station found out the guy's name this afternoon. The one and only Beau Braden, contractor extraordinaire from rinky-dink Pleasant Hill, Maryland."

"Becca tracked down the goods on him." Presley grabbed Charlotte's arm, and they headed for the elevator. "He's got quite the résumé. He makes *huge* profits, and from what Becca said, the guy never stops working. She followed his trail. So, if by *busy* you meant you were *on your back* with Beau *hot and hard* on top of you, then you're forgiven."

"Or on your knees," Aubrey said. "Hard to talk with your mouth full."

"Have I told you lately how much I love your trash mouths?" Charlotte sighed and put her arms around them. "I miss my contractor extraordinaire. I had a shit meeting with Chelsea, and Becca said Aubrey's been stressed, so let's go drown our sorrows."

"I'm always a bitch," Aubrey said.

"Yes, but a likable one," Charlotte added.

"What about me?" Presley complained. "I need a reason to drink, and my life's been pretty good lately."

"You're our support system," Charlotte said as they rode the elevator down to the lobby. "Besides, when I tell you how my meeting with Chelsea went, you might need that drink." As they headed out to the street, she asked, "Can we go to Quarters, *please*? I'm in need of cheese fries."

As they walked the five blocks to Quarters, a classy pub that served amazing food at the corner of High Street and Mighty Avenue, they reminisced about their college years. Port Hudson was a small college town located fifty miles north of Manhattan on the Hudson River, with rolling hills, babbling brooks, coffee shops, and a wealth of wonderful memories. The house they'd rented in college was just a few blocks away from Quarters and was now owned by LWW Enterprises.

"Carter Banks bought this bar," Aubrey said as they walked in. "Do you remember him? He was a year ahead of us, super competitive, insanely hot?"

"How can I forget? He was your first kiss," Charlotte said.

Presley raced off to find a table, and they followed. They settled in and ordered drinks and dinner. After the waiter brought their drinks, Charlotte toed off her heels.

"What are you doing?" Presley asked as she peered under the table.

"Taking off my heels. I have no idea how you can wear those things every day."

"Charlotte," Presley said in a hushed, firm voice. "You don't know what's on the floor in this place. You can't just take off your shoes."

Aubrey stifled a giggle.

Charlotte picked up her drink and said, "I just did, Mama Bear."

"Don't give her a hard time, Pres, or she'll never leave the inn again." Aubrey winked and said, "Now tell me all about Beau and why he hasn't taken the contract yet."

"How about I cover the reality show job first, because there's going to be a lot of swooning to do when I tell you about him." Charlotte explained that he was leaving Thursday afternoon for L.A. and would be signing the contract Friday morning.

"You know that position will keep him on the road for the length of his contract, right?" Aubrey asked.

"I know. But if he wants to do it, who am I to stand in his way? He loves to travel, and you already know how good he is at his job. You should see how much he's done at the inn. There were a million little things and he not only fixed them all, but he found problems I didn't know about and fixed those, too."

"I like a man who's good with his hands." Presley took off her designer blazer and hung it on the back of her chair.

"Trust me, he's good with *everything*." Charlotte waggled her brows. "And he's careful and smart and loving. He worries about me in ways no one has for a very long time. You know how I sometimes leave my doors open?"

"Sometimes?" Audrey scoffed. "When do you ever lock them?"

Charlotte gave her a deadpan look. "He put up the prettiest security screen doors on my bedroom and painted the decorative swirly things pink. He's the most thoughtful man I've ever met. He doesn't mind that I don't cook, and he doesn't get jealous of my writing time, which is crazy considering how many hours I worked to get the chapters to Chelsea, which we also have to discuss."

"Beau first, work second," Aubrey said.

The waiter brought their meals, and Charlotte waited for him to leave before saying, "He's just..." She tried to think of the right words, but none seemed big enough for how he fulfilled her. "We click on every level. He even helps me brainstorm ideas and work through scenes."

"Thank God. I was starting to worry that your blow-up dolls were going to become a fetish," Presley teased.

"Ha ha." Charlotte ate a few fries. "Talking about him makes me miss him even more than I already do." She and Beau had texted earlier, and she'd called him between meetings. He sounded stressed, and she wondered if his brothers were pushing him about going home, but she didn't ask. She didn't want to bring it up if they weren't. He could have just been missing her, like she was missing him.

"You're *really* falling for him," Aubrey said incredulously. "I've never seen you like this."

"I am," she said a little giddily. "He makes me happy. Truly, deeply, *insanely* happy. And it's not just what he does. It's the things he says, the way he looks at me. And this sounds dumb, but it's what he doesn't say, too. He doesn't bullshit, you know? I can feel the truth like his words are bathed in it. He's romantic in a broody kind of way, and he's got this big, loving, funny family, and they welcomed me with open arms." She ate another fry, smiling. "Did I tell you he fixed up the barn and *brought in* horses for us to ride one weekend? It was like something right out of a—"

"Fairy tale," they said in unison.

Aubrey and Presley exchanged a concerned glance.

"He sounds incredible, Char. You deserve a guy like that."

"Agreed, but what are you not telling us?" Aubrey asked. "Nobody is perfect. Give us the dirt on the guy or I'll have Becca dig deeper."

"There's just a little dirt," she said uneasily. "If I had the right broom I could clean it up, but I don't, so I probably need your help." She hadn't stopped thinking about Beau's guilt over Tory, and she still wasn't sure how to handle it. But she knew if they really wanted to make this work, it *could* be a problem. She looked at her friends and hoped they might have some solid advice.

"He had a long-term girlfriend who he really loved, and she was killed in a car accident about ten years ago. He seems to be over the rough stuff, but he wears his guilt on his sleeve, and I know it's eating him alive."

"Why?" Presley asked. "Why does he feel guilty? Was it his fault?"

Charlotte shook her head and relayed what Beau had told her about missing Tory's texts. She told them how he'd changed since then and said, "He grew up in a small town, and he thinks everyone blames him. The anniversary of her death is this Saturday and, from what he says, like every year, he's made sure he's not going to be there. He's leaving for L.A. Thursday."

"How convenient," Presley said.

"Pres, please don't. I know you're right. It's convenient and he doesn't deny that. He's been nothing but honest with me about this, so please don't be sarcastic. I'm pretty sure that's why he's taking the job in L.A., so he won't have to think about when to travel or where. It'll all be planned for him. But the whole reality-show thing makes no sense. He's such a private person, and hosting something like that is the equivalent of standing on a street corner naked."

"Oh, Char." Aubrey sat back with an empathetic expression. "This breaks my heart for both of you."

"I know. That's why I need some advice." She swallowed hard and said, "I know life is not a fairy tale, so don't worry. I'm not romanticizing what's going to happen. If anyone knows how hard it can be, it's me. But I *love* him, you guys. Everything is so good and feels right, but I think his guilt is like a mountain between him and true happiness. It's like he wants to be happy, and he is *right there* with me when we're together, but I can't ignore the truth. His guilt interferes with other parts of his life. He went to her funeral, but from what he says, he hasn't talked about it since, until he told me, of course. I keep wondering what that must feel like. They grew up together in a small town, saw each other's families every day, and after the funeral, he never had another conversation with them. He didn't just lose *her*. He lost a whole part of his world. That's why he travels all the time and works his fingers to the bone."

"To outrun his demons," Aubrey said. "How weird that you wanted to surround yourself with memories and he can't even be near them."

"I know." She felt the burn of tears and took a drink, willing them away. "What am I going to do? I know what he's going through. I want to help him to the other side, and I can't figure out how."

Presley touched Charlotte's arm and said, "You can't play second fiddle to a ghost. That's not fair to you."

"I know, and I'm not," she assured them. "I never feel like Tory's there with us, or between us. This isn't about her. It's about the guilt he carries from the night it happened. I honestly believe him when he says he's moved past missing her. Well, as much as anyone can be expected to. If you saw the way he looked at me, felt the way he touched me, you would believe it, too."

"That'd also make us pervs, but we won't go there," Aubrey said.

Charlotte laughed softly. "Thank you. I needed that. Now please help me figure out how to help him."

"He needs to deal with the guilt. That's the only way." Aubrey pushed her salad around on her plate, then set her fork down. "When you wrote your grandparents' story, it was cathartic. It helped."

"Tremendously," Charlotte said.

"He needs that kind of closure. He should talk to her family," Presley suggested. "Otherwise, what are you going to do? How will you see his 'big, loving, funny family' that welcomed you with open arms'? Schedule your visits around this time of year? That'll get old quick."

Charlotte's gaze swept over the busy bar. They were telling her everything she already knew. "Thanks, you guys. I'll figure something out."

"Have you two talked about the future?" Aubrey asked carefully.

Charlotte nodded. "We both want to make it work. We'll see each other as his schedule allows. And I can write anywhere, so I'm sure at some point I'll visit him when he's filming." She knew she had to try to talk to Beau about this again.

They finished their drinks and ordered another round, which Charlotte skipped since Beau wasn't there to love her through a hangover.

"Do you want to talk about your meeting with Chelsea?" Presley asked.

"No, but yes," Charlotte said. "You're her boss's boss. I'm sure you already know what she told me, right? That I'm probably working too hard, *blah, blah, blah.*"

"More importantly, I'm *your* friend," Presley said. "She told me, and I read the chapters you gave her. I know you don't want to hear it, but I think Chelsea is right. The love story is awesome, and the sex? Hot as fuck. Especially that scene in her office? Damn, if men like that existed in real life, we'd all be happy women."

Charlotte bit her tongue. She didn't need them to know Beau had played out that scene touch by scorching-hot touch.

The waiter brought their drinks, and Aubrey held up her glass. "To well-hung men and happy women." She lowered her voice and said, "I read it, too. I might have taken it to bed with me."

Charlotte happily clinked glasses with her. "TMI, babe."

"Me and Mr. Buzz." Aubrey snort-laughed.

"Ew." Charlotte wrinkled her nose. "How can I delete that visual?"

"You write that stuff," Aubrey reminded her.

"But not about my friends. Anyway, Chelsea told me the story wasn't *raw* enough. She thinks I've lost my edge because I'm working too hard. But I *love* the story so much. It feels right for the characters, and every character is different. They're not all going to want to be handcuffed, or have anal sex, or be taken against a brick wall."

Aubrey raised her hand. "I'll take it. All of it. Who can I work the scenes with?"

Presley glared at her. Then she shifted her attention to Charlotte and lowered her chin, looking very serious, every bit the powerful executive. "For the record, I don't agree with Chelsea's reasons about why your story isn't raw enough. I don't think you've lost your edge. But I have seen this happen many times. A writer gets married and she writes about marital bliss. She gets divorced and suddenly all men are scum. She has a midlife crisis, and her characters are cougars. It's natural, Char. Before this afternoon, I didn't know that you and Beau were together. I only knew that you had a hot contractor at your house with a big cock and a chip on his shoulder."

"Thanks, Aub," Charlotte said.

Aubrey winked. "I aim to please."

Presley leaned toward Charlotte, the way she did when she wanted someone to really listen to her, and said, "The reason your writing isn't as raw as your other books is because you wrote the others when you had stuff still bottled up inside you—sexual urges, fantasies, anger over being alone even though you chose to be. And based on the look in your eyes, you hate hearing it. But I think that was part of it. You were pouring your heart and soul into each and every word. You still are. That's the good news. But this is the book you're writing while you're falling in love. You don't feel *raw*. You feel warm and mushy inside, and that translates onto the page."

"Great!" Charlotte threw her hands up. "So now my relationship with Beau is ruining my writing?"

"No, Char. Your writing is impeccable," Presley assured her.

"But it has a contemporary romance feel rather than erotic romance."

"But I *like* it this way. They're *my* characters, *my* voices. I can't just tell them to be another way. It'll feel forced."

"She's right," Aubrey said. "But if you make it into a trilogy—show a wedding, babies, tone down the awesome sex, it'd be perfect to turn into a script for our new Me Time channel." She sat up straighter. "Hey…"

"No," Presley said. "She has a publishing contract for erotic romance."

"Wait, what?" Charlotte's gaze moved between them, trying to follow their cryptic conversation.

"So what? Rewrite the contract," Aubrey suggested.

"Aubrey," Presley warned. "It's not that easy."

"What are you saying?" Charlotte asked.

"Bullshit it's not that easy," Aubrey said sharply. "We own the company. You run the publishing division. You control this, Presley. The book isn't even up for preorder yet."

Charlotte wasn't sure she was following, but she was getting excited at what she *thought* they were saying.

Presley glared at Aubrey. "The contract is legally binding. Can you imagine if other writers got wind of this and thought they could write whatever floats their boats despite their contracts?"

"I hope you know I didn't do that, Pres," Charlotte insisted.

"I know you didn't," Presley said with a kinder tone. "That's not what I meant. The contract is legally binding. I need to tread carefully if we go in this direction. I'm not saying it's a bad direction. Aubrey is right, and she heads up the media department, so if she didn't think it would work, she'd never have said it. It's just that this is a bigger issue than friends making concession for each other."

"You're right," Aubrey agreed. "We need more information. Charlotte, can you write two more in this series? Not erotic but contemporary?"

"Yes! I know I can. I've already dreamed about it. My characters, Roman and Shayna, have a beautiful outdoor wedding. They have two babies, twins, I think, and a dog…" She hadn't realized how much she'd thought about their future. And now she wasn't sure if she was thinking about Roman and Shayna, or her and Beau.

Aubrey smirked at Presley, then said to Charlotte, "And do you think with your new stud muffin in your life, or if it doesn't work out, *without* him in your life, you will be able to write edgy, erotic romance? The type your fans expect from you?"

"With him *in* my life, with different characters, yes. I think so. I know what you were saying about it being harder if I'm in a happy relationship, and I know that's true on some level. But I really enjoy writing erotic romance, and I love the grittiness of it." And after yesterday morning's incredible sex, she knew she and Beau would be pushing even more boundaries in the future. "I've already thought up a new BDSM story that is super edgy and just dark enough, and I have been taking notes about it. Roman and Shayna's story has me hung up because it feels personal, like my grandparents' story did."

"Oh Lord." Aubrey finished her drink. "Now I'm picturing you and Beau having sex at your desk."

Charlotte felt her cheeks flame, remembering that steamy afternoon. She pointed her finger at Aubrey and said, "Do *not* go there."

"It totally happened! You're Shayna! You're beet red." Aubrey leaned in, holding Charlotte's gaze. "That sex was scorching hot."

"Okay, sex kitten and penis pusher," Presley said with a stern voice. "Let's get back on topic, shall we? Char, what if you and Beau break up? Do you think you'll still be able to write erotic romance?"

Charlotte's heart sank at what she knew might be a real possibility. What if Beau couldn't fully move past his guilt? Could they be happy avoiding his hometown at certain times? Avoiding the people who had known them as a couple? His family definitely didn't want him to live such a separate life from them. Would that cause stress for *their* relationship? She wanted to stand by him no matter what, but what if they only worked away from his hometown? The other thing she was trying not to think about rose to the surface. She wanted to support his new career, but what if he moved to L.A. and things changed between them?

Her stomach knotted up. She looked at her friends, wishing she could avoid telling them the truth, but she'd never been able to lie to them. "If we broke up, eventually, *maybe* I could write erotic romance again, but not right away. It'd be like losing my family all over again, only different. I'd probably write something dark and depressing while I mourn."

Presley shook her head. "I love you, but writers make me crazy. I can't get you out of your contract. There's too much red tape, and it would be setting a precedent."

"I'm not asking you to do that. I can go home and write a new erotic story if that's an option. I'll finish this one no matter what, even if we don't publish it. But I can go home and write my dom/sub story if you give me a little extra time."

"*Charlotte's* not asking you to do anything, Pres," Aubrey said. "But I am. Now that I thought about the Me Time channel, I can't *stop* thinking about it. Me Time is like Lifetime, only steamier. That story is perfect. It's sweet, loving, and passionate. Fans love her voice, regardless of how much hair pulling there is."

"I know they do." Presley sighed, the stress of the conversation evident in her serious expression. "Charlotte, you're an incredible writer, and your voice is what makes you special. I don't want to pressure you to write anything you don't want to. But you need to fulfill this contract with an *erotic* romance one way or another. Why don't you let me and Aubrey think this through and see what we can work out? You can take a few days to think about things and talk to Beau. I have to watch our asses legally, but honestly, babe, you come first. I can see how in love with him you are. And as you said, if things go bad and he can't be all in with you, then this might be the beginning of a change in your writing for a while. So, let's all take a breather, enjoy our evening together, and regroup on this topic in a week."

Aubrey leaned in, mimicking Presley's serious expression, and said, "You're our sister, and we'll always have your back. If you need help dragging Beau's ass to his hometown, I'm your gal."

Chapter Nineteen

BEAU STOOD ON the ladder late Monday night, touching up paint on the shelf he'd put up along one wall to hold some of the special things he'd found in a box in Charlotte's closet. He and his brothers had taken a break earlier to grill steaks and shoot the shit, and as he'd known they would, they'd busted their asses without complaint all day. The study was done, the furniture was in, and by the time he was supposed to pick up Charlotte from the airport tomorrow, her room would be done, too.

"Want me to toss a few Twix wrappers on her comforter so she feels at home?" Nick teased.

"Don't forget the water bottles," Graham said as he sank into one of Charlotte's pink chairs. "How'd Mr. Neat and Organized end up with a woman who has other priorities?"

"A better question is, how'd you end up with a woman at all? You're surlier than I am," Nick said as Beau climbed down the ladder.

"Not around Charlotte," Graham pointed out.

As much as Beau wanted to own the truth of Graham's statement, he didn't respond. He'd been wrong about Nick wanting to harass him, but he still didn't want to spark a conversation that would stir things up. Nick had made a few comments about Beau moving, implying that he was avoiding the obvious, but he hadn't pushed the subject. Then again, Nick had a way of saying just enough to get under Beau's skin, making the uncertainty of his impending move rub like sandpaper.

Beau set the paintbrush on the paint can and said, "Are you guys up for one more job?"

His brothers exchanged an incredulous glance.

"You don't even have to move," he assured them. "I installed a driveway alarm, and I haven't had a chance to turn it on and test it."

"Dude, what are you doing?" Nick asked just as Beau's phone rang.

Beau grabbed his phone, smiling at Charlotte's name on the screen. "Making sure she's safe. Give me a sec." He answered Char's call and stepped out the French doors to the yard. "Hey, babe. How's it going?"

"Well, it's after eleven o'clock at night and you're too many miles away. How's it going for you?"

She sounded tired and sweet. He wanted to climb through the phone and gather her in his arms. "The same. I miss you." He glanced inside, catching his brothers watching him, and paced under their scrutiny. "How'd it go with your editor?"

"She was blatantly honest, as always. My story isn't erotic enough. It's too loving. The sex is good, but erotic romance needs to be grittier. Basically, she wants me to rewrite it with less love and more sex."

Beau grinned. "Guess we'll have to work on that, huh? If anyone can nail a scene, it's you, babe."

A tired sigh came through the phone. "I think *we're* the

problem. Remember how I told you that I had writer's block before you showed up? And then it was like you'd punctured a vein, and I could write again? Well, don't get upset with me, but I think Roman and Shayna ended up being more our story than the one I was supposed to write."

Beau gazed out into the darkness, unsure if that was good or bad, given that her story wasn't what her editor wanted. But he couldn't deny the pleasure he felt in knowing their relationship had affected her as deeply as it affected him. "Char, I don't want to screw up your writing. Tell me how I can help, and I will."

"Hm. Let me think." The tease in her voice made him smile. "Lots and lots of amazing hot sex."

His body heated up as he pictured her lying naked on the bed, her beautiful hair spread over the pillow, her eyes lulling him into a Charlotte-induced trance. *Fuck.* Now he was getting hard. He adjusted himself and said, "You're on, babe, and if my brothers weren't watching me like a hawk, I'd flip on the video chat and take you to heaven and back right now."

"Beau," she whispered with a giggle. "I've never done that."

"I look forward to popping your video-chat cherry, and before you ask, yes, you'll be popping mine, too." He heard Nick say something and said, "But not tonight. Not with these guys around."

"I can hardly wait! Want to hear my good news?"

"Absolutely. Anything to get the image of you naked out of my head."

"You're thinking about…?"

"Don't. I'm already sporting wood just thinking about talking dirty to you. Tell me your good news, and for God's sake, do *not* use any dirty words."

She giggled. "Aubrey heads up the media division of LWW,

and she's thinking about using the story I'm writing for their new Me Time channel, which is a hotter Lifetime-type channel."

"Seriously? That's awesome."

"Who knows if it will come through. And part of me feels like it's too private to share like that."

"But you gave it to your editor, and if she had loved it, it would get published anyway, right? Besides, what choice do you have? Aren't you under contract for this manuscript?"

"Yes, but I think they might let me swap another book for this one. And you should know, I gave it to my editor before I realized there was so much of us in the story."

"Aw, babe. If you want to tuck it away in a drawer, publish it, or make it into a movie, I'll support your decision. Do what makes you happiest. Just know that no matter how much of *us* is in that manuscript, it doesn't show *all* of us. My love for you grows every day, so if you decide to do this Me Time thing, by the time the story gets out there we'll be on a whole new level. Think of the inspiration you're giving to all your fans who are hoping to find love."

"I never thought of it that way."

"Can't say I have either," he said, and glanced into her bedroom, where Nick and Graham were busy cleaning up.

"Did you have fun with your brothers?"

He didn't want to tell her about her surprises, so he said, "Yeah, we had a good time. How about you and your friends?"

"It was great seeing them. I wish you were here to meet them."

"One day we'll take a trip out there together. I want to see where you grew up, and I'd love to meet the friends who have been there for you."

"I'd love that. I talked to Aubrey about the reality show. She said your life is going to be very public, even if you don't want it to be. She gave me a list of things she said you should look for in your contract that protect you. I'm sure you have a lawyer, but I was glad she offered some suggestions."

"My cousin Savannah has been handling the contract, but I'd still like to look over Aubrey's list. Please tell her thanks for me." Savannah was Hal's daughter, and a high-powered entertainment attorney.

"I will. I'm having breakfast with them at seven tomorrow morning."

"Enjoy your time with them. Sweet dreams tonight, baby. And, Char?"

"Yeah?"

"I think your parents and grandparents would be very proud of everything you're doing."

She was quiet for so long, he thought he'd said something wrong. "Babe? Are you okay?"

"Yes," she said shakily. "Thank you for that. In the back of my mind I always hope they'd be proud of me. How could you know that I needed to hear it?"

He couldn't tell her that he'd spent so much time among her and her family's things today that he just knew they'd want her to hear it, so instead he said, "Because they're never far from your mind. Just like you're never far from mine."

They talked for a minute longer, and after saying good night, he headed back toward Charlotte's room. Nick was leaning against the doorframe blocking his way. Beau's muscles constricted.

"Let me just finish cleaning up, and then I'll head out to test the driveway alarm."

"What are you doing, bro?" Nick asked.

Beau pushed past him. "Did I mumble?" After talking to Charlotte, the last thing he wanted was to have a pissing match with Nick. He glanced at Graham, who held his hands up, like he didn't want to be involved. Beau knelt to close the paint can and gathered the tarps.

"Talk to me, Beau." Nick grabbed his arm, stopping him from doing any more work.

Beau rose to his full height, meeting his brother's steely gaze. "What do you want to know? Just tell me, because I don't want to play games."

"I know. There was a time when you could banter like a pro, but that was a long time ago."

Beau ground his back teeth and set down the painting supplies. "I knew you not giving me shit was too good to be true."

"Here we go," Graham said exasperatedly. He moved beside them, close enough to intervene while Beau and Nick faced off.

"What are you doing with Charlotte?" Nick asked. "Do you even know? Does she?"

"What are you talking about?" Beau waved around the room. "What do you think I'm doing with her?"

"What matters is what *you* think you're doing," Nick challenged.

"Then we have no problem, because I know what I feel. I *love* her, man. I fucking love everything about her. I love that she eats candy for breakfast and gets so drawn into her work that she doesn't notice anything else. I love that she doesn't let go of the memories of the people she loved most and that she lets herself dream of a fairy-tale life and really fucking believes it can come true. And you know what else? This is what you really want to hear, so listen carefully." Beau stepped closer, unable to keep from raising his voice. "I love that she loves me. All of me, including the fucked-up broken pieces. I love that we are so good together I can't imagine a single day without her. You got a problem with that?"

"No, bro. That's what I *want* for you," Nick said sternly. "I came here expecting to see the same surly brother I've seen for years. Instead I found a guy who's all googly-eyed over a chick. It's fucking awesome."

Beau's breath rushed from his lungs. "Then what the fuck, Nick? You just like making me crazy?"

"Yes," Graham said.

Nick smirked. "No. But I worry that you like making yourself crazy. You think you don't deserve to really be happy. I saw you last night. You were so fucking happy, and then you looked around, and I saw guilt consuming you."

Beau had done that more than once. But he didn't think anyone had noticed.

"Then you looked at Charlotte, and guilt swallowed you whole. Damn it, Beau, I wanted to dig you out of that fucking guilt hellhole you've buried yourself in."

"Don't you think I want to dig myself out?" Beau snapped. "Do you think I like feeling that no matter where I go or what I do, Tory's death will always haunt me?"

Graham put a hand on Beau's shoulder, slowing him down enough to take a breath.

"We worry about you, Beau," Graham said calmly. "We know that's why you're taking that job in L.A., to run away from it all."

"You have to deal with this shit, Beau. Moving isn't going to settle your ghosts." Nick's voice escalated. "What if Mom or Dad get sick and it happens to be this time of year? What if

Charlotte wants a real life? One that's not controlled by when you can visit?"

"She *understands* my shit," he said angrily.

Nick's shoulders dropped and he shook his head. "Of course she does," he said more empathetically. "She loves you. Any fool can see that. Beau, we lost a big part of you when Tory died, but at least you're around sometimes. We don't want to lose more of you. If you want that job, take it and we'll support it, but first just ask yourself this. *Why* do you want it? You hate attention and you already make seven figures. We both know it's not the money." He held Beau's stare. "When are you going to stop running? You're not a dumb kid who made a mistake. You've got to let that guilt go, deal with it once and for all."

"Why?" Beau seethed, hands fisted, jaw clenched, and his heart ripping to shreds. "So Tory's family and everyone else in the fucking town can think I've forgotten her? So they can talk about how unfair it is that I get to be happy when she's dead?" Tears burned his eyes, and he turned away.

Nick circled him with a determined and sad look in his eyes. "You still don't get it, do you? Nobody blames you. You'd know that if you ever talked to people about this. But you didn't give anyone the chance, Beau. You were too hurt and too damn stubborn, and you've been stuck in self-imposed hell ever since."

Beau stalked away, all of the emotions of the past few weeks coming to a head.

Nick grabbed his arm and stepped in front of him so he had no choice but to look him in the eyes. "You have a second chance at happiness in your hands. Don't screw this up by making Charlotte live within your fucked-up boundaries."

"You want me to walk away?" Beau was as angry as he was

confused.

"No," Graham said, stepping between them. "He—*we all*—want you to come back home and face your issues. Live your life where you were meant to live it once and for all. Let us stand by you, Beau. You're not alone in this. You've been alone for too long."

Chapter Twenty

"REMEMBER THAT TIME we went into the city before Christmas break and Pres puked in that tattoo parlor?" Aubrey asked Tuesday morning at the Pit Stop Café, one of their old favorite haunts.

Charlotte was too excited to see Beau to eat anything, but Aubrey and Presley had no problem gobbling down the muffin she'd bought. "And you got your belly button pierced while she was puking her guts up!" Her phone vibrated with a text from Beau. "I still have the pictures of us with Tom Selleck," she said absently as she opened the message. A picture of Beau holding her rooster popped up with the caption. *How's my girl? Your big cock misses you. Xox.*

"Oh my God, we were so drunk!" Presley said. "Remember how Aubrey kept yelling, 'Just one picture for my mom! She has the biggest crush on you!'"

"We got the pictures, didn't we?" Aubrey leaned closer to Charlotte, looking at the text from Beau as she took a drink. She choked on her coffee, then burst into giggles. "I *need* to meet this guy!"

"Why?" Presley leaned across the table, and Charlotte showed her the text. "Oh my gosh. I *so* love him!"

"Send him a picture of your cleavage," Aubrey said. "Tell him he can play with your eggs anytime."

Presley rolled her eyes. "Gross. Eggs are balls, not boobs."

"I've got this." Charlotte navigated to a picture of a kitten and then typed, *Not as much as your...misses you!* She showed it to the girls.

"What the hell is that?" Aubrey grabbed her phone and replaced the ellipses with the word *pussy*.

"No!" Charlotte deleted it. "I don't talk that way."

Aubrey looked confused. "You write it in your books. It's totally the same as what he sent you."

"It's gross when you're saying it to someone you love, unless you're in the heat of the moment talking dirty. I think this is cuter." Charlotte pressed send.

"It's also *you* and not Aubrey." Presley blew Aubrey a kiss.

"Whatever," Aubrey said. "My way is more direct."

Her phone vibrated again, and they all huddled together as she opened the text. A gif of a cartoon wolf popped up. It had big dark eyes and was panting, its tongue hanging out of its mouth. They all laughed. Charlotte sighed longingly. She couldn't wait to be in his arms again.

"Did you just sigh *dreamily*?" Presley arched a brow.

"Maybe," Charlotte said, scrolling through gifs to find something cute to send him.

"You're so different. I noticed last night," Aubrey said thoughtfully. "But we were talking about such heavy stuff half the time it wasn't as clear. You're not just happier, and I don't want to sound cheesy—"

"Go for the cheese, please," Charlotte encouraged. "If you *see* what I feel, then it is cheesy, dreamy, swoony, *and* hot and bothered at the thought of him." She clicked on a gif of a woman wearing a low-cut blouse and fanning her face and showed it to the girls.

"Now, *that's* cheesy," Presley said. "I'm so happy for you. You know we worry about you, and that's the only reason we pushed so hard for you to try to get him to find closure, right?"

"I know," Charlotte said as she deleted the gif of the woman.

"We want you to follow your heart," Aubrey added. "You think you've found Mr. Right, and we want him to be that for you *so* badly."

"I get it, and you guys didn't say anything I wasn't already thinking. It's not like I'm going to give him an ultimatum. I *love* him, and I *want* to be with him, even if it means working through this together over a period of time. It's not like there's a deadline or we're running off and getting married tomorrow."

"But you want to," Aubrey said in a singsong voice.

With every iota of my being. "Shut up. I need you to take a video of me." Charlotte handed her the phone.

"A video?" Presley waggled her brows. "Maybe we should go someplace private?"

"Not *that* kind of video. He sent me that wolf picture. I was going to send a gif, but this is better." She pushed up the arms of the cute green button-down she wore over her white scoop-neck T-shirt and angled herself toward Aubrey. She leaned back and adjusted the neckline of her T-shirt, exposing the swell of her breasts. Then she shifted her necklaces so the longest rested in her cleavage, and said, "Okay. Ready."

"Nice," Aubrey said as she aimed the phone toward Charlotte. "Tell me when."

"Okay, go." Charlotte fluttered her lashes seductively and slowly, purposefully fanned herself. "Whew! Just the thought of you lights me up like a volcano." She flipped her hair over her shoulder and leaned forward "I can't wait to get caught up in the lava with my big, strong man." She blew a kiss, and Aubrey clicked off the video.

They all squealed.

"That was *perfect!*" Presley said.

"You were right, babe," Aubrey said. "You don't need the p-word. You're so freaking adorable!"

"And late!" Charlotte jumped up, scrambling to gather her things. "I have to go."

She quickly sent the video to Beau with the message, *On my way to the airport! Love you!* And after too many hugs, *I love you*s, and promises to call, she ran for her rental car, excited to see her man.

AFTER NICK HAD raked him over the coals last night, Beau hadn't been sure what to expect from his brother this morning. But Nick and Graham had been waiting for him in the kitchen. He and Nick bristled at first sight, and then Nick had punched him in the arm and said, *Get over it. We love you.* They had gone with him to collect eggs, and by the time they returned to the inn, they were joking around. The hours passed in slow motion as Beau put the finishing touches on Charlotte's bedroom while his brothers teased him about *playing house* and suggested they might buy him a stroller or a minivan for Christmas.

By the time they finally arrived at the airport they were all in good moods, and Beau wasn't anxious to see his brothers go, but he was excited to see his girl.

Nick embraced him and said, "Don't forget to give Char my number. You know, in case she needs a *real* man."

"You realize you're an asshole, right?" Beau said with a slap on the back.

Nick shrugged. "An asshole who loves you, man."

Why did it always cause his throat to thicken when Nick said stuff like that? "I love you, too." He embraced Graham and said, "Thanks for sticking around."

"I'd like to see your ugly mug more often." Graham tugged his MIT hat lower on his forehead and said, "Think about what we said, okay?"

"It's all I've thought about since last night." Beau glanced at the clock. "Well, almost all."

"Mr. Lovesick needs to get over to his woman's gate, and we have sexy stewardesses to hit on." Nick nodded at Beau. "Give me a holler when you touch down in L.A."

"Sure thing." For some reason, Beau was feeling nostalgic, remembering when he'd gone off to college, and Nick had told him not to worry, that he'd take care of Tory for him. He'd kept his word, stopping by her house during those first few weeks when she'd been so sad about Beau leaving. When Nick heard she was going to be at a party, he always made sure to stop by and see if she needed a ride.

As Beau watched his brothers move through security, he realized Nick had tried to take care of him in the same way the weeks after Tory's death. But Beau hadn't let him, or anyone else for that matter.

He chewed on those memories as he headed into the gift shop. He bought a bouquet of roses, a Twix, a protein bar, and a bottle of water, because if he knew Charlotte, she was probably too busy writing on the plane to eat. He made his way to the gate, his anticipation ratcheting up as the minutes ticked by. He couldn't wait to see her, to hold her in his arms and kiss her beautiful lips. They had only two more days until he was leaving for L.A., and he planned to make the very best of each and every minute.

He anxiously scanned the passengers coming through the arrival gate for Charlotte.

"Excuse me! Excuse me!"

He heard her voice before he spotted her pushing through the crowd like a woman on a mission. Her eyes found his, and he rushed forward as she ran toward him and leapt into his arms, wrapping herself around him like a monkey to a tree. He captured her lips, and they made out like they'd been apart for years. He was vaguely aware of the crowd moving around them, while the chaos and the stress of the last two days faded away. His world shifted and settled, and he reveled in their closeness. She was the balm to his guilt, the goodness to all that felt wrong.

She was all that he wanted.

"Two days was too damn long," he said between kisses. Her eyes glimmered with love, and he couldn't get enough of it.

"Kiss me," she pleaded.

He pressed his lips to hers again, pouring all of the longing he'd felt into their connection. Their kisses went on and on, but if they didn't stop now, he never would. He drew back with a series of softer, more tender kisses. "I'm so glad you're home."

Home. The word had taken on a whole new meaning over the past few weeks. *She* had become his home.

"You know how you call me shortcake?" She didn't wait for an answer before saying, "I figured out what I want to call you."

"What's that?"

"Mine." She lowered her lips to his.

His heart beat so hard he thought it might pound right out of his chest. When he finally set her on her feet and tucked her against his side, he handed her the flowers.

"They're so beautiful. Thank you."

"I'd buy you the world if you wanted it." He reached into his pocket and pulled out the Twix and protein bars. "Hungry?"

She snagged the Twix and said, "Starved. You?"

"Famished." His gaze coasted heatedly down her body. "But not for food."

Her cheeks flushed, and the familiar, adorably sexy reaction made his chest feel even fuller. "I missed everything about you. Your voice, your sweet face, the way you're looking at me right now. I need to get you home so I can show you just how much."

Her eyes flamed, and she said, "I'd say let's go find a secluded spot to park, but cops seem to have a homing device for horny couples."

They kissed as they hurried through retrieving her luggage and drove home, kissing, holding hands, and wanting so much more. When they reached the inn, he opened her door to help her out, and their love took over. He leaned in as she wound her arms around his neck, and their mouths crashed together.

"*Inside*," he panted out. "I want to love you until the sun sets, and then I want to watch the sun roll over the hills and make love to you again and again, until those two days apart seem like they happened ages ago."

"I've always loved coming home, but I really love coming home *to you*."

They kissed and groped their way into the inn and down the stairs. In the hallway, Beau's heart thundered against his ribs as he backed her up against the wall, tearing off her green button-down as she pushed at his shirt. He ravenously devoured her neck. She tasted of hope and desire. She was his sweet salvation, his *everything*.

She arched off the wall, rubbing against him the way she knew drove him crazy.

"Fuck, baby, I need more of you." He lifted her into his arms, and her legs circled his waist.

"Hurry!"

He pushed the door to her suite open, reclaiming her mouth as he strode toward the bedroom. She pushed her hands into his hair, holding his mouth captive as he lowered them both to the bed. He kissed her jaw, her neck, and she arched back, giving him better access.

"Beau," she panted out.

He lifted her T-shirt and kissed her belly. He loved her belly, so soft and tender. He imagined it round with their babies and was shocked that the thought didn't scare him, didn't make his body go cold. He wanted that with her—a life, a family.

"Beau?" she said again, pushing up to her elbows.

He lifted his gaze and saw her looking around the room. Holy shit. He'd forgotten about her surprise. Tears welled in her eyes, and his heart sank. *Shit.* He'd overstepped, and now she was upset. He climbed off the bed as she pushed to her feet, her gaze skating over the new white bedside table and the bronze fairy lamp he'd found at an antique store in town.

"A fairy lamp," she said breathily. Her gaze moved to the fabric roses he'd strung around the bedposts and up to the chandelier and the star medallion he'd made and painted white with gold glitter. A tiny gasp escaped her lips as she took in the small silver and gold stars arcing out from the medallion like they were shooting across the sky.

"Stars," she said softly. "You made me glittery stars."

He touched his fingertips to hers, feeling her trembling. "I wanted to surprise you. I hope it's okay."

"Okay? This is better than I could have dreamed." She moved silently around the room, one hand covering her mouth as she gazed at her reflection in the ornately carved full-length white mirror on a stand by the French doors. Then she looked up at the high shelf holding the Hopes and Dreams jars he'd found in a box in her closet, each filled to the brim with notes.

"They're all there," he reassured her. "All twenty. I didn't open them. I just didn't think your dreams belonged in a box."

"Neither did I, but I didn't know where to put them. There's one for every year since that first time my family made me the dreamscape. I can't believe you did all of this." Her gaze moved to the Hopes and Dreams jar she'd made him, sitting beside hers.

"I hope you don't mind that I put mine with yours."

"Mind? I *want* yours with mine." Charlotte turned with rivers of tears streaming down her cheeks. Her eyes landed on the leather-bound fairy-tale book lying on her hope chest.

"I found that in your grandfather's desk when we were renovating the study for you."

"The study?" She gasped. "You renovated it for me?"

"Yes. It's all pink and white, even brighter than your office down here. I replaced the furniture with white. But don't worry. I moved your grandfather's desk and the shelves upstairs until you decide where you want them."

"Ohmygod," she said, drawing another rush of tears. She reached for the leather book.

"There are loads of drawings in there that you must have

made for your grandfather. Pages and pages drawn in crayon, pencil, and ink, along with letters from you to him. He probably kept every single one of them."

A tortured sob fell from her lips, and she sank down to the edge, clutching the book to her chest. "I thought they were gone forever."

He gathered her in his arms, holding her until her sobs eased. He knew what he wanted, and he wasn't going to take a chance of losing her. "I was thinking, if it's not too presumptuous, maybe I'd stick around and help make your dreams for the inn come true."

"Wh-what about L.A.?"

He cradled her face in his hands, brushed away her tears with the pads of his thumbs, and gazed into the eyes of his angel, his princess, his other half. "I'm canceling the trip and turning down the job. I don't want or need a reality show. I'd like a shot at a real-life fairy tale here with you."

Her lips curved up, but more tears fell. "But what about seeing your family? I really like them, and if we're together, I'll want to see *more* of them, but…"

"But you're worried I can't go back this time of year, or that I'll avoid going out while we're there."

She nodded solemnly.

"I'd never put you in that position. It might be hard at first, but nothing would be more difficult than living life without you. I don't want to run anymore, baby. I want to put down roots, and once you're done with your book, I was hoping we could go to Pleasant Hill so you can meet the rest of my family."

Fresh tears slipped from her eyes, and he brushed them away. "I was also thinking we might eventually choose to spend some time there, and some here. I know you won't want to leave the Chickendales, but I'll build a chicken coop and we can bring Channing and the crew with us." That earned a soft laugh. "I'll build you a beautiful, sunny office, so you always have a place to write, but I think we both need to be around family."

She set the book on the bed and climbed into his lap, her tears landing on his cheeks like rain. "I want that. I want that so much. I love you."

"I never imagined wanting to dream again, much less fall in love. You've not only changed my world, but you've become it. I love you, shortcake, and I never want to spend a single night without you again."

Chapter Twenty-One

"BE RIGHT BACK," Charlotte called out from the other room as Beau finished unpacking his bags in the bedroom of his Pleasant Hill home. It was July 4th and they were meeting his family for dinner at his parents' house. After that they were all going to the fireworks, a Braden family tradition that he'd missed out on for too long. Even Zev was going to make it home for the event.

He heard the side door open and looked out the window, spotting Charlotte hurrying down the stairs to the yard. It had been several weeks since he'd turned down the job in L.A., and one week since Charlotte had finished and turned in her manuscript, which she'd finished writing in her newly renovated study at the inn. Aubrey and Presley had struck a deal allowing Charlotte to finish the book she was writing for LWW's new Me Time channel, and they'd come up with the title *Anything for Love*. It was perfect, because he would do anything for her. In exchange for the concession, Charlotte agreed to add a fifth book to the contract for her Nice Girls After Dark series, and they'd given her extra time to write the first book in the series, which she was supposed to have written to fulfill her contract. He and Charlotte had been busy working on edgier, more erotic scenes, and she was more than ready. The blow-up dolls were no longer necessary, although they were great conversation starters when friends visited. Okay, it was mostly his cousins and their wives, and of course Cutter, but they were getting there. They were slowly building a life together.

Beau put his suitcase in the closet, warming at the sight of Charlotte's dresses hanging beside his clothes. They'd arrived at his house only three hours ago, and it already felt more like a home than it ever had. The first thing Charlotte had done was set out notebooks and pens in each of the rooms. Her pink cowgirl boots were by the side door. Nick had offered to let them borrow his horses anytime, and Charlotte had already arranged to ride at sunrise. She was a whole different woman when she wasn't under a deadline. They sat outside on the terrace at night talking until all hours, sharing even more about their favorite things and their pet peeves. There was nothing about his Twix-eating girl that he didn't love, and the more he learned about her, the harder and deeper he fell.

Beau followed the scent of Charlotte's perfume to the door she'd left open. She still wasn't good at closing or locking doors, but at least he knew she was safe. He'd worked through the repairs on Snow White's cabin and fixed the barn roof. When Charlotte was ready, they'd move into the cabin. There was no rush to do anything other than enjoy their lives as they renovated the inn. He wasn't going anywhere.

He closed the door behind him, watching her from the landing as she twirled in her pretty off-the-shoulder blue blouse and skinny jeans, picking wildflowers. He made a mental note to look into planting more gardens. If her relationship with Jillian was any indication, they'd be spending a lot of time in Pleasant Hill. Jillian called Charlotte nearly every day, and they'd become as close as sisters. Even his mother was making a habit of calling on a weekly basis and talking not just with him but with Charlotte. Beau no longer avoided his family's phone calls. His brothers were right. He'd been alone long enough. He just had to want something more than he needed to hold on to guilt.

Charlotte headed back toward the house, her arms full of bright flowers. She smiled as he came down the steps to help her.

"How's my beautiful girl?" He kissed her, then took the flowers as they went upstairs.

"Nervous as a virgin on her wedding night." She smacked his butt and ran up to the landing. "I'll get a vase."

He chuckled and followed her into the kitchen.

She opened one cabinet after another. "Where are your vases?"

"I'm a guy, Char. I don't have vases." He set the flowers on the counter.

Over the last week he'd learned that she didn't pick flowers when she wrote because she didn't get to enjoy them, but the day she'd finished her book, she'd filled vases and put them out all over their suite.

"Well, we need to fix that. In the meantime"—she reached into the cabinet and took out every glass he owned—"we'll use these." She began filling the glasses with water and dropping a few flowers into each.

He moved behind her, kissing her shoulder as she arranged the flowers. "You already met my parents on FaceTime. They love you. Why are you nervous?"

"I don't know. Meeting them in person is different. And I haven't met Jax or Zev, either. I hope they like me."

She was his silly girl. Everyone loved her. He wrapped his arms around her and said, "They will love you, but I can think of one way to ease your jitters."

She turned in his arms and pressed her lips to his. "We're supposed to be there in twenty minutes and there's no way I'm showing up after having been utterly and completely ravaged by my man. I'd have noodle legs all night long, and I'd worry they'd know why." She pressed a kiss to the center of his chest and said, "Can we stop on the way to get a card?"

"A card?"

"I have a gift for your parents, but I forgot to get a card. It'll only take a minute."

"Sure, although a trip to the bedroom would be more fun. For a woman who can't remember to feed herself, it's astonishing how often you think of others. Why did you get my parents a gift?"

"They raised you from a little bean of a baby. They need to know I'm worthy of you. I don't cook and I'm pretty sucky at cleaning, but there are some things I'm really good at, and this gift will show them that."

He lifted her onto the counter and wedged his body between her legs, earning a bright, sexy smile. "I thought you didn't want them to know about our bedroom activities."

"Their gift has nothing to do with sex." She wound her arms around his neck, put her mouth beside his ear, and said, "We should go, but I promise to make it up to you after we get home."

He growled, and she bit his earlobe. "You know I love that growl."

"And you know I love when you bite me." Which they'd discovered in their edgier sexual adventures. He clutched her ass, holding her tight against him.

Her eyes sparked with seduction. "Why do you think I did it?"

"You are such a tease."

His lips descended hungrily upon hers just as his cell phone vibrated. He groaned, but he didn't relent. They were about to be inundated with family, and he wasn't ready to share her yet. He took the kiss deeper, and she moaned into his mouth. He ground against her, loving the sinful sounds he earned and the way she arched against him, wanting him as badly as he wanted her. His phone vibrated again, and she giggled.

He reluctantly tore his mouth away, cursing under his breath.

"It's probably Jilly telling us to hurry up. I need to grab my bag anyway." She touched her lips to his and pressed her hand over his zipper, palming his erection as she slipped off the counter. "I'll take care of this bad boy when we get home. Promise." She made a big show of swaying her hips as she disappeared into the bedroom.

The text was from Jax, not Jillian. *Fair warning. Mom and Jilly are bouncing off the walls, practically planning your wedding. Don't be late.*

Beau grinned as Charlotte came out of the bedroom with a big blue leather bag over her shoulder.

"What are you grinning about?"

He grabbed his keys from the hook beside the door and hauled her in for a kiss. "I've got the sexiest, sweetest girlfriend in the world. What's not to grin about?"

They drove into town to get a card. Charlotte gazed out the windows at the brick buildings and upscale shops and the flowering dogwoods lining brick-paved sidewalks along the main streets.

"We've been here only a few hours, and I already love it. It reminds me of Port Hudson, the way the town itself is surrounded by rolling hills and sprawling pastures."

"It has a nice mix of rural and city life," he said as he circled the beautifully landscaped roundabout in the center of town. He pulled her against his side, glad to be in his own truck without the console between them.

"Look!" She pointed to Emmaline's Café. "That place is so cute. Can we go there for coffee one day?"

"Sure. The card store is a few doors down. Why don't we park so you can see it when we walk by?" He drove around to the parking lot and found a spot.

"*Emmaline's.* I love that name." She climbed out of the truck after him and bounced on her toes. "I have a good feeling about this place."

"A *story* feeling?" He kissed her grinning lips. She got inspiration everywhere they went, from people, signs, businesses. Her mind was a creative playground.

"Probably a story," she said. "You never know when a character or setting is going to come to life."

"Beau? Is that you?"

Beau turned, and a chill prickled down his spine at the sight of Duncan Raznick and Carly Dylan, Tory's best friend and the love of Zev's life. Carly's blond hair was pinned up in a ponytail, and her eyes lit up like she was genuinely happy to see him, while Duncan's jaw was clenched as tight as Beau's.

Duncan and Carly's gazes moved between him and Charlotte—Duncan's serious, Carly's sparkling with delight—and guilt tightened like a noose around Beau's neck. Charlotte slipped her hand into his and held on tight. If they were ever going to have a normal life without him feeling like he was on the verge of a heart attack when he saw people who knew Tory, he had to man up and deal with it.

"It's *so* good to see you," Carly said as she embraced Beau. "And *who* is this? Hi. I'm Carly."

"Charlotte, this is Carly Dylan, and this is Duncan Raznick. Carly, Duncan, this is—"

"Charlotte. Got it." Duncan nodded, flashing a feigned, tight smile. "Nice to meet you."

"You too," Charlotte said sweetly, but Beau could hear the tension in her voice.

"It's so nice to meet you, but I'm a hugger." Carly leaned in and hugged her. "We all go way back. You know, small town, known each other since grade school. Beau's brother was my first...*kiss*. So, Beau. How have you been?"

"Good." Beau looked at Charlotte and said, "Great, actually."

"I didn't expect to see you," Duncan said coldly.

Beau had seen Duncan in movies and magazines, but as he stood before him, Beau didn't see the square-jawed, chisel-faced actor. He saw the brown-haired, blue-eyed kid he'd grown up with who had lost his sister. The guy he'd respected and loved so much like a brother, he'd approached him before asking Tory out for the first time. *Listen, dude. I'm asking out your sister.* He'd never forget the look on Duncan's face when he'd said, *It's about time. You've only loved her since we were kids.*

Charlotte looked up at Beau, a silent offer of escape in her eyes. "We're supposed to meet your family. Should I run in and grab the card, or...?"

"That'd be great, babe, if you don't mind. We don't want to be late." He kissed her and reached for his wallet.

"I've got it," she said.

"Carly, why don't you…?" Duncan suggested.

"You suck at subtlety." Carly looped her arm through Charlotte's. "Come on. We can get to know each other, and you can give me all the dirt on you and Beau. I miss the big guy."

As they walked away, Beau's gut clenched. He didn't have any idea where to begin, so he went with the easiest, most obvious topic. "So, you and Carly…?"

Duncan scoffed. "No. You know she's been like a sister to me since she was a pain-in-the-ass little girl. She's just here for the weekend and we're hanging out."

They held each other's cold stares, and Beau wondered how he'd let so many years go by when he and Duncan used to be inseparable. "Listen, man. I'm really sorry about—"

"Abandoning me?" Duncan said coldly. "Leaving me to grieve for my best friend *and* my sister? Do you have any idea what it was like to lose both of you at once? What the hell, Beau? I called you and came by a hundred times. What the fuck was that?"

"What did you expect me to do?" Beau shot back, hands fisted by his side. "It was my fault she died. I couldn't face you, your family, *Carly*. Everyone who knew her blames me, and they should, because I'm the reason she's no longer here."

Duncan's brow knitted. "*What* are you talking about? She died in a car crash, and you weren't anywhere near her."

"But I should have been! She texted me to pick her up at the airport. She was coming back to surprise *me*, Duncan. If she hadn't wanted to see me…if I had seen her texts…"

A disbelieving look came over Duncan, and he shook his head. "Beau, this is *Tory* we're talking about. Do you remember what she was like? She was not a girl who waited around for *anything.* I don't know if she texted you first or what, but she texted me, and she called my parents who were an hour and a half away at a dinner party. She called Carly, who was too drunk to go pick her up. *None* of us could have known what was going to happen when she got in that cab."

Beau tried to piece together what that meant. "Just because no one else could get her doesn't mean it wasn't my fault."

Duncan's expression softened. "Then we're all equally guilty. Nobody blames you, Beau, and nobody ever has." He glanced at the café, his eyes tearing up. He gritted his teeth and blinked the sadness away. "She'd be happy for you, you know. She would be pissed at how you left me hanging, but she'd want you to be happy. You know that, right?"

Emotions clogged Beau's throat, making it impossible for him to speak.

"Tory loved you, and I know how much you loved her," Duncan said. "I never got to thank you for that. You made her life great, Beau, and my family will always be grateful for that. My mom talks about you all the time. She worries about you. Her *other* son."

Beau felt an unexpected smile tugging at his lips, the knots in his chest loosening. "I miss your mom."

"She's going with us to see the fireworks. She'd love to see you."

How much could one man's heart take? *They don't blame me.* "We're heading over to my parents' house for dinner before the fireworks. Why don't you guys stop by?"

"Carly has to swing by her friend's house for a bit, but maybe I will."

They stared at each other for a long moment. Beau didn't think as he opened his arms, and they fell into a manly embrace as he said, "I'm sorry, man. I'm so damn sorry."

"Me too. Don't fucking abandon me again," Duncan said as they parted. He nodded toward the café. "Charlotte, huh? Is it serious?"

"Yeah, it's serious. By the way, she's got a chicken named after you," Beau said as the girls came around the corner. Charlotte's eyes found his, soothing the remaining knots right out of him.

"Seriously? You must *love* that."

"I love her, man," Beau said as Charlotte and Carly joined them. "Nothing else matters."

ON THE WAY to his parents' house, Beau told Charlotte about his conversation with Duncan. She heard a difference in his voice. He sounded lighter, as if at least some of his burden had been lifted.

"How do you feel about it?" she asked as he parked in front of his parents' enormous brick and stone manor-style house.

"Strange but good. It'll take some time before the visceral response of seeing certain people goes away, but I'm glad he told me she'd texted him and the others. It doesn't take away my guilt, but talking with Duncan eased the weight of it. Did you like Carly?"

"Yes. She's funny and smart, and she really misses you. Did you know she lives in Allure, Colorado, not far from the inn? We can see her when we're there." She filled out the card for his parents and tucked it into her bag with the gift.

"Nice change in subject by the way," she said. "I know you

don't want to talk about it anymore, but I just want you to know I realize how hard that was, and I'm glad you did it."

"Thanks, babe." He pressed his lips to hers, hearing Bandit barking. "Here come the troops, but I need one more kiss." He took *several*.

Bandit bounded over as they climbed from the truck, and they knelt to love him up. He had thick black fur with a white stripe on his snout and a red bandana tied around his neck. He was the cutest bundle of energy Charlotte had ever seen, and the way Beau buried his face in his fur and Bandit wiggled, whimpered, and licked spoke of their love for one another.

"Hello, pretty boy. Thank you for sharing your daddy with me. I'm so happy to finally meet you," Charlotte said as Bandit moved between her and Beau, licking their faces. "He's so soft."

Beau kissed Charlotte, and Bandit pushed his nose between them, giving them both more kisses. "Hey, buddy. Char's pretty great, huh?" He winked and said, "I think you got his stamp of approval."

They'd left the Chickendales with Cutter watching over them, but they'd be back in Colorado soon, and they were excited to introduce Bandit to his new friends.

"Finally," Jillian said, running toward them. She hugged Charlotte. "You look amazing! I've missed you so much!"

Beau kissed Bandit's head and rose to his feet. "You talk to her every day."

"Says the brother who, according to Nick and Graham, nearly lost his mind when his girlfriend was away for two nights." Jillian took Charlotte's arm and headed for the backyard. "Come on and meet Jax and Zevy."

"I didn't lose my mind! I *found* it," Beau called after them.

Charlotte blew him a kiss. "Love you!"

His parents were holding hands as they came around the side of the house. She'd met them over FaceTime, but in person Lily's shoulder-length straight hair was even blonder, and her hazel eyes were warm and welcoming. Clint's hair was mostly gray, cut short like Jax's and Beau's, and he had what Charlotte's father would have called *wise* eyes. Charlotte and Lily had gotten close over the past several weeks. Lily called often, and she made Charlotte feel as though she were part of their close-knit family, catching her up on the happenings of each of Beau's siblings and wanting to know what was new in her and Beau's life. It had been so long since she'd had a mother, she felt drawn to her. His father had also gotten on the phone to chat with Charlotte a few times, and before they hung up, Clint and Lily always said, *We love you both. Talk soon.*

"Hello, sweetheart," Lily said warmly. "It's wonderful to finally meet you in person."

Lily embraced her for so long, it reminded Charlotte of how her own mother had sometimes embraced her for long stretches out of the blue. *Come here, ma chéri*, she'd say, and then she'd hug her for no reason other than loving her daughter.

Bandit pushed his nose between them, and Charlotte loved him up, too.

Clint embraced Beau, and then he drew Charlotte into his arms. "I finally get to hug the woman who brought my boy back into the world. Thank you. I might never let you go."

"I'm not above taking my father down to get my woman," Beau teased. He reached for her hand as a whistle sounded, and Bandit took off toward the backyard. "That'd be Nick. The man can whistle like a train."

As they entered the backyard, Charlotte saw Nick holding up a piece of meat while Bandit sat anxiously waiting, his tail wagging. Nick threw the meat up, and Bandit sprang off the ground, catching it in his mouth.

At the other end of the yard, Graham was playing basketball with two guys she recognized from pictures Beau had shown her of Jillian's twin, Jax, the wedding gown designer, and Zev, the treasure hunter who had taken off after Tory died. Jax was clean-cut, with short brown hair and the classic looks of a movie star, while Zev's hair hung almost to his shoulders, and his beard was thick and unkempt.

Zev looked up and lifted his chin in what Charlotte had come to know as the Braden greeting. "About time," he said in a deep, serious voice.

"You grungy bastard, look at you." Beau opened his arms and embraced Zev. "Good to see you, bro. It's been too long."

"I don't know what your girl's been telling you, but there's no such thing as *too long*." Zev winked at Charlotte and said, "Hi, *cutes*. I'm Zev, the good-looking brother."

Charlotte liked his affable personality. "I've heard a lot about you."

"I'm shaving his head tomorrow," Jillian said.

Zev scoffed. "In your dreams."

As Zev and Jillian argued over his hair, Graham sidled up to Charlotte. "Good to see you again, Charlotte. Have you met Jax yet?"

"I'm the only sane one in the bunch," Jax said with a wink. He had his father's wise eyes. "My sister hasn't stopped talking about you since she came back from Colorado."

"I'm sure I've been driving Beau crazy, too," Charlotte said. "I'm so happy I'm finally here and get to meet everyone."

"I'm glad I got to see you two before I leave for Oak Falls," Graham said. "My buddy Reed is getting married, and I'm going to take a look at an old theater he just bought. You'd love it, Beau. The architecture is incredible."

Charlotte's ears perked up. "Oak Falls, Virginia?"

"The one and only," Graham said.

"One of my LWW sisters lives there! Amber Montgomery. She owns a bookstore."

"Her sister, Grace, is marrying one of my college buddies, Reed Cross."

Charlotte gasped with surprise. "Grace is getting *married?* I'll have to call Amber. That's exciting."

Nick headed over with a plate of steaks. "Who's hungry?"

Everyone chimed in, and they headed for the table, which was set for dinner.

Zev put his arm around Charlotte, guiding her toward the table. Fresh flowers sat in a gorgeous pottery vase in the center of the table, surrounded by platters of vegetables, bread, and several side dishes. A bottle of wine was placed at each end of the table. Charlotte recognized the label from Lily's family's winery, Hilltop Vineyards. Beau had shown her the website online and had pointed out the vineyard in which his father had proposed to his mother.

"So," Zev said casually, "erotic romance, huh? I hear you have a handcuff fetish."

Charlotte laughed. "I guess you heard about Beau's first night at the inn and the blow-up doll?"

All eyes turned to Beau. Beau swore under his breath.

"Why haven't I heard that story yet?" Nick asked as he set down a platter of steaks.

"Speaking of erotic romance," Lily said. "Would you mind signing my books? I loved your Wicked Boys After Dark series, and I'm waiting with bated breath for the first book in your

Nice Girls series."

"Geez, Mom," Nick said. "I don't want to know this about you."

"Oh please." Lily waved her hand dismissively as they all sat down at the table. "Where do you think you kids came from?"

"Mom!" the guys said in unison.

Jillian cracked up. "You guys, it's only fiction!"

"There is not enough tequila on the planet to erase this conversation from my mind," Beau said as he draped an arm around the back of Charlotte's chair and leaned in for a kiss.

Dinner was delicious, filled with comfortable conversation and lots of teasing. Bandit sat by Nick, who snuck him bits of food, earning glares from his mother and laughs from everyone else. Beau held her hand, kissed her, whispered explanations of inside jokes, and gave his siblings as much of a hard time as they gave him. But it was easy to see how much he and his family loved each other. It was present in every glance, every joke and taunt. Lily and Clint stole so many kisses, Charlotte knew Beau was right. They had a love as deep and true as her own parents had.

As deep and true as we have.

As the sun set, Beau scooted closer and spoke directly into her ear. "Feel like you've entered Crazyland yet?"

She whispered for his ears only, "I love your family so much. I never want to leave!"

He pressed his lips to hers. She thought Beau had filled her heart to the brim, but as her mother used to say, the heart was an amazing organ, and as she looked around the table at his family, she was filled with love and joy and a sense of peace she had only ever dreamed of.

"I think we'd better get this cleaned up if we're going to

make the fireworks," Beau said as he pushed to his feet.

Everyone got up to help, and the table was cleared in no time. Charlotte stepped up to the sink to wash dishes, and Beau turned her in his arms. "No way, baby. We've got this. It's our thing, you know, since Mom spent so many years doing everything for us."

He was such a good man, he reminded her of all the parts of her father and grandfather she adored. *And so much more!* "I love you. Do you know that? Do you have any idea how much?"

"I think I have a pretty good idea." He kissed her again.

"Okay, lip-lockers." Jillian pulled them apart and dragged Charlotte toward the patio door. "The guys always do dishes. This is girl time!"

"I've got the wine!" Lily exclaimed as she snagged a bottle from the counter.

They settled in at the table, and Lily filled their glasses.

"I almost forgot! I have something for you and Clint. I know I have a weird lifestyle, and I'm sure you have heard that I'm not great at domestic things. But I'm really good at one thing." Charlotte withdrew the gift and the card from her bag and handed them to Lily.

"You didn't have to bring us anything," Lily said as she opened the card.

Charlotte watched her read what she'd written. *Thank you for sharing your amazing son with me. Love, Charlotte.*

"Oh, Charlotte." Lily hugged her, and then she unwrapped the picture Aiyla had taken of Beau reaching a hand out toward Charlotte with a smile so big and real it lit up his eyes. Lily pressed her hand to her chest. "My boy looks so happy. Thank you!"

"Let me see!" Jillian leaned in. "Aw, I remember when Aiyla

took that. He is so in love with you."

Lily lifted her glass and said, "To the woman who gave me my son back."

They clinked glasses.

Clint stepped out onto the patio. "Hey, Lil, can you come in here for a sec? Sorry, girls. But you know, men don't always know how to do everything right."

"You can say that again!" Jillian teased.

"Honey, look at this." Lily showed Clint the picture.

He put his arm around her as he looked it over. Then he lifted a soulful gaze to Charlotte and said, "Thank you, sweetheart. I can't think of anything more wonderful than seeing you two so happy."

When her parents went inside, Jillian scooted closer and said, "I hope I find what you and Beau have one day."

"Want to know the secret?"

"Heck yes!"

"I think you have to become a reclusive woman who hangs out with fictional people."

They both laughed.

"Jilly?" Jax called from the doorway. "Sorry, Char, but do you mind if I borrow her for a sec?"

"No. Go ahead."

Jillian pushed to her feet. "I'll be quick. Feel free to finish my wine."

As Jillian went inside, Bandit ran out and went paws-up on Charlotte's lap. He had a pair of sparkly red slippers in his mouth. Charlotte took them from him and loved him up. "Who did you steal these from, you sneaky boy? Did you steal them from Grandma?"

She pushed to her feet. "Come on, sweetie, let's go give

these to Grandma Lily."

She stepped inside, and Bandit took off through the dining room. She followed him in. "Beau? Lily?"

Bandit barked and ran back to her, pacing between her and whatever room he'd just come from. She'd only been in the kitchen and had no idea where to go. A loud whistle sounded, and Bandit took off again. She followed him into a gorgeous living room with vases of red roses covering every surface. Beau walked in through an arched entryway and stood before her. His family followed him in, standing off to the side and watching them expectantly. Nick held on to Bandit's collar.

Charlotte's nerves prickled. "Beau? What's going on?"

He took her hand and dropped down to one knee.

"Beau," she whispered, tears spilling down her cheeks.

"Baby, before you came into my life, I didn't know what a dreamscape was or a Hopes and Dreams jar. I didn't know that I could forgive myself for my mistakes or that others would do the same. I never imagined wanting to live a fairy tale, but I want it all with you, Charlotte, and those are your ruby slippers."

He rose to his feet, and she could barely breathe, could barely stand on her jelly legs.

"I've saved a hell of a lot of money over the years and I never knew why. Now I do. My slate is clear for two years, and I figure that's about the amount of time it'll take to create fairy-tale rooms at the inn and find someone to run it. I'm so in love with you, Charlotte. I want to live in Snow White's cabin, ride horses, and have a family with little girls who have your eyes and boys who have your smile. I want to keep your family legacy alive, and I want you to be part of mine, here, whenever we want to come. Will you marry me, baby? Be my wife, my forever love?"

"Yes!" She could barely see through the blur of her tears as she leapt into his arms. "I love you!"

They kissed as his family cheered and clapped. And then he slipped the most stunning diamond ring she'd ever seen on her finger. Several small diamonds encircled a large round one, and rubies cascaded down the slim, elegant band.

"I love you, baby," he whispered. "I'm going to make all your dreams come true."

"You already have," she said, and kissed him again.

They were passed from one embrace to the next as his family congratulated them and welcomed her to the family. Bandit ran around the room, sniffing the roses and barking. Charlotte could barely catch her breath.

"I'd be honored to make your wedding gown," Jax offered.

"Both of us!" Jillian said.

"Actually, would it be rude of me to ask if you guys would alter my mom's dress for me?" Charlotte asked.

"That's even more perfect," Jax said.

They both hugged her, like they were two sides of one person, and said, "We'd be honored."

"I'll get the champagne!" Zev disappeared into the kitchen.

Beau drew Charlotte into his arms again. "You did all this with your family for me? The roses? Bandit?"

"This is just the start, baby. There's nothing I won't do for you."

There was a knock at the door, and Lily went to answer it. A minute later she returned with Duncan. "Look who showed up to visit."

Nick sidled up to Beau. "Shit. I'll get rid of him."

"Don't," Beau said. "I invited him."

Nick's eyes filled with disbelief.

Beau's eyes met Charlotte's, and he said, "It was time."

"Champagne!" Zev exclaimed as he burst into the room holding a bottle over his head. His eyes locked on Duncan, and he froze. "What the hell are you doing here?"

Duncan held his gaze. "Drinking your champagne. Are you pouring, or am I?"

"I'm not sticking around."

Graham grabbed Zev's arm. "Yeah, you are. Let's go out back. It's time for a clean slate."

"I like my slate dirty." Zev wrenched his arm away and took a swig from the bottle.

"Oh boy," Beau whispered to Charlotte.

"He just needs a little lesson in forgiving himself from my big, burly Beau."

As the others headed for the backyard, Beau didn't look convinced. "Or maybe I wasn't thinking straight."

"Did you see the look on Graham's face? He's not going to let them walk away without a resolution." Charlotte wound her arms around his neck and said, "Besides, after that incredibly romantic proposal, I'd say you're thinking perfectly."

Ready for more Bradens & Montgomerys?

Fall in love with Graham Braden and Morgyn Montgomery in
Trails of Love

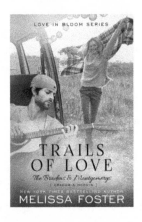

When Graham Braden travels to Oak Falls, Virginia, to attend the wedding of his buddy Reed Cross to Grace Montgomery, he sticks around to help with renovations to Reed's new theater. The last thing he expects is to be asked to assess and possibly invest in Grace's sister Morgyn's business endeavors. Graham is a careful, keen businessman, and Morgyn is impulsive, disorganized, and more interested in the energy flow in her eclectic retail shop than in the accuracy of her records. While Graham isn't ready to open his pockets to the sassy, sexy business owner, he may be ready to open his heart.

Have you read STORY OF LOVE,
where readers first met Charlotte Sterling?

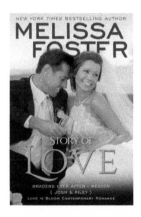

A Braden wedding!

Family and babies abound during this fun-filled weekend of
love, laughter, and happily ever afters! Join Josh and Riley on
their big day and fall in love all over again with each of the
Bradens at Weston, and their children, in this sweet and sexy
wedding novella.

How can two famous fashion designers pull off a wedding
without the paparazzi involved? The Braden family knows no
boundaries, and they will stop at nothing to give Josh and Riley
their magical moment at the altar. But no wedding is perfect,
and the Bradens find unexpected mayhem around every corner.

There's a special surprise in this book for loyal Braden fans, and it comes directly from your favorite patriarch, Hal Braden! You'll also meet Charlotte Sterling, a sassy, sexy erotic romance writer who runs the inn where Josh and Riley are getting married. Charlotte is Beau Braden's love interest in Anything for Love, The Bradens & Montgomerys.

New to the Love in Bloom series?

I hope you have enjoyed getting to know the Bradens at Pleasant Hill as much as I've loved writing about them. If this is your first Love in Bloom book, you have many more love stories featuring loyal, sassy, and sexy heroes and heroines waiting for you.

The Bradens & Montgomerys (Pleasant Hill – Oak Falls) is just one of the series in the Love in Bloom big-family romance collection. Each Love in Bloom book is written to be enjoyed as a stand-alone novel or as part of the larger series. There are no cliffhangers and no unresolved issues. Characters from each series make appearances in future books, so you never miss an engagement, wedding, or birth. You might enjoy my other series within the Love in Bloom big-family romance collection. You can start at the very beginning of the Love in Bloom series absolutely free with SISTERS IN LOVE or begin with another fun and deeply emotional series like the Remingtons, which begins with GAME OF LOVE, also free.

Below is a link where you can download several first-in-series novels absolutely FREE.

www.MelissaFoster.com/LIBFree

More Books By Melissa

LOVE IN BLOOM SERIES

SNOW SISTERS
Sisters in Love
Sisters in Bloom
Sisters in White

THE BRADENS at Weston
Lovers at Heart
Destined for Love
Friendship on Fire
Sea of Love
Bursting with Love
Hearts at Play

THE BRADENS at Trusty
Taken by Love
Fated for Love
Romancing My Love
Flirting with Love
Dreaming of Love
Crashing into Love

THE BRADENS at Peaceful Harbor
Healed by Love
Surrender My Love
River of Love
Crushing on Love
Whisper of Love
Thrill of Love

THE BRADENS & MONTGOMERYS at Pleasant Hill – Oak Falls
Embracing Her Heart
Anything For Love
Trails of Love

THE BRADEN NOVELLAS
Promise My Love
Our New Love
Daring Her Love
Story of Love
Love at Last

THE REMINGTONS
Game of Love
Stroke of Love
Flames of Love
Slope of Love
Read, Write, Love
Touched by Love

SEASIDE SUMMERS
Seaside Dreams
Seaside Hearts
Seaside Sunsets
Seaside Secrets
Seaside Nights
Seaside Embrace
Seaside Lovers
Seaside Whispers

BAYSIDE SUMMERS
Bayside Desires
Bayside Passions
Bayside Heat
Bayside Escape

<u>THE RYDERS</u>
Seized by Love
Claimed by Love
Chased by Love
Rescued by Love
Swept Into Love

SEXY STANDALONE ROMANCE
Tru Blue
Truly, Madly, Whiskey
Driving Whiskey Wild
Wicked Whiskey Love

BILLIONAIRES AFTER DARK SERIES

WILD BOYS AFTER DARK
Logan
Heath
Jackson
Cooper

BAD BOYS AFTER DARK
Mick
Dylan
Carson
Brett

HARBORSIDE NIGHTS SERIES
Includes characters from the Love in Bloom series
Catching Cassidy
Discovering Delilah
Tempting Tristan

More Books by Melissa
Chasing Amanda (mystery/suspense)
Come Back to Me (mystery/suspense)
Have No Shame (historical fiction/romance)
Love, Lies & Mystery (3-book bundle)
Megan's Way (literary fiction)
Traces of Kara (psychological thriller)
Where Petals Fall (suspense)

Acknowledgments

I hope you enjoyed Beau and Charlotte's story and are looking forward to reading about the rest of Beau's siblings. In *Trails of Love*, the next book in the Bradens & Montgomerys series, the two families will come together in their big, new, close-knit world.

I am thrilled to announce a special surprise for fans! If you have not heard the news yet, I am now part of a fantastic group of romance authors called the Ladies Who Write (LWW), and we have created a fun, sexy world just for you! In *Anything for Love* you've met several fictional members of LWW, each of whom will have their own book written by me and the other authors of LWW. For more information on our group and to stay up to date on the release of LWW books, visit www.LadiesWhoWrite. com and sign up for our newsletter.

A special thank-you goes out to Brittani Jolley, who entered a contest on Facebook and provided the name of the reality show *Shack to Chic*. If you haven't yet joined my fan club on Facebook, please do. We have a great time chatting about our hunky heroes and sassy heroines. You never know when you'll inspire a story or a character and end up in one of my books, as several fan club members have already discovered. facebook.com/groups/MelissaFosterFans

Remember to like and follow my Facebook fan page to stay

abreast of what's going on in our fictional boyfriends' worlds.
facebook.com/MelissaFosterAuthor

Sign up for my newsletter to keep up to date with new releases and special promotions and events and to receive an exclusive short story featuring Jack Remington and Savannah Braden.
www.MelissaFoster.com/Newsletter

And don't forget to download your free reader goodies! For free family trees, publication schedules, series checklists, and more, please visit the special Reader Goodies page that I've set up for you!
www.MelissaFoster.com/Reader-Goodies

As always, loads of gratitude to my amazing team of editors and proofreaders: Kristen Weber, Penina Lopez, Elaini Caruso, Juliette Hill, Marlene Engel, Lynn Mullan, and Justinn Harrison. And, of course, I am forever grateful to my husband, Les, and the rest of my family, who allow me to talk about my fictional worlds as if we live in them.

~Meet Melissa~

www.MelissaFoster.com

Melissa Foster is a *New York Times* and *USA Today* bestselling and award-winning author. Her books have been recommended by *USA Today's* book blog, *Hagerstown* magazine, *The Patriot*, and several other print venues. Melissa has painted and donated several murals to the Hospital for Sick Children in Washington, DC.

Visit Melissa on her website or chat with her on social media. Melissa enjoys discussing her books with book clubs and reader groups and welcomes an invitation to your event. Melissa's books are available through most online retailers in paperback, digital, and audio formats.